T0150825

the shakespeare conspiracy

sandra hochman

the shakespeare conspiracy

A HISTORICAL FANTASY

TURNER

Turner Publishing Company
Nashville, Tennessee
New York, New York

www.turnerpublishing.com

The Shakespeare Conspiracy

Cover design: Maddie Cothren
Book design: Glen Edelstein

Library of Congress Cataloging-in-Publication Data available on request

9781683365402

Printed in the United States of America
18 19 20 21 22 9 8 7 6 5 4 3 2 1

To my best friend, Rigmor Newman, and
Gary Kupper, a musician with many talents

contents

Editor's Note

In the venerated tradition of historical fiction
(including many works by Shakespeare himself),
accuracy with regard to certain events, dates, and
personalities has been superseded by elements of
the fantastical plot.

A Poet's Prologue

This summer, by accident, the way most things happen in the life of a poet, I came upon what may be the Rosetta stone of Shakespearean studies. I discovered the secret diary of William Shakespeare's wife.

Because of this diary, I have come to believe that William Shakespeare, in his need for attention and creative feedback, was no different from other male literary geniuses. He needed a woman to prompt, fashion, and validate his creativity. James Joyce and his wife, Nora, come to my mind, as do Vladimir Nabokov and his Vera, and even Marcel Proust and his cook, Francoise. From my own experience as a poet, I know it takes a great deal of love to gain confidence in one's work. Could it really be that William Shakespeare had no collaborators at all? Or could it be that the sole person to help him with his writing, his plays and plots, with the learning of his lines, with his endless business problems as a theatre owner, was none other than this wife? Could the bard have had, at his side, a *bardolina*? Could it be that a woman by the name of Anne Hathaway, Shakespeare's wife, contributed her feminine intelligence and wove her own wit into the DNA of Will's genius?

The diary says yes.

I cannot help but refute the bogus scholars who assert that Will hated his marriage and left his wife at home in Stratford-upon-Avon while he went off to fornicate and triumph in London. All this "antimarriage" theory is based on two facts that do not compute. "Fact" one: upon his death, Shakespeare slighted his wife and dishonored his marriage by leaving Anne only his "second-best bed" (that is to say his marriage bed; the best bed was used for guests). So long held, so long unchallenged, the assertion renders scholars nearly incapable of entertaining the possibility that such a bestowment was a simple token of love, like a charm bracelet, like those little gleaming rings he left to friends in his last will and testament. Nor do scholars seem able to accept the unwavering reality that, by English law, Anne also inherited one-third of her husband's considerable estate, that extraordinary home of New Place and the wide swath of land, and of course, all his poems and plays. Later, upon publication of these literary jewels, she became the richest widow in Stratford-upon-Avon.

"Fact" two of the Shakespeare-the-Misogynist theory is grounded upon a broken, ageist assumption: that Will could not have fallen in love with Anne because she was eight years older than he. As a woman who has often found herself with younger men, I find this theory ridiculous. So much did Shakespeare dislike his old and lonely wife, apparently, that one prominent scholar suggests that the epitaph in the Trinity Church of Stratford-upon-Avon—"Cursed be him who moves my bones"—was inscribed for the possible purpose of keeping his bones from being jumbled with his wife's. Somehow such speculation, having gained the momentum that only large, strong voices can lend, is read as fact, though pure fiction.

Picture this. A beautiful midsummer day. The hills of Stratford-upon-Avon, Shakespeare's birthplace, rolling from the river to the horizon of trees. The statuary enshrined in Holy Trinity Church. And here I am, strolling in the cemetery outside the church, winding among the stones, feeling like an old soul come home. Suddenly, and quite miraculously now that I consider it, an ancient gardener pops up, interrupting my daydreams with his remarkable and uninhibited chatter. He is the last of a family of stonemasons, he claims, dating back to the fifteenth century. A remarkable fact, I think, to have such precedence. Not as remarkable, however, as what he says next.

"When they were takin' down the house of New Place, Shakespeare's home, a stonemason in my family found in the beams of the rafters the diary of the missus."

"The missus?"

"Mrs. Shakespeare."

"Pardon?"

"Mrs. Shakespeare. Anne of Shottery."

"Mrs. Shakespeare? Anne Shakespeare? Her diary?" I am stunned. Who wouldn't be?

"Of course, m'lady! In the rafters it was! And now it's for sale."

Ancient and historic as it is, Stratford-upon-Avon bears the marks of the modern world. Vendors and trinkets line its streets with cheap hotels and plastic replicas of Shakespearean busts. But an interesting scheme this one. Hawking fabricated diaries in a cemetery? This seems to me to be far-fetched.

"Where is this diary?"

"It's right 'ere, m'lady, in my wheelbarrow."

As a poet, I am a believer; as an American, I'm a fallen

innocent, a cynic. But as my stomach flutters, and like a child I smile in astonishment, I want the poet to win.

I think of how much we don't know—that of the over three thousand books written about William Shakespeare, we have learned so little of him, and so much less of his wife. The greatest writer in the English language remains yet a sphinx.

"How—how much are you selling the diary for?"

"Two hundred pounds—and worth every penny," he says convincingly.

"Why so little?"

I look down at his wheelbarrow filled with peat moss, rusty tools, and, according to him, Anne Shakespeare's secret diary.

"Dearie," he says softly and without shame, "I need the money."

It is a dream to believe this is real, and that such a miracle might happen, but what do I have to lose? I have read and acted the works of William Shakespeare all my life; there were times I love him as dearly as a husband. I fish two hundred pounds out of my handbag—the emergency money I keep hidden from thieves and from myself. So be it. This is a literary emergency.

The gardener reaches into his wheelbarrow stash, pulls out a dirty, gray, flannel burlap, and with great care unwraps a precious diary. He dusts it off, holds it out, and places it in my hands with a sense of ceremony I do not expect from him—he might as well have been handing me the Dead Sea Scrolls—and then immediately disappears. I haven't even time to ask his name.

Two hundred pounds gone. A worn leather book in hand. Worst-case scenario: I am taken, one more time in my life, for a sucker; best-case scenario: I have just purchased the Ark of the Covenant of Shakespeareana.

Have I found, by some absurdity, a genuine key that can unlock the secrets of the life of Anne and William Shakespeare?

Am I holding it now in my hands, the remarkable result of my foolish lifelong habit of talking to strangers? Who knows? Sometimes even fools luck out.

I flew home the next day, and, without stopping by my apartment, took the train to Cambridge to visit a good friend, a poet and Elizabethan scholar at Harvard University. He has a day job as a librarian at the Lamont Poetry Room in the Widener Library, where a Mr. John Sweeney had once displayed my own poetry manuscripts. My friend agreed to translate the diary for me at once, from Elizabethan English into contemporary English, so I could read it more easily. (The translated version is what is reproduced in this book.) Of course, once he finished, I began reading it at a feverish pitch.

The copies of his work in hand, I gave the original diary to scholars and forensic scientists at Harvard, who are now working on verifying its authenticity. They are testing the carbon, the chemical quality of the ink, poring over the musty yellow papers, measuring Anne's diary against the elements used in England four hundred years ago. I know from that, the ways of scholars and scientists take a long time. It might require years to find out if the secret diary is authentic. And while they are doing all this scholarly authenticating, I can't help but wonder if I have slipped, by mistake, on the banana peel of truth in the vaudeville of Shakespearean scholarship.

We know almost nothing about the man named William Shakespeare. We have, thank God, his plays, his magical poems and sonnets, but about the man himself, all we really know is written in the records of the court and the church. The Elizabethan Age was extremely litigious, thankfully so, as the courts and the lawyers remain the only places of official records. There are no letters about Shakespeare, no sketches of Will and Anne, and oddly enough, no letters to them or from them. They existed at a time when lives were spoken, not written.

But of course there are the rumors. Some say Shakespeare didn't exist, that he was a composite, an amalgam of the creative energies of many or a few. The mystery is attractive, even if the idea is proven untrue by the records of copyrights of his work entered in the courts. Some say he was a lover of many, though we have no proof whatsoever that Will was ever unfaithful to his wife, that he had a black mistress, or that he was a homosexual. This is only so much speculative musing on the part of writers and scholars, dreamers like Oscar Wilde, who believed (or so said) that Shakespeare's love sonnets were written to a young actor named Willie Hughes. That fantasy, like so many others, is not backed up by records, but by Oscar Wilde's imagination.

According to Anne's diary, her husband was a family man, a secret Catholic, a man who knew how to keep his money in his pockets, a man who dearly loved his parents, his children, his wife, and his friends. He was also a very private man and wanted nothing of his to remain except his land, his heirs, and the writings of his plays and poems. We suspect that as a young man he went to the north of England to be a tutor when he graduated from the King's School, and we learn from court documents that he married Anne Hathaway when he was eighteen.

There are seven years before he went to London, called "the lost years," which have remained unaccounted for until now. According to his wife's diary, Will and Anne spent those seven years raising their three children in Stratford-upon-Avon, reading books borrowed from the local bookseller, Richard Field, and making day trips to Oxford University's library. There, Will taught himself everything—science, art, medicine, astronomy, astrology, military tactics and history, and mathematics. Ever the autodidact, ever the genius. They were seven years spent making money, spent waiting for their children to be old enough so the couple could take their nest egg and go off to test their luck in London, while Will's parents, John and Mary, tended to the children in Stratford, two days' ride by horse from the great city.

Anne is a writer, a delightful documentarian, a poet and songwriter. She tells us how Will wrote, how he felt sorrow at loss, joy at success, how he lived with élan, and why he finally retired, after a triumphant career, to live in glory in his hometown and busy himself with nature, his children, and his home. Her diary, after all, is a love story. I dare to say that some of the Shakespeare gossip-mongers have had such fun in assuming that Will was a woman hater, but that indulgence ends here. Though his poems and his plays are often used to back up the myriad absurd assumptions about Will and his personal life, nothing can truly be discerned from such material about who Shakespeare really was.

We can tell nothing about Shakespeare or his wife from his plays or poems because William Shakespeare wrote about everything and its opposite. His work was all ambiguity. He delighted in doubles. You can point to passages in the plays that say he loved women, or you can find other passages that say he hated them. You can find passages that say he loved men or passages that say he hated them. His work can show a deep compassion for the human condition and a great love for humanity, or they can be read to show that he was a misanthrope. Will Shakespeare's plays were not written as confessional works. How, then, can they be read as such? His plays and beautiful poems were entertainments, conceits. They are always the work of an actor. In Anne's diary, she records him saying, "When I need to play a part, I call on that part inside me. I am an actor. I have all humanity within myself."

Yes, Will, above all, was an actor, or, to use an Elizabethan term, a "shadow." Like Ariel in *The Tempest*, he is here, there, everywhere. As a writer, he is a spirit, like Ariel, yet we feel that William Shakespeare was a passionate man. I believe, from

7

my reading of the diary, that he was in some ways quite ordinary and in other ways the most exceptional of all writers.

Every now and then God throws us a bone. A universal genius. A poet like Saint Theresa. A novelist like James Joyce. A scientist like Copernicus. A Saint Joan, a Mary Baker Eddy, a Bach, a Mozart, a William Shakespeare. It is almost unfathomable to imagine what these genius men and women, touched perhaps by God, were really like, but I do imagine them, dear madam, dear scholar, dear madman. That is my job as a poet: to imagine them. To imagine their successes and failures, their friends and enemies. Yes, their enemies. Genius always has them.

"Law, say the gardeners, is the sun."

That line from W. H. Auden influenced me when I was a young poet. Now it reminds me of a new illumination that arrived in a soiled wheelbarrow. Reading about Anne and Will has been the most interesting experience of my literary life. You can say, as the late Dylan Thomas claimed, that "all poets are liars," but I believe that Anne and Will's great love affair was real. I see the life of Anne Shakespeare as shiny and dark at the same time, but like many women poets I have known, she refused to die in spirit. I must admit that as I read her diary, I often felt Anne Shakespeare was I, and that I was reliving my own life through her language.

Anne's secret story of Will and the conspirators who tried to kill him have pricked my own neurosis. A poet can never be too paranoid and, of course, should Mrs. Shakespeare's diary prove to be, by any stretch of the imagination, *real*, it will assure us that Will really existed and that he didn't write alone, but wrote with the help of his wife. In a moment of perfect irony, it will take the diary of his long-silenced wife to finally convince us he was real. His genius, according to this journal, inspired enemies envious of his talent and his money, his patronage and success.

In the meantime, I have read Anne's diary in facsimile over and over. I cannot put it down. Will becomes my ideal man. And Anne? Her blood is in my own. Her fear of enemies was not unfounded. This document, if authenticated, shows the life of a man and woman we do not know. If it is authenticated, it puts to rest the Oxfordian and Francis Bacon theories that always seemed to me, and many others, to be unbelievable. No one ever had Shakespeare's "voice." Bacon was long since dead when Shakespeare wrote his greatest works. Anne's secret diary also puts to rest rumors about his wife, for all time. If the diary is real, we know she was more than a stay-at-home wife and the mother of his three children. She was his mistress, his wife, his inspiration, and his closest writing partner, being a writer herself.

Part One

Elizabeth

March 11, 1601

Oh, what do we fear with reason?
How many men will die tonight,
Their heads lopped off,
Killed by lust for power?
Good-bye Essex. Good-bye Kyd.

Yes, not everything is what it seems.
Thank God our patron is the queen of curds and creams.

April 15, 1601

I pretend to be Will's cousin, not revealing I am his wife. Final rehearsals? 'Tis enough to drive one mad. They sit at the pivot of weariness and success, and all one's fears are spun into a center, black and damning. And yet quietly on the stage, among the expectation and uncertainty, is the feeling of nearly limitless hope.

Master John Dowland, the composer who Will trusts above all, was tuning his finely crafted, mother-of-pearl-inlaid lute tonight at the final rehearsal, and I could not keep from listening in wonder to the tune he wrote to a poem which is now Ophelia's song. 'Tis a beautiful piece, and his masterful playing very nearly does it justice. Like all the other musicians, he is thrilled to be part of *Hamlet*. Out of the hundreds of musicians in London, only eight have passed the audition to play songs, flourishes, and fanfares for the tragedy.

The trumpeters, with their heraldic banners hanging from long, thin, golden-brass horns, were dressed in red and white, and standing there together, playing music, they seemed a row of kings of hearts from a fine deck of playing cards. As they stood proudly, each holding his instrument, the other musicians gathered early at the Globe. A short, fat lute player with red hair and freckles was running to the theatre, late, and beside himself for his tardiness. I smiled at his urgency as the viol player with the gold earring, and with a small red-velvet cap draped over an eye, said to me in a reverent voice, "Your cousin is at the height of his powers. *Hamlet*—and we all agree—is a bloody great tragedy."

Cousin? They should only know who I am.

A flute player and a man known for the sound of his loud drum both took their places on the balcony along with the other musicians. The flute player asked the drummer, "'Ave you see this *Hamlet* play in rehearsal?"

"Yes. As good as *Julius Caesar*," said the drummer. "Now there's a poet who's not puffing with the wind and rain."

The musicians' gossip had its own rhythm, and as I stood by the balcony near the trumpeter, I listened to musicians warming up their instruments, the sounds blending with the scattered voices. Ophelia's song was being rehearsed, sung by the fair young actor whom Will had plucked out of the children's theatre and then paid a fortune for him to abandon the juveniles and join the Lord Chamberlain's Men.

Our queen's patronage and Will's skill have made it the finest group of actors and the wittiest group of playwrights in all of England. To see this young boy, I wondered if he knew yet that he was a part of a brilliant and creative family.

Will appeared suddenly. He was, as always, well dressed, and his white ruff was, by my own hand, well starched and pressed. He strolled forward, his strides long and quick. The musicians cut short their gossip. They are in awe of Will. They and England all.

"Ophelia's song once more," Will said in his quiet, intense way, his dark hair perfectly a mess, his large brown eyes above the bags of skin beneath. He's not slept in weeks.

The lutenist then began to play. The blonde actor sang his words, written for the sad Ophelia:

And will a' not come again?
And will a' not come again?
No, no, he is dead,
Go to thy deathbed,
He never will come again.

His beard was as white as snow,
All flaxen was his poll.
He is gone, he is gone.
And we cast away moan.
God ha' mercy on his soul!

I try now to remember the first time Will used my songs in his plays—I cannot.

So many of them now, I cannot trace them back. The feeling is the same each time: when the young actor sang, he became our Ophelia.

"I am proud of you," Will said.

The young actor pushed his very light blond hair from his

face, and I saw small beads of perspiration on his nose. "The day you discovered me was the luckiest day of my life."

I wanted to tell him I felt the same. At this moment, Richard Burbage, dressed in green velvet, now the greatest actor in London outside of Edward Alleyn, joined us and ran through a few of his lines as Hamlet, adding a few lines to a speech, a few words of his own mixed with Will's. To all the great actors does Will give this license.

"Burbage," I remarked. "From now on your name will go down in theatrical history." He was Hamlet, standing there before me. As I had seen him in my dreams, the young prince now took flesh.

"The name of Burbage will be known for a few years, but the name of your cousin, William Shakespeare, will be known for a thousand," he replied with humor and modesty.

"Oh, Richard, you are too modest!" I said, laughing. The old actor's large brown eyes still held the innocence of a child, the wild wonder, and yet had the sadness of the prince of Denmark. Burbage always becomes the person he plays, even offstage, even before the opening. I could sense in him a deep sadness that was familiar to me. It was the despair of the prince.

Burbage said softy, "The part of Hamlet is an actor's dream, and it will be played by great actors as long as there is English theatre. And judging from the enthusiasm of the audiences, every time one of Will's is presented, great English theatre will be with us for a long, long time."

'Tis thrilling to hear the voice of Burbage, even in conversation. As the lute player and Ophelia rehearsed the songs, Will and I exited the theatre and stepped out into the London darkness, leaping the final three steps to the earth. Pleased by the enthusiasm of Burbage, he threw his arm around my neck and pulled my head to his chest. Edward Alleyn, his rival, has the airs of an aristocrat, but Burbage has a touch of the common man, which, 'tis true, is why we love him. He has not

16

the canker of an actor's arrogance.

"Were I not this black-fogged night the writer, and were you not my thin-limbed helpmate, I should throw you in the bushes and show you things I cannot tell!"

We both laughed and embraced. Like every playwright, Will thrives on admiration. And I, this wife cast in a poet's role, this woman, bold as a man, thrills to see him. On nights like these he floats.

In one day's time *Hamlet* is to be performed at the Globe. I should even now be hearing the fore-echoes of the applause, the sound of a crowd laughing. I should be dreaming only of the way the city shall throb with excitement when the playbills are posted. Yet I am weary with worry. And there is blood in my dreams.

The queen does adore my husband. But by my truth, the beauty of Will's talent is both worshipped and despised. Will's God-given gift has produced ungodly malice, a hatred and envy in the hearts of many. They stare in anger, their eyes dancing behind their clapping hands.

And on the morrow, I shall see them all, friend and enemy, as they hear the great language of *Hamlet*, a music that no one, save Marlowe, could ever create for the stage.

APRIL 16, 1601

This is the life I was born to live—the life of playacting, poetry, and playwriting; not only as a wife, but as a member of the rowdy crew at the Globe. Always I am taking on the ruse of cousin or servant. And yet the deceit, the living lie, is my means to this end, of sharing every moment of life in the hurly-burly of the London theatre with my husband. That I could not do this as his wife revealed—my bosom not wrapped tightly, my hair not trimmed, my dresses worn proudly rather than hidden in a trunk—is not a thing changeable. There is, I know, no other way. I choose subterfuge and secrecy for love, and for him. My husband is a man of solitude, but in a strange ambiguity he does not like to be alone. I am always at his side.

In truth, most days I do not mind. There is a thrill in an always-lie. It is only the trouble of readying myself that troubles me. The "cousin" costume makes me always late. It takes me at least an hour to properly disguise myself—though it once took longer. Now, when I look in the looking glass at my short hair and firm jaw, I see only Arthur Headington, my assumed "cousin" name.

This afternoon at exactly two o'clock, the queen's coachman, the whiskered Mr. Buckman, called my false name from outside our modest lodging. The stout coachman yelled to me from the dark street. Will was already at the Globe, and now I would join the mob and sit in the audience.

"Mr. Headington, come down, sir! The traffic on the street piles heavy, and we must leave lest we be late!"

As usual I was punctual, as one has to be in the professional London theatre. I was dressed in my best man's clothes: a golden shirt, velvet breeches, a white ruff, and a gold bracelet. Some of this finery, I must admit, I borrowed from Will. I soon ran down the steps in my leather boots and out to the carriage (again, the queen provided the finest of all her carriages). A strange, cold air slapped my face. Even the usually composed Mr. Buckman seemed on edge, jittery with anticipation, I supposed.

Will does appear in his own play tonight—the ghost—so we have arranged that I am to sit in the audience and, as always, pen notes in my mind. I become his body in these moments. I am his "eyes," looking from a distance at the plays, judging, in my own mind, how the audience is reacting. I am also his "ear," listening for the lines we've written, picking up the broken cadence. The occasional improvisation, the here and there of dropped lines, who performed well and who needs more coaching. I am above all his "surrogate spy," eavesdropping on the tittle and tattle of the audience during the intermission. I am in a true snit of anticipation, but my mask is that of the male cousin, servant to the master and calm.

What is the life of a playwright? An agony. Enough pain for both of us to share.

As his muse, researcher, collaborator, and lover, I know there is always someone else in the room: the work, the character, the genius. And I am there to see it, to criticize the work that the brain of the Writer, Will Shakespeare, creates with godlike intuition, with passion, while magically his mind conjures up all the feelings humanity has ever known.

Last night, as he lay staring into the warm night, his mind full of worry over what might be, the lines and songs sounding flat and thin in his mind, he told me that if I were not at his side— to research stories, listen to the soliloquies, help him plot the beginnings, middles, and ends, discover new words, improvise lines and scenes while he is in a fit of writing—that never in his wildest dreams could he be the success that he is now.

"You are," he said to me yesterday, "my feminine soul."

I am as ambitious as he is, perhaps more. I always wanted, once we met and were betrothed, to be in the center of the theatre world. And indeed here I am—at the center, swirling in the success—and yet on the edge, the outer rim. I am Mr. Headington, here to take great pride in the financial and artistic success of a cousin; Will is, after all, the most popular and highest paid playwright in London, and the queen's favorite as well. There is no one in our company of the Lord Chamberlain's Men who can both act and even begin to write as he. *He.* He and I.

I admit that *Hamlet* has been, of all Will's works, the most difficult for Will to complete. He has rewritten it three times over the years, and in his roguish fits he has killed it and created it one thousand times. But today it came to full life, a

19

completed, birthed body. And the Globe will hear its first cries of life.

Will is always nervous when any of his plays are performed before the fickle public for the first time, and he has been particularly nervous about *Hamlet*. Will believes it his finest tragedy. Somehow, by the grace of God, he has discovered the very soul of Prince Hamlet of Denmark, and then penetrated that spirit in a way he has never been able to—to pierce the soul of a man, to strike his arrow of imagination into the bull's-eye of a tormented prince's life. And yet he breathes insecurity. Inhale: will the mob in the pit throw vegetable and eggs? Exhale: will they applaud and throw flowers? Inhale: will they walk out? Exhale: will they come back, time and time again? Inhale: will *Hamlet* appear once on the boards, never to be seen again, the playbills littering the streets? Exhale.

A playwright is insane. If he is not insane he is an arrogant fool. But a natural-born poet, with no desire to be a university wit or, God forbid, a lawyer, has no choice: there is no other profession for him. He knows that from birth he has been blessed by God and the muses. And Will has not just eked out a living in the playwright's profession. He is now at the top of his game; now, he triumphs.

And after only nine years. Nine years ago we arrived in London town, determined to succeed in what was then such a new theatrical industry no one except Christopher Marlowe had yet laid claim to its territory. Will has now planted his flag on its beach. To the queen, a favorite. To the people, beloved.

And to a few, hated.

Because he is now the queen's pet, the man with the mystic talent has hundreds of enemies. Robert Greene was the first I remember who loathed my husband. Greene's wild resentment of Will's popularity gave me my first taste of the anger born of envy and classism. I hated his cheap little pamphlets saying Will had stolen all his ideas from university men like himself. Will has told me never to talk about or even mention Greene's name, as Greene, who is now dead, had nothing to recommend him but his slanderous tracts and his envious quill.

Besides, everyone knows, in London theatre plagiarism is the highest form of flattery. Will does not steal; he borrows and betters characters and heroes from English history. How he adores the *Holinshed's Chronicles*. Ovid and Plutarch are there, though I doubt they would complain. Nor any of the others who wrote what he now puffs up and changes or twists and turns into a play. Making large a story once small into a comedy for the ages, or a tragedy so universal that all who scrape together a few pence for a ticket identify themselves therein.

But London is full of small stories and small talents. And from miniature minds, the angry and envious send thoughts of anger: for his large talent, for his size upon the landscape. I can see it so clearly in their fawning handshakes and glasses raised. I can see it on nights like this one, when Will as an actor once again struts on the stage in one of his plays, such as *Hamlet*, which every playwright envies and wishes he had the noble talent to write.

For years Will has worried that no one in the Globe audience will give two pence to see the problems of a Danish prince struggling with insanity and procrastinating about revenge. His opinion is a catastrophe of his nerves. Hamlet is not just a Danish prince; he is an Everyman. Surely, Hamlet's inner struggle is one that all have experienced during the vicissitudes of life.

There is more of Will in this play than in any of his others. The soliloquies we sketched will move the mob and the nobles to tears—I am sure of this. *Hamlet* will be his greatest success. Success: it is what a playwright worships. The sound of laughter, the gasp of fear, the constant clapping, the spike of applause—it is like sex, or air, a necessity to every playwright's soul and body.

This afternoon, as I stepped into that lacquered black coach with the queen's gold crest emblazoned on the doors, I felt such conflicting emotions: the nearness of success left me with the residue of elation, while the knowledge of the jealousy of enemies left me aching for home. *Hamlet* would live for the first time no longer solely in the mind of the playwright, but on the stage, which is another kind of life, a life that only Will can create, with his own magic, his own language. And I am always by his side to listen and help him perfect his characters, songs, dialogue, and soliloquies.

Today, my carriage rides through the filthy, fog-filled streets of London to the suburb of Shoreditch. The trip to the Globe will take us more than half an hour. These crowds that once appalled me now seem familiar; the beggars, the old soldiers home from war, the vagabonds wheeling their carts, the ragamuffins twisting and turning as they chase after each other no longer amaze me. Nor does the black-hooded hangman, his victims like ghosts on the gallows of wood, awaiting the rope that will choke them to death. The cheering crowds excited by death. The innocent eye—mine once but no longer—is offended at every corner.

The executioners lopping off a head, the torturers who delight in pressing the bodies of recusants, those stubborn few Catholics who will not follow the queen into Protestantism. I am always sickened in my stomach by the huge, iron presses, which crush the spine. As the carriage proceeds to the Globe, I cannot help but smell the dog urine, the dung from vagabonds on the streets of Shoreditch, stinking of slop and garbage; I sniff, in disgust, manure, sewage, and dead bodies that have not been swept away to the charnel house.

We pass the huge arena where one hears the screams of the poor bears whose eyeballs are stuck by men in sport. I hear the loud cheers of the citizens of London, whose love for grotesque entertainment finds humor in the stomach-curdling sport of bearbaiting. London may love the theatre, but more than this they love death. It is their way of laughing at their foes. And they laugh most heartily at Shoreditch, a bawdy whorehouse of life and death on the outskirts of London, and yet Shoreditch is a haven for artists, exiles, and the unfortunate misfits who regenerate culture. In Shoreditch, nobles and beggars piss in the same alleys.

Suddenly there rises from this filth the glory, the Globe, a holy octagon in a depraved suburb. Around her buzzes the energy in the hands of pickpockets, or the slick, quick talk of conmen at their vocation, of scoundrels laughing and screaming. The Rose Theatre is nearby, but it is the Globe that casts its tower-shadow on the streets, a promise of better things for the imagination than bearbaiting. The thousands of theatregoers come by ship, horseback, carriage, or foot to worship at this new church of drama.

Mr. Buckman lurches the carriage towards a side street, four blocks from the theatre, and halts the horses by an empty inn. He jumps down from the carriage and, landing miraculously on his feet, motions for me to listen. His eyes are wide, his body full of energy. Signaling for me to be silent, he looks once more down the street in both directions. I put my head next to the carriage window and give him my ear.

The past comes round again. Buckman, I remember, was with us when our son died, and the scene of our son Hamnet's death flashes through my mind. Mr. Buckman, for a moment, proved to be not just a coachman but a consoling and compassionate friend. My heart aches as I remember how the queen, a few years ago, gave us her carriage when she heard the news of Hamnet's sickness from the plague. Her coachman, Buckman, drove us home to see him. On the journey, there was no time or reason to keep up the charade of my being a cousin to Will. And since Buckman stayed for several days, he saw and knew our secret. Headington disappeared.

We could not hide my gender or the sadness of a mother of a dead child. And so Mr. Buckman, the carriage driver, became our close friend, our confidant. He behaved with tact then, and has since been always a gentleman. He always addresses me as Mr. Headington in public, without a hint of performance. Will has said repeatedly, and I agree, that if he weren't a coachman he could have been in Will's company as a great actor.

To distract ourselves momentarily from our grief, we all played cards together—Will, Mr. Buckman, and I. I remember what Mr. Buckman said to Will one night. It was after Hamnet's funeral, at the card table, after the temporary diversion of winning at a trivial sport had worn off, and Will was crying, tears running, his white cheeks drained of their usual ruddy color. Buckman said gently to Will, "We cannot determine the course of human events, for they are beyond us. Accidents of time and chance will always happen. It is not the accidents, but what we shall make of them. You mustn't become angry in your despair, Mr. Shakespeare. The death of your son is one of these accidents. But what you do now will be of your own making; your own courage must carry you through. Be calm. And carry on."

These wise words from a coachman stung our hearts. From that moment, I have considered our carriage driver—with his big red nose, his fat hands, his Cockney accent, and his small cornflower eyes—our friend. Despite the occasional sip or two from his silver flask, a gift from the queen, the coachman has a great deal of dignity. We love him dearly and appreciate his loyalty. We trust him completely.

I must kill those memories. Now the always-composed Mr. Buckman is standing outside my coach, my ear to his lips, as he whispers, "I am not one to bend truth for interest's sake, or for personal gain, my lady. And I do never wish to upset you or Mr. Shakespeare without cause and purpose. And so you may trust that what I speak to you now will prove itself of import."

I bid him go on, my interest piqued.

"The Writer is not exempt from the hatred of normal men. Perhaps indeed it is the opposite. And now I hear the whispers of those whose envy would bid them act upon it. There are those now who speak not of hatred but of action. These are knavish, evil-eyed, swag-bellied men."

I speak to him truth: "There has been blood in my dreams."

"I doubt it not, my lady. I suspect Edmund Tilney, the Master of the Revels, of a murderous intent towards the Writer. He has, you well know, an aristocratic and peevish resentment towards all who write for a living. Although he chooses the plays for the queen, and has helped in selecting actors, he has no friendship with your husband. Tilney? He is a deviant, fool-born murderer. The Writer's success is a threat. Never has one so won the queen. Before the Writer, there was only Tilney. Never has he witnessed one become such a success in London. His job, his position, I dare say his life, seem threatened."

"But what cause have you to assume that he now speaks of...*action?*"

"Yesterday, as he was riding with the queen in this very same carriage, he said that your husband had gotten so much money out of her that he appeared to any outsider to be a spongy sucker. That if anyone other than the Writer had taken so much from the queen he'd be rendered a thief, put in the Tower of London as a scoundrel. He laughed, but it was not a laugh of good humor. Mr. Shakespeare is now the richest man in the theatrical world, and Tilney is jealous, my lady, of your husband's influence with the queen. Your husband has both money and power. This has upset the sour-faced, dim-witted Tilney."

I listen in fear as he continues whispering.

"Tilney would not dare speak so boldly as yesterday, if

he were not already contemplating evil against Mr. Shakespeare. Behind his smile is a doubtful character. Remember that Marlowe was stabbed in the forehead, above the right eye, a difficult position to give a fatal blow. It was no accident, as has been said. This you know. Tilney found him dangerous—an atheist, a powerful playwright, a bawdy, political thinker—and had him killed. He is of a cruel heart, a scoundrel. If he worried about—and acted against—Marlowe, what do you think this toad-spotted, folly-fallen devil will do to your husband?"

A cold wind blows in my face, and I touch Buckman's arm and assure him he has spoken enough. He has. And he has spoken it well. I lean back in the carriage, my heart racing and my breath labored. I hear the long, black whip click on the white horses' backs, hear the clap of carriage wheels—my senses awakened, my mind now recalling all looks, gestures, words from the Master of the Revels. I am afraid I will see him today. And I do not doubt he is greatly duplicitous and capable of worse than his smooth voice and highbrow taste suggest.

Nearly daily we see Tilney. If not at the Globe, at the Blackfriars. But forewarned is forearmed. Tilney is a dangerous man, and though my feminine intuition has always told me thus, I had neglected to follow its voice. Tilney is too important to us. Yes, he has long been rumored to have been directly responsible for the murder of the playwright Kyd, whose *Spanish Tragedy* once made such an impact on Will and myself. Rumored, but never proven. And then Tilney, it has been said, arranged for the death of Marlowe. This was the rumor.

A pattern arises, and its figure fills me with fright: first the murder of Kyd, then the murder of Marlowe. The Master of the Revels has acted before. There is no reason to think he will not again. And with Will, the stakes are much higher, because the queen is besotted by his genius. Now the fool-born Tilney is a sour-faced, nasty-witted enemy.

How lonely I would be without Will—it is my first thought. And how, in those bygone moments—the first time I read Greene's pamphlet, the occasional word of spite from an angry actor overlooked at audition—I wished Will had remained in Stratford-upon-Avon and not waded into the cesspool in which we now swim and bob. Theatre writing is an ugly, bloody sport. And yet it is Will's ecstasy.

The sight of the Globe saves my thoughts, as it often does, from collapsing into despair. A great octagonal miracle of wood the theatre is, with all the seats empty until the afternoon brings thousands of people to fill those seats. Now, all the spectators' pockets are jangling with coins for tickets. Two-penny seats? Three-penny? A pound? Or the best cushions on sale on the stage? The best seats that money can buy? The theatre servants throw me cheerful glances of respect, cousin to the great William Shakespeare.

After showing my ticket and climbing the wooden stairs, I take my seat on the second floor. Sir Walter Raleigh, dressed as usual in his fashionable purple crushed-velvet suit with a spanking white ruff, is waiting for me. The theatre, he tells me, is sold out this afternoon. More than three thousand impatient spectators waiting for *Hamlet* to begin. Feet are stomping, young and old cawing and cheering like baby birds, impatient to be fed. The nobles, sitting beneath us on the stage on pillows, cracking nuts, jabbering with each other, showing off their fashionable clothes and feathers, remind me of peacocks and sparrows who preen and twitter. Mobman and nobleman equal in their excitement for the show.

I thank God the rain is waiting; the afternoon's pleasant weather is a good omen. All the playwrights are sitting together, the custom, but Will has asked me to sit today only with Raleigh because Will had him listen, at our house, to each line read out loud, listen very carefully, so we might pick his brain later on. Raleigh has given us excellent suggestions through *Hamlet*'s many revisions, and excellent support, marveling always at Will's ability to break the rules and write his tragedies with sexual puns and complicated twists of fate that produce the opposite of what the audiences expect. Raleigh has the brain of a rebel and a poet. Will and I not only quote his poetry to each other but we respect his adventurous and unconventional mind.

Sitting at the Globe with Raleigh, I suddenly remember one comment he made at the end of the last act that had influenced Will. When we read out loud the grave-digger scene, towards the end of the play, we asked Raleigh if this comic interlude slowed things down too much before the tragic conclusion. But Raleigh, when he heard Will and me read the scene, clapped his hands and told us that the grave diggers, whose business it is to deal with death in a very matter-of-fact way, are a marvelous touch, a brilliant contrast to the murders and gore that follow their comic moment. Will wanted to scratch the scene, but after hearing Raleigh's praise he wrote them back into the play.

At rehearsals, we both saw and heard how right that touch of comedy worked to bring in the lowest language of the common man before the tragic, high-flown rhetoric of the king. In the end, the grave diggers were brought back from the dead, Yorick living on. All thanks to Raleigh's opinion and taste, which is not the taste of most of the rabbit suckers and hacks who call themselves "playwrights."

This afternoon at the premier of the play, when Hamlet speaks his fourth soliloquy, I do not breathe from its beginning to its end. I do not realize I had stopped my breath, but when he concludes, "To be or not to be?" I gasp loudly, as though emerging from the water after too long below. No heads turn to judge me, since all around me have gasped as well. A breath-taking soliloquy.

I cannot help but take pride in the moment. I suppose that

is why my breath was caught. It was I, not Will, who wrote several lines. He had written something quite different, less melodic, and more complex in another version.

> *To be or not to be; ay, there's the point,*
> *To Die, to sleep, is that all? Ay all:*
> *No, to sleep, to dream, ay marry, there it goes,*
> *For in that dream of death, when we awake,*
> *And born before an everlasting judge,*
> *From whence no passenger ever returned,*
> *The undiscovered country, at whose sight*
> *The happy smile, and accursed damned.*

I didn't like "ay, there's the point." I told him I felt simpler lines would be more

powerful. He listened to me as usual, like a child listening to his mother. At those moments, when he learns something from another, when a truth strikes him from the lipsof someone other than himself, he becomes so vulnerable, so beautifully open to newness. And so the lines were changed. And so I suggested this second version:

> *To be or not to be, that is the question:*
> *Whether 'tis nobler in the mind to suffer*
> *The slings and arrows of outrageous fortune,*
> *Or to take arms against a sea of troubles*
> *And by opposing, end them. To die, to sleep—*
> *No more, and by a sleep to say we end*
> *The heartache and the thousand natural shocks*
> *That flesh is heir to; 'tis a consummation*
> *Devoutly to be wished. To die, to sleep—*
> *To sleep, perchance to dream—ay, there's the rub,*
> *For in that sleep of death what dreams may come,*
> *When we have shuffled off this mortal coil.*

At the intermission, applause. Some of the well-dressed, gossipy spectators on our level walk up and down, laugh, joke, argue, spit, piss, drink, and eat. But many more are thrilled by the incredible dark beauty of Hamlet's words and sit staring at the stage, still absorbing the lines as if they have been transported themselves, for just a moment, to the one undiscovered country of Hamlet's mind.

"To be or not to be? That is the question." Burbage delivers it so movingly that all three thousand spectators have been enthralled, completely silent as the shadows break through the wall of the stage and speak directly to each one of the men and women, both highborn and lowborn, in the audience. What person alive has not asked himself or herself in a moment of human madness, when reality is too much to bear, the same question?

Yes, memory kills all things. There still remains the never-resting mind so that one cannot escape; the past comes back again. Suddenly, memory whisked me from my seat in the theatre, back to meeting Will in Shottery, near Stratford-upon-Avon, for the first time. No longer at the Globe, I am a shy farmer's daughter, miserable and filled with despair. And yet, my fears of Will being murdered seem to me to be a shade pretentious. We are writers and lovers, living in a fabulous lie, and I should laugh at my fears.

Memory: before meeting Will I had often thought of jumping in the waters of Avon and ending my life—I couldn't imagine life as a spinster on a farm without anyone who could read or write or talk to me. These were the suicidal feelings I described to Will when he created the character of Ophelia. When she ended her life as I had thought of doing, I felt so far from her, so far from the darkness that had once been so attractive to me. Now I remembered that desperate feeling I carried around inside of me until I met by some miracle this man they call the Writer. An old maid of twenty-four. What did I know of old? I knew of loneliness, which at the time felt so much like aging. My farm days rushed back into my brain with the pleasant smell of wild lemongrass and succulent apples that grew on the trees of my father's farm.

I was, without wanting to be, enveloped in one of my many epiphanies as I sat with an ear bent to the past while my eyes looked upon the stage. Memories, like fingers plucking the lute, began the strange music of all the covered-up remembrances stored in my head. I suddenly was deaf to the actors speaking and gesturing upon the stage. I heard, instead of soliloquies, the sweet sound of rain on the farm, the searing, sharp sound of scissors during sheep shearing, the sound of the distant bells at Guild Hall, the faint shouts of the quarrelsome drunks ousted from the Boar Inn down the road from my childhood farm, the distant sound of bees in the lavender fields. I am no longer who I am now, but for a few moments, I am who I was then.

I turn back my thoughts to young Anne, the only woman poet of Shottery, writing in the tall, sweet grass, seen by no one, sitting in the field of oxlips, daisies, bees, and buttercups. Anne Hathaway, the secret woman poet who was so isolated in the world of illiterate farm people. The Anne I used to be.

I was not uncomely. I had always heard rumors buzzing like bees in the wax of town gossip that with my long brown hair, pretty face, and thin body, I was one of the most desirable young ladies in Shottery. It was perhaps because I was the only woman for miles around who was educated and was also able to read and write that I couldn't find the right husband. When the simple people of Shottery heard of my unheard-of education, I was seen so strangely.

I was stared at by the townspeople. My mother had taught me to read books at the age of eight and had made me a poet frozen in the world of milk pails, pig troughs, and breeding young women. Being well educated: that was my curse. Now, like any woman with brains and a true soul, I wanted to marry for love. Not for prestige or, worse, for money. But marry whom? None of the young men I knew were educated.

Who were the many male dullards in the village of Shottery that had courted me? The slob of the cobbler's son, whose nose kept running, and he wiped it with his arm so that snot got all over his shirt. He had dirt under his fingernails, and etched into the lines of his hands was the polish from thousands of boot-shines. I never even wanted him to touch me. How could I lie with such a filthy dunce?

The skinny and bearded coffin maker? He smelled of bones and the charnel house, and looked like a corpse himself. Dressed like an undertaker, he was missing many of his brown teeth. I could have never considered bedding him, let alone marrying him.

The pig farmer? He looked like the company he kept: fat and pink. I could have stuck an apple in his mouth and served his head on a plate for the Yuletide holidays. Married men with their drowsy eyes and perverted intentions ran after me when I went shopping every day in the Shottery village market. With my jaunty step, I could tell they fancied me. So sad they seemed, lust burning beneath their skin. But I ran from all of them.

And then, my drunken father, always dressed in the filthiest of farm clothes, cow dung on his shoes, told me one morning that the mayor of nearby Stratford-upon-Avon, his Catholic childhood friend, old man John Shakespeare, was coming to call on him with his young son, Will. I cannot say it sounded promising. In my memory this afternoon, I could hear my father's boozing words buzzing in my ear and me answering him with a slight arrogance, as I believed God had me born in the wrong place, to the wrong parents, at the wrong time. I would much rather have been the Greek poet Sappho, whose poems my mother had read to me in Greek. I would have fled England as she did Greece, to live with other women poets.

But I was not Sappho. I was Anne of Shottery, whose beloved mother had died of a beating from my drunken father. My father hated educated people, especially an educated woman like his daughter, unfit for farmwork, all my talents immeasurable in his language, invisible to his heart and eye.

"Your dead mother did you no favors," he would say. "No favors. Would that you had a man's making."

"Then I shall make myself a man, dress in trousers, and go to London, and there I will have other things to do besides pulling the slippery pink teats of cows or shoveling the stinking dung of horses."

"Keep dreaming, my dear Anne," he said, spraying his alcoholic breath on my face, "and you'll end up like that young woman who threw herself in the Avon last week."

"Being without a man is no reason to despair. Being with a sot would be."

"The devil has plans for you if you don't get married."

"Do you and he talk often?"

"'Tis enough from your tongue!"

"An educated woman now sits on the throne! Soon all the women in England will have an education, and you will be left behind."

"Why are you so peevish, sullen, and sour?" my father asked in his loud, drunken voice. "It is I who will give you a dowry, Anne. It is the golden rule that he who holds the gold rules."

"Keep your dowry," I said, sweeping the barn as he cawed like a blackbird in my ear.

He laughed at my idea to run away from the provinces. Of course I would miss the smell of hay, the geese, the cows, and the beloved horses that had become my only family, but I would never miss him. He kept talking, unaware of how much I detested him, how much I loathed his ideas about everything, especially women. The large, black-and-white-dappled cows, with their long-lashed bovine eyes, swatted flies with their tails and stared at me with their dumb humanity. 'Tis true. I loved animals more than people.

"You're scornful of the eyes of every farmer who desires you."

"I have not only a body but a mind. I am a poet and shall marry one."

"What kind of mind can a woman have? You sound just like your mother."

I *was* just like my mother. My mother, whom he beat like an animal until she died. He would not beat me further. I soon would be gone.

Wishing I could sweep away the horror of my life into the dust of another, better world, I prepared the house for our guests. I pulled several lace slips over my long legs and let my blouse stay open at the top so I could see the cleavage of my breasts. I looked in the mirror. I saw a face that, I had been told, was extraordinarily pretty, and I saw how large and blue my eyes were, how fair my skin, and how small my nose.

I laughed to myself because, wearing new perfume oil I had bought at a fair, I had a fantasy of seducing the young son of the mayor of Stratford, if for no other reason than because my father mumbled drunkenly that William was crazy and a poet. He felt sorry for his old friend John Shakespeare, cursed by God to have a dreamer, not a glover, as his oldest son. It was rumored that John Shakespeare's son was a genius and recited poetry in Latin.

I didn't listen to my father's drunken drivel. Before Will and Master John Shakespeare arrived, I ran behind our farm and threw myself on fields of sweet-smelling grass. I loved wildflowers. Near our farm in Shottery, you could walk to the forest of Arden and what I called the "fields of heaven." Lady's smock herbs were everywhere, along with Jack-in-the-hedge mustard plants. Fragrant wild mignonettes, sweet violets, and common rockrose with huge yellow flowers grew next to bright blue cornflowers. I walked through the fields of common mallows, wood sorrels, and touch-me-nots. The wildflowers were tall plants; many of them were self-pollinated, while others, when you touched them, would separate their valves and coil inward, thus violently ejecting mottled brown seeds. They seemed so allusive, these flowers, always meaning more than themselves. And I constantly wrote about them.

Paper was expensive, but I had a small amount of money left to me by my mother, and I always spent it on paper. I carried a secret notebook wrapped carefully in a beautiful, soft leather bag that hung on a strap around my neck, along with a pot of ink and a quill. That bag my late mother had given me, along with dozens of sheets of precious paper, when she showed me how, as a child, to paint with words. That morning I sat in the field of tall golden lilies, hidden from the world, a lonely girl poet, nearly a woman, scribbling this poem:

> *I have made love to the yellow lilies,*
> *Turned my face against their cool skin*
> *Led my own lips and eyes to their stamens*
> *Cried to see anything as bright*
> *As these golden lilies.*
> *How I look for them*
> *There are people who do not explore the inside*
> *Of flowers, kissing them,*
> *Resting their own tongues on their petals,*
> *I must tell them.*
> *Where will I begin?*
> *I love*
> *Earth violently and vegetables,*
> *Stars and all things that will not break,*
> *My hair smells of melons, marl, jasmine.*

When I wrote, I was in ecstasy. I read the lines aloud. The Shottery church bells chimed twelve o'clock, bringing me back to the earth, back to my body, and more than a little sorry to return. I put my poem in my leather pouch, and touched lovingly the feather of my quill that came from the swans near our property. My mother had shown me how to cut and forge quills with a sharp knife. Quills from swans remain my favorites. They carry the gift of flight.

"Who wrote those lines?" he asked.

"I did," I said.

He spoke first. And from nowhere. From the grass, I thought. From the wind? After a late morning alone, I thought the voice from the sun, the trees. I turned. And there he stood. Young, tall, slim, with long black hair and large brown eyes. He looked at me directly, into my blue eyes.

"You are a poet," Will said when we met. Not a question, but a statement.

He smiled, without pitying me. That was his opening line. His entrance to the stage of my life.

"Yes."

"Show me another poem," he quietly commanded. Despite his young age, he had a rich voice and a deeply masculine attractiveness. Although paper was so expensive, I tore a page out of my notebook and gave it to him immediately. I had never done such before. He took my hand and kissed it before reading aloud my poem in his mellifluous voice:

I shall meet you at the instant of rebirth.
In the green leaves
Dripping with the sweat of our skin.

You have been lonely too,
Inside the salt weeds,
Under the red leaves
Many mornings
Of my life

36

Have I been sleeping
Under the oak trees,
My veins splayed
Like the veins of leaves,
Reaching beyond me
And caught in the air
For I have always
Wanted to be born, to be
Reborn each morning,
And in that beginning
I find my own meaning.
What can I say?
What shall I tell you
When I meet you for the first time?
We will meet
Face to face
In the great, burning,
New-leaf beginning,
The first
Red-leaf
Moment of our lives

After finishing, he stood silent, smiling. Then he looked at me—the way he looked at me when we were rewriting Hamlet's soliloquy—with those open eyes, and said, "It is good." We were immediately on fire.

We made love in the forest of Arden, the forest Will's maternal ancestors once walked when in generations past the Arden family owned the land. It was a moment of return and beginning. There we were. We kissed. Then Will stepped away and smiled.

We had consummated our mutual attraction in a whirl of lust. His teeth, I noticed, were very white, and he had a few early crinkles around his dark, almond-shaped eyes, which drew me into his soul. We lay back, the grass for our pillow. Naked, he was now Adam to my Eve, we in our own Garden of Eden.

We babbled to each other for hours. Words replaced kisses, coming as hastily to both of us. We were dizzied by each other.

I remember so well that warm summer day. Will told me he was sixteen. I was already twenty-four. But it didn't seem to matter to him at all. "We were both born rebels, Anne. Time is only a word; nothing matters but life, and we're equal in that, so you must be my wife."

He laughed at his own rhyming of our future. Even then he was a delighted child-man for whom rhyme was a game he often played during any moment of serious thought.

"We must leave Stratford," Will said. "I refuse to remain locked in the stocks of our genealogy."

Memory stopped. And now I am back at the Globe with Burbage, who spills out with a perfect pitch the words that Will, in another of his moments of brilliance, had written for *Hamlet*:

> *Oh, what a rogue and peasant slave am I!*
> *Is it not monstrous that this player here,*
> *But in a fiction, in a dream of passion,*
> *Could force his soul so to his own conceit*
> *That from her working all his visage waned,*
> *Tears in his eyes, distraction in 's aspect,*
> *A broken voice, and his whole function suiting*
> *With forms to his conceit? And all for nothing!*
> *For Hecuba!*
> *What's Hecuba to him, or he to Hecuba,*
> *That he should weep for her? What would he do*
> *Had he the motive and the cue for passion*
> *That I have? He would drown the stage with tears,*
> *And cleave the general ear with horrid speech,*

Make mad the guilty and appall the free.
Confound the ignorant, and amaze indeed
The very faculties of eyes and ears.
Yet I,
A dull and muddy-mettled rascal, peak
Like John-a-dreams, unpregnant of my cause,
And can say nothing—no, not for a king,
Upon whose property and most dear life
A damned defeat was made. Am I a coward?
Who calls me a villain, breaks my pate across,
Plucks off my beard and blows it in my face,
Tweaks me by the nose, gives me the lie i'th'throat
As deep as to the lungs? Who does me this?
Ha, 'swounds, I should take it; for it cannot be
But I am pigeon-livered and lack gall
To make oppression bitter, or ere this
I should ha' fatted all the region kites
With this slave's offal. Bloody, bawdy villain!
Remorseless, treacherous, lecherous, kindless villain!
Oh, vengeance!
Why, what an ass am I! This is most brave,
That I, the son of a dear father murdered,
Prompted to my revenge by heaven and hell,
Must like a whore unpack my heart with words
And fall a-cursing like a very drab,
A scullion! Fie upon't! Foh!

When the speech ends there is deafening applause. Raleigh shouting. The nobles jumping from their seats. I am caught between the past and the now; lingering, these memories of the past glide into the present—this fragile wheel of time. The letters that Will wrote to me from the north, when I was that lonely young woman in love with him. And now him there, bowing, the energy of the Globe drawn to him, who held it fast.

What eyes look to Will as the ghost with murder in their line?

I recall a long letter Will had written to me from the north, where for a time he had gone to tutor Lord Houghton's children: "As far as I can see, the only good thing you can say about the princes and nobles who masturbate and play with their penises in public is that they use the excess of their money to patronize drama and make the art of comedy and tragedy happen. Never before have there been intelligent plays written as there are now under Queen Elizabeth. The gossip up north is that all the poets with talent are drawn like a magnet to London, and poetry is flowering like a new art form. I want us to go to London one day when we feel we are ready."

I remember kissing the letter, putting it near my breast, and carrying it with me in my bodice. It was delivered to me by a special messenger from Lincolnshire, from the huge, secretly Catholic estate of Lord Houghton. Will's teacher, from the King's School in Stratford-upon-Avon, had the ear of Lord Houghton and had found Will, a brilliant young man with deep Catholic roots, as a history tutor for his children. Will left for his first and last tutoring employment.

Will wrote in his first letter to me from Lincolnshire, "Acting is sort of war. To be a player in Lord Houghton's company is extremely competitive, and all the players are envious of each other, jostling for the best part. Each actor collaborates on the writing of plays; soon 'twas obvious to me that my talent as a writer outshone that of all the other players. Because of this, I am in demand, even here, to appear often in more plays."

Memory again swivels in my mind. I am no longer celebrating *Hamlet*. I am young Anne, waiting every day for another letter to arrive by messenger, for news from the north. Will wrote in another letter, "We are all nervous when we try out for different parts. It is up to Lord Houghton to decide who he thinks best fits the part. This gives him a great deal of power, which makes me think it is why he supports an acting company in the first place. As a patron he can control the destiny of human beings, even if they are only actors and playwrights. Power is art—above it, through it, around it. To have your own plays is to be a king."

In the next letter to me, so precious, he wrote, "Actors are no longer vagabonds, but trained servants whose vocal and physical accomplishment are much prized by wealthy patrons, hungry for protecting their prestige."

Memory stopped. I am floating back to the present. The audience is shouting, except for the nobles, who are much too snobbish to show their enthusiasm in a vulgar way but applaud with their gloved hands softly as they rise from their pillows on the stage to stand up. One can sense a change even in them, a new, subtle vigor in their clapping, stunned as they are by the power of the stage and the language.

I scream too—unladylike and undignified, but what was I but an un-lady? With the quirks of my help, Will has written a masterpiece. I must remember to gather the sides from the actors tomorrow, lest they lose them and we have no means to collect them. Will believed that no script of a play should be allowed to circulate, lest some playwright steal the idea or even the words or claim the play as his own. Also, Will doesn't want to spend the extra money on scripts. Will always cares about the cost of everything. He is nothing but frugal.

As an actor, Will is glorious as the ghost, and frightful. Edward Alleyn is excellent as Claudius. When the play is over, the actors dance a jig. The jig was created to bring us back to reality: the play was just a play. Real life begins again. The memory of the jig sings, "It's only make believe. Cry no more."

And if real life is more terrifying still? And if tragedy awaits on the doorstep just as it slithered cross the stage?

Raleigh and I ride together to the Mermaid Tavern, Buckman pushing the queen's prancing white horses through the mob. Staring out the carriage window, feigning good spirits as I feign a male personage, I think of loss. I suddenly recall, with untold sadness, the one morning far ago, while Will was writing *Hamlet*, when we heard a terrifying knock on the door. Then another. I would not answer, as Will was working—we had told ourselves when he entered a productive session that I would not allow him to be disturbed, "not even if it's the queen herself." The knocking persisted. Shouts from the street. And the pounding, pounding. God, I still recall it. It rattled the house, and my heart. Something in its urgency.

Mr. Buckman stood at the door in the rain. His coat was soaked, he was wet and chilled. But his mournful look was of another source. He was in tears.

"Come in," I said, "where it's dry, and have some sherry."

"Oh no, Mr. Headington. Thank you." He then very politely addressed my husband. "The queen has sad news, sir. It seems that the plague has broken out in your town of Stratford-upon-Avon. Many have died, sir. And your son…," he paused, "…I'm afraid your only son has fallen ill."

The woolen cloak by the door was not on my back when I ran to the carriage. Will carried it behind me, he told me later, shouting for me to put it on. I painfully recall this moment. We left immediately, without even packing any clothes. On the way, we spoke little. We were desperate to see Hamnet, pausing not to stop at the inn at Oxford. The dangerous and slippery roads I did not notice; they could not keep us from riding on.

When we arrived, Mary Shakespeare's eyes—they were as I'd never seen them—were swollen with red bags. She opened the door with John behind her. He could not lift his eyes from the floor.

She spoke softly what I've never written till now. I have only allowed her to say it again in my mind, and again and again. "Too late." That is all she said. "Too late." It is a terrible phrase, too short to mean so much. And then I heard only his name. Will was calling it, as though Hamnet were late for chores, as though he'd turn the corner in a moment with a tale of lizards and trees or a story he'd been thinking of. Hamnet, my son, was dead. That was my only thought.

Will called out his name in grief.

I am told I went directly to the kitchen to prepare a meal. I do not recall this. I recall not the weeping of Will, the touch of Mary's hand on my arm. They have told me the house was loud in the following days—the family, the church elders, the food from hither and yon, the packages of care. I do not recall this either. I recall only the terrible silence of the house, the absence of a young boy's voice, the missing of the steps upon the floor. Our son. Dead. The girls had gone off to grieve in the woods by themselves.

Will was not there. His body, yes. But not else. His whole existence was wrapped up in his love for his only son. Hamnet his only heir, and his claim to a certain immortality of name. Soon, he later said, he too thought only of silence, of a name gone from the world.

"Never, never, never, never, never..."

These words rang in my ears like the chimes of doom. Will said them more than any others—the words that are the presence of absence. He said them as John Shakespeare reminded him that he would meet Hamnet in paradise. He said them when the elders assured him he would heal. He said them when I told him we could still have another child. He said them to himself. When the silence needed a word for itself, he gave them this nothingness.

We saw our son laid out in the bed. His color had faded. Dead for a day, and his face was already chalky white. The plague we knew of, but as a distant tragedy. Hamnet, just a few days ago, was alive, playing in the garden with his grandfather. Suddenly the hated disease had struck him down. The

Protestant ceremony of burial was to take place the next morning—not even a Catholic burial for our son. No monks at prayer. No alms. Not even last rites. Will could not speak. Silence was now his religion.

Only later, only often: "Would that I had died instead of him."

White crosses in the churchyard and many more coffins lowered into the earth. My own father had passed away without Catholic rites, but he was too drunk when he died to know the difference. I never felt that I loved him because of how cruel he had been to my mother, so his fate in the afterlife did not disturb me. But Hamnet...he was the love of my life. For our loving family to have the only male heir go into the ground without the Mass, last rites, and the right blessing was an unspeakable sadness. There were no last rites with a Protestant priest. This troubled Will profoundly.

I scribbled a death song in my notebook.

It hurts like a terrible slap,
These frightening words of good-bye,
And it shatters my world,
Where you no longer are,
You were too young to die.
I will see you always in the eye of my heart,
I will hear your voice in the ear of my soul,
I will trace your face on a path of the sun
To the bells of my own death toll.
It hurts like a terrible slap
These frightening words of good-bye
And it shatters my world, where you no longer are
You were too young to die.

After the Protestant funeral, Will was in despair; all the things he enjoyed—reading, planting in the garden, chatting, drinking sherry with our neighbors the Sadlers, horseback riding—were rejected. Silence partnered with stillness. His sister, whom he loved, had died when she was seven. Hamnet now departs. The two losses merged: the child and the adult. Without a Catholic funeral, our son—his soul may always linger in that awful half place, that dark purgatory.

"Speak to no one about this when we return to London," Will said to me in a quiet but firm voice. How many times did he say this? "I do not want to be pitied. Sympathy from others is nothing but poison to me. I am not Ben Jonson—he writes many sorrowful laments about the death of his child, always sharing his personal tragedies with all of London. I prefer—"

"Silence," I said.

He did not answer.

Once we were back in London, we fell into our usual patterns of dinners with the queen, who seemed infatuated with Will; nights in the taverns talking theatre gossip; cooking; shopping in the large food markets; preproduction on plays that had to be cast; scenery production and costumes and advertising with posters that I devised myself because I had a flair for design. Under all the gaiety, Will was in silent despair. He often stared at me, his eyes full of tears.

Will began writing comedies again to forget his suffering, studying clowning and pratfalls with his friend and teacher, Kempe the clown. Will finished *Love's Labour's Lost* and *The Merry Wives of Windsor*, which gave birth to my favorite character, the bombastic and witty Falstaff. He was a corpulent and clever clown. We both loved him and talked as though he were a common friend. As though we'd drink with him at the Mermaid. Falstaff was inspired not only from Marlowe but by Will's enemy, the pompous Master Oldcastle, who had arrested Will when he was a youth for poaching deer on Oldcastle's private property with other schoolboys. Falstaff was originally called Oldcastle, but the family threatened to sue Will because the character was vulgar and not at all flattering to Oldcastle. So we renamed him Falstaff. Falstaff? Hamlet? They all belong to Will's imagination before they are born onstage.

Still, the writing of *Hamlet* was always on Will's mind. Soon he went back to writing the tragedy with a vengeance. It was almost as if this play—in which Hamlet takes revenge on his uncle Claudius, who killed Hamlet's father—was a way for Will to take revenge on the plague that had killed Hamnet and taken him from us forever. He fought with an invisible enemy, and fought only with imagination and ink. He fought death.

Hamlet was healing the death of Hamnet; it was a vessel into which Will could pour the wine of anger that tormented him. The universal system of life and death was going to be questioned in this tragedy, the course of nature reversed. "Time is out of joint."

I sat with him, helping him ready the ink and the quills for the next writing session, and waited patiently for him to recommence work. All revenge plays were written in a certain pattern, but *Hamlet* broke the rules. Will does love to break rules. Instead of going directly to the gory end, he held back the final tragedy with the humor of the grave-digger scene, a cynical contrast to Hamlet's melancholy, his tragedy belittled by the grave diggers, to whom revenge or death means only work. Everyone, sooner or later, it says, goes into the grave.

Melancholy meets joy as I witness the amazing reception of Will's great new tragedy. Such is the power of Will's imagination that he has conjured from a twelfth-century Danish story written by Saxo Grammaticus, translated by our bookseller friend Richard Field, this tale of a Danish prince seeking revenge. Hamnet is dead, but *Hamlet* remains. In many odd ways *Hamlet* is the ghost of our dead son. Hamnet buried, *Hamlet* rising immortal. Such is the power of art to heal and to remain, like air, in the universe, and for words to float, like clouds in the universal blue silence.

The large, yellow playbills announcing *Hamlet* are attached to tavern doors and houses all over town. A few hours ago, they triggered anxiety and anticipation. Now they seem to join in celebration with the rest of London, singing my husband's praises among the hazards of the world. His name, in full, is everywhere the eye can see.

As I step down from the carriage with Sir Walter Raleigh beside me, he says, "Your cousin Will is a man of shining luck. In less than a dozen years, he has sculpted the Lord Chamberlain's Men into the best company in all of England and has worked his magic, stuffing poetry into prose the way one stuffs a goose. His work on this night was a glorious feast."

Everyone at the Mermaid Tavern greets us with high spirits and toasts to my famous "cousin," who will soon be joining us. I know it will take him much time to remove his makeup and costume and brief the other players on their parts in preparation for tomorrow's rehearsal. Still, I watch the tavern door in despair, trying to appear joyful, while fearing always that he will not be the next one through.

To see the Mermaid is to see London in a room. Dominated by its large oak bar, it is the home of wits, playwrights, craftsmen, and nobles. Whiskey washes away day as it washes clean the class system. On any given night you can see Francis Bacon, the proficient writer in many genres and a maker of cheap poems, stuffing his face with pickled herrings and cheap Rhenish wine. One can hear the laughter of W.H., that silly noble William Herbert, who adores Will's sonnets. The chatter of regulars: Thomas Nashe, Henry Wriothesley, the young Earl of Southampton, and another patron, Thomas Lodge. Not only can you find tipsy patrons of the arts, but gaggles of playwrights such as Michael Drayton, Chapman, Ben Jonson, Middleton, John Donne, Raleigh, the Earl of Oxford, Dekker, Beaumont,

Fletcher, Kempe the clown, as well as actors such as Alleyn and Burbage, who will turn up soon.

And there among them all is the ghost of Marlowe.

How he used to drink here until he could not walk, and then would pick a brawl with anyone who annoyed him, daring them to pummel his face.

A hundred people mull in the Mermaid's pit, and each knows each. The crowd of shadows, set designers, wig makers, costume makers, playwrights, poets, nobles—also travelers and explorers, telling tales of the New World. It is as if the Mermaid is the center of the universe. For us it is.

And those beautiful barmaids, whose pink breasts show through their peasant bodices, who clean up vomit and serve the wine and shoot whiskey out of spigots. The tavern is a second home, its wooden tables and stools, barking dogs, patrons, and whores the furniture of our life. The talk is always of the stage, of plays, of us who are lucky enough to be alive and at the center of inebriated Elizabethan London.

Raleigh, unlike most of the poets, is not at all jealous of Will's success. He is wealthy, witty, daring, and adventurous in his own right. Perhaps because the queen counted him a daring explorer and a pleasant sonneteer long before Will and I came to London, there is not in him the livid anger displayed by many men over the fact that it is Will, and not them, who now stands aloft in London.

The Mermaid Tavern is lit with more than the usual number of candles, and I see a feast laid out upon the bar. All kinds of hams, Stilton cheese, cheddar cheese, black bread, and fruits from the New World are being devoured by the guests who have already arrived. The food and the drink were given freely by Lord Chamberlain, and I felt in good spirits, letting the singing and laughter lift me as the ale lifted the wits in whose midst I stood. Dekker ran up to me and congratulated me on my cousin's play. Already a bit drunk, he nearly knocked me over.

"Stay steady now, Arthur! And tell me your cousin has not brilliantly reworked *The Spanish Tragedy*!"

Just then a waitress with a low-cut bodice walked by with a tray of drinks from which I helped myself to a glass of port. She passed so close to me that her hips rubbed against mine while she held the tray. I turned at once to Dekker, who, already drunk on whiskey, could not see her inflamed desire. So comic it was, and I no one to laugh with.

"Arthur! Listen! *Hamlet* has a revenge plot!" Dekker said as he kept stumbling all over me, quite inebriated. "And so does the *Spanish Tragedy*. *Hamlet* has a ghost; so does the *Spanish Tragedy*. *Hamlet* has a drama staged by an avenger— and listen!—so does the *Spanish Tragedy*! *Hamlet* has a philo- sophical concern with the afterlife—" he could barely say it—"and again, so does the *Spanish Tragedy*. *Hamlet* has episodes of violence culminating in a murder for revenge...." He was really tipsy now.

"So does the *Spanish Tragedy*," I interrupted, laughing. "So what?"

"Well, other than that, there are no similarities," Dekker said sarcastically. "So you see Will has lifted his play directly from Kyd!" He finished dramatically, and looked around for applause, like an actor finishing a soliloquy. No hands clapped.

I spoke up. "There is the slightest of difference. *Hamlet* holds great poetry and the *Spanish Tragedy* holds none. It is a small variation that makes Will Shakespeare a genius and Kyd a hack. Quite a difference."

I had made a public fool of Dekker. Now came the hands applauding, and Dekker walked away, having forgotten likely what it was he wanted to say. But I knew: he felt Will a thief, a lifter of lines and stories. But the deeper point he wanted to make I felt deeper still: that Will deserved not the place he had won. I fear, with reason, that Dekker would be only too happy to slip poison into Will's glass of sherry. I will make sure Will stands away from Dekker.

Some of the actors have arrived from the Globe. They form a circle near the great Burbage. Burbage, slightly tipsy, speaks to the clown Robert Armin, who congratulates him on his performance as Hamlet. Burbage was as tall as Armin is short, and the two have the most difficult time hearing each other. So much singing, cheering, screaming, and drinking.

"What a party this is!" says the handsome Edward Alleyn, who had been cajoled by Will to play one of the grave diggers as well as Claudius. "I have had seven glasses of port and have not paid for one!" Alleyn was soon surrounded by a gaggle of overrouged whores.

As Burbage and I drank together, I observed Philip Henslowe, the red-nosed, wealthy theatre owner, talking to a circle of ladies and ambassadors of foreign countries who wore magnificent, bright brocade clothes covered with jewels, now slumming at the Mermaid Tavern. Many noblemen who had time on their hands attended all the performances at the Globe, and then attended the performance parties as guests of Lord Chamberlain. The parties, I often thought, were the only reason they went to the theatre. The upper crust of society mixed with the lower crust of actors and playwrights; the Mermaid is the only place in all of London where every level of society, from groundlings to nobles, meet and drink together. Here at the Mermaid, the class of each person floats away with the whiskey.

Suddenly I saw the dramatic entry of that pompous fool Tilney, his head tilted back in laughter and his arm around the waist of a whore he had invited from a Shoreditch brothel. I shivered. He glanced my way, nodded, and I returned the distant greeting. Buckman's words whispered in my mind: "There are those now who speak not of hatred, but of action."

Tilney is gatekeeper—there is no dispute—of every

playwright's career. He holds their destiny in his sullied little fingers, as the queen never appears at the public theatres, and Tilney decides the plays that come to her. Once she has seen a play and approves, only then may it appear "in rehearsal" at the Globe.

And Tilney is always by the queen's side, drinking deeply of that power. Tilney was, as usual, dressed fashionably. He wore a pink-velvet jerkin and a green-velvet blouse with a white ruff. I saw cruelty in his false smile. I moved away, towards Beaumont and Fletcher, the two as inseparable as twins, and dressed, as always, alike.

"Where is wondrous Will?" Beaumont asked.

"Yes, where wondrous whimsical Will?" echoed Fletcher.

"He'll be here shortly," I answered. "And I'm sure you'll be his first companions."

"We shall hope!" they answered in unison.

At that moment Will entered the Mermaid, as triumphant as a homeward-bound hero in his blue-velvet suit, carrying his dag pistol and wearing his huge smile, which could charm, as Alexander's, an empire. He hopped upon a table, stole a glass from Dekker's hand, and raised it high.

"To the shadows who danced upon the lighted stage—"

A roar of applause.

"To the musicians—"

A roar once more.

"The stagehands—"

A roar, a shout.

"And to the Lord Chamberlain himself—"

Great applause.

"And most of all, to the barman, whose magic milk will carry us to Heaven or to Hell!"

Burbage interrupted, his hand on Will's knee.

"And to the Writer, who makes a new world for those of us who tire of the old!"

The Tavern erupted in applause, and Will's eyes met mine.

I swear to highest heaven, I do love no one more.

Will joined our circle and placed his hand upon my back, and I saw it plainly— his joy mixed with sorrow. He was thinking as I was: *Hamlet* is Will's greatest moment, and yet beside him Marlowe is not standing.

No, right now Ben Jonson is at Will's side, the most self-opinionated and self-advertising of all the playwrights, and yet a dear, good friend of my husband's—and a glorious gossip. Only God's ears hear more than his. But he is, in my eyes, the opposite of Marlowe, poor fellow, who never promoted his reputation. Jonson is much like Will; he did not go to university, is self-educated, and too has lost his only son. Because of all these things we feel a common bond with him. But the connection can only be drawn so taut. Will has loved only one person in London, has only wept for the loss of one other: Christopher Marlowe. Will thinks Marlowe's death too sudden, despite a life that invited such an end, and there are days we speak of him as though he walked with us still. Will does sometimes agree with me that Marlowe was murdered, and that perhaps it was a conspiracy that swept his life away. First Kyd, the queen's favorite. Then Marlowe. And now?

Again my memory runs back—I am living always in two places—more than ten years ago when we came to London and watched in wonder Marlowe's *Tamburlaine the Great*. It was 1590. Marlowe had been very important to us back then. His *Tamburlaine* was the first written play either of us experienced on a stage. And what an experience it was.

I remember that when we first arrived, two provincials in London, with an eagerness a child could not rival, our life had one object: the theatre. We had, of course, never been to a playhouse. Marlowe's new drama was playing at the Globe. I remember when first we stepped into the Globe's wooden womb, how shocked we were to see its size—a huge octagonal wooden building with a thatched roof and hundreds of people pushing each other, almost to death, to get inside.

The open-air theatre was jammed with every kind of sweating man and woman you could imagine, all making such noise that we could hardly hear our voices. There were old people, poor people, rich people, and rowdy drunks, all stomping their feet for the play to begin.

The odors of the Globe suffocated us. It smelled of rank human smells—sweat, vegetables, eggs, and cheap food and drink—but we cared not. It was as though we had entered the belly of existence: humanity was here and nowhere else. The spectators came to shed their lives like old shoes and enter into the slippers of those on stage. They were the same Londoners who went to the arenas for bearbaiting; now they came to see theatrical presentations and to experience the thrill of life and death. With Marlowe they were not disappointed.

Marlowe's brilliance blinded us, struck us dumb. His musical language we never had heard before—he was a master of English speech. The effect on us was immediate and profound. We sat spellbound in our seats as the players spoke the tongue Marlowe had created, a new music from the most beautiful flourishes in the English language.

All the dramas that we had seen—the religious shows and mystery plays back in Stratford or Coventry—had been visual, but Marlowe changed all. He introduced a human voice, the voice of Tamburlaine, a hero and a monster of ambition. He excited the audience with his thumping rhythms. His was a new voice, and I could see that Will was already working in his mind to create iambic pentameter lines of his own, as Marlowe did. The musicality of the verse shocked his ears as it shocked my own.

I hold the Fate bound fast in iron chains,
And with my hand turn Fortune's wheel about;
And sooner shall the sun fall from his sphere

Than Tamburlaine be slain or overcome.

I remember, at that moment so long ago, Will looking at me, his eyes all openness: "Before hearing Marlowe's verse I knew nothing. Now I know everything."

Marlowe's *Tamburlaine the Great* concentrated the world's ambition into one character. He was grotesque, full of savage brutality. Tamburlaine's world was a mad world where order broke down and all strove to be like him, a hero cruel but magnificent, with unstoppable grandeur, the embodiment of Herculean power. Like a god, Tamburlaine did whatever he wanted. Born a poor Scythian shepherd, he dreamed "to march in glory through Persepolis."

As we watched him, that became the dream of every spectator. We all identified with this giant, Tamburlaine, whose wish was to parade his power. He was a lovable monster, dizzy-eyed with ambition. I must admit that in Tamburlaine's character I recognized none other than Queen Elizabeth.

When the spectacle was finished, we went to the actor's exit at the back of the stage to introduce ourselves to Edward Alleyn, who had played Tamburlaine.

Will was unabashed: "You are a great actor, Master Alleyn. My cousin and I would like to invite you to our home and perhaps share in the wisdom of your art. We should be honored by your company."

Alleyn was flattered by Will, and obviously taken. What actor does not crave adoration?

As we were walking away, Will commented, "He is the finest actor who ever lived and probably the handsomest man as well."

"Oh, I had not noticed. Only that he's quite tall," I replied. Though in fact I had noticed him indeed. But I desired not to let Will know I noticed. Will was not fond of me praising any actor but himself.

Will chuckled. "Yes! He is an oak tree in a forest of fools."

My mind was still spinning from the play. That night we spoke of the magical spell that *Tamburlaine the Great* cast upon us. In bed, I told Will, "You too can write history plays, but you needn't write about the exotic East. Consider *Holinshed's Chronicles*— would it not be brilliance to write of England's history! Plays of the troubled fifteenth-century reign of, say, King Henry VI? Begin with a historical epic, like Marlowe, but make it an English epic, a bloody and vivid account of the troubles that preceded the order brought by the Tudors. England's own past will capture the interest of the audience, and especially of the mob. It will interest the queen, I am sure, who loves her own country's history."

"And my characters—they shall not be only heroes, but mortals, the vulnerable," Will said. "Mortals who sit in the audience, reflected in the looking glass of my histories."

I added to this thought by saying, "Your history plays will be all about little vicious people who surround kings, not just great Tamburlaines."

We prattled all night about the harlots and heroes of English history who Will, with his talent, could bring to life for the first time on the English stage.

The next week Will and I were drinking ale together at the Mermaid Tavern, engaged in conversation with Kempe, the clown, when a thin and rather handsome red-haired fellow, about Will's age, with a pockmarked face and a clumsy gait, pushed his drunken way over to our table and heavily placed a hand upon its top, shaking our drinks. He spoke to us belligerently. It was he: the famous Christopher Marlowe.

"So you are the new playwright in town—you who aims to take up arms against this Marlowe?" he said. I sat drinking and played my part of Will's male cousin to deceptive perfection. I remained silent but my eyes were filled with wonder.

"I am an actor"—Will took the tone of the innocent—"and playwright from Stratford-upon-Avon, and this," he gestured towards me, "my cousin Arthur Headington, who serves me well. Please sit down. It would be an honor to have you join us." Will completely ignored Marlowe's hostility. "I stand in admiration of you, and I hope with a whole heart that we may be friends. You, Marlowe, are a genius, and I hope you mind not that I'm stealing all your ideas about history plays and writing my own. I only do battle with the best."

Marlowe's furrowed brow relaxed, and he shouted a great throaty laugh across our table. "Steal, my Shakespeare, as much as you want! Competitors should not be friends." He paused, and leaned in towards us. "But to hell with that!" He sat down to join us with a clumsy laugh and slapped me so hard I nearly lost my breath. "Let me buy you both drinks. There's nothing I like better than a good enemy"—I looked at Will, who looked back, his eyes twinkling—"whom I can raise a glass with!"

That moment, I could tell, was the beginning of a great friendship between two horn-mad geniuses.

"So you're writing history plays about England, Shakespeare? Bravo! Now I plan to do the same myself and I'll steal from you. Perhaps we can borrow stories and swipe words from one another, and I can copy you the way you have copied me." Marlowe laughed. "Then we shall both be thieves!"

We soon found out that Will and Marlowe were the same age, Will being two months older. They also shared the same lowly origins. Marlowe's father was a cobbler, a huge strike against him in class-conscious England. Despite his poor origins and upbringing, Marlowe had managed to go to Corpus Christi College at Cambridge at the very young age of thirteen. Thus he hung a few rungs higher on the ladder as a university wit than Will. Isn't it odd how a university education can turn a rabbit sucker into a gentleman? I'm afraid 'twill always be true.

Everything in London, I soon realized, has to do with social class. There is a direct order of things, the entire world of English society a hierarchy. The social elite live in a mannered world of deference, bowing, kneeling, doffing hats, curtsying, and cringing before those higher than oneself. This is, in an odd way, mirrored by the world of theatre. All the playwrights are social climbers. Each wants to scale the ladder and then, as it were, hide the ladder. And more than anything, everyone wants the ear of the queen.

Marlowe was the king of the counterworld of theatre for two reasons. One: his great success. The other: he had once been a spy for the queen in France and had traveled all over Europe on her command to uncover plots by Catholics against her Protestant reign in England. This gave him a certain notorious glamour that Will didn't have as a married man, a father, and an unknown scribbler. No one was exactly sure how Marlowe had become a well-paid spy for the queen—his courage, ambition, education, or affinity for danger perhaps. He was, as many called him—but Will first—the "Merry wanderer of the night." One night, Christopher wrote a song about his life. He was drunk with ale and friendship, and he laughingly sang to both of us.

As a clever success in London's excess
I went through the upper-class follies
What was deep inside—I thought I could hide
Secretly getting my jollies—
I decided to come out at this time of my life
I'm really loose-wristed—and who needs a wife?
So don't shed a tear
I'm quare, my dear
Sing Hey nonny non hey nonny non hey nonny nay
Sing Hey nonny non hey nonny non nay.

Is every playwright, except Marlowe, a Brutus pretending to be Caesar's best friend while holding a sharpened knife under his cloak? Greene accused Will openly of being a fake, but what of those who envy Will's popularity, his talent, his success, his royal crest? "Beware of friends," I tell Will every day, and perhaps that is why he distances himself from the mob of admirers and plays the scribbling sphinx.

April 18, 1601

When we hear of news at the Tavern, some bit of gossip or tittle of stirring, Ben is never surprised by it. As Will says, "Ben jumps not at the news, because he knew it forehand, four days ago perhaps—nay, even before it happened!"

According to Ben Jonson, Lord Burleigh and our new friend Edward Alleyn met by chance just a few days ago at the most expensive tailor in London. Haughty and vain Lord Burleigh is a fashion plate and spends many pounds every year on clothing himself. Edward Alleyn, as all London knows, recently received an enormous dowry for marrying the daughter of the theatre owner Henslowe. And he, too, adores spectacular tailored clothes.

Burleigh and Alleyn each has his own style. Alleyn is the more flamboyant one. Both men that day were coming for fittings of embroidered jackets with fashionable shoulder padding and pearl bone buttons. Both of them, I am told, also have their codpieces especially sewn by this mutual tailor. The tailor in question is a tall, balding man with the most nimble fingers in London who insists on doing all his own embroidery and stitching.

Jonson told us that at this fitting Lord Burleigh pranced around in front of a mirror, admiring himself in a narcissistic jig of self-regard. Burleigh and Alleyn—one would be hard pressed to find two more snobbish fops in all London. Like most wealthy men in London, they consider the tailor in a class beneath them, an invisible servant, a nobody, a blob with hands. For this reason, as they talked to each other they ignored the tailor, as if he didn't exist. Or even if he was there, they falsely believed he would not betray the confidence of his clients. But the tailor has good ears and better friends—among them Ben Jonson, a charismatic gatherer of gossip who reported to Will and me. For a fair sum, the tailor was only too willing to spy for those who favor him as a source of information. The money Jonson paid for information as well as his nimble wit were always appreciated by the tailor. As his two clients talked, the tailor pinned their clothing, reaching from time to time into the bracelet round his wrist stuffed with pins.

"Are you going to the Globe this afternoon to see William Shakespeare's performance as the ghost in *Hamlet*? You know Queen Elizabeth considers Shakespeare a genius." Alleyn spoke to Burleigh, looking down on him as a giant might look down on a mere man of ordinary height.

Just then, Ben Jonson entered the tailor's suite. To my fear and Will's delight, Jonson had overheard them speak against Will. Now he addressed them, telling the two that he was creating a masque for the queen and her courtiers and that both men were invited to participate. This was a joke of Ben's—to flatter and mock at the same time. It was perfectly executed.

Lord Burleigh was not at all flattered by Jonson's theatrical invitation. "I'm not an actor," he said in his haughty voice, "but thank you for the kind invitation."

Of course, he is a huge landowner, a member of Parliament, and advisor to the queen, and he looks down on actors as paid vagabonds necessary to amuse the queen and keep the mob pacified. He continued preening in his new clothes in front of the mirror, like a parakeet, unknowing that Ben would dine with us that evening.

Will laughed when he heard all this gossip—because he knows that the power of the queen is now in his hands. I did not see the humor, or the confidence. Power breeds more enemies, and in a London full of villains, one need not increase their numbers. Will shrugged off their villainy.

Ben lifted a glass and said, "The meaning of genius is to be detested by the mediocre. We minds of men mind not the maladroit malevolency of the mundane."

Ben chuckled heartily and we all raised our glasses in a toast to the queen. I told Will that he should go to the same tailor for some new clothes. God knows that with the commissions coming in for his comedies and tragedies he could afford to look less provincial and more aristocratic.

"I'd sooner have a tail pop out my arse than a feather don my cap!" he said plainly.

Jonson painted the canvas: "The three greatest playwrights in London are I, whose father was a bricklayer, Marlowe, the greatest of them all, whose father was a cobbler, and you, whose father is a glover. 'Tis a jolly coincidence that Queen Elizabeth prefers us over all the snobbish, highborn playwrights. You and I didn't even go to university, and here we are, competing with some of the most educated and highborn gentlemen of London, who have come from excellent families and have wasted many years at the universities."

"Yes, they have wasted years, but we will lay waste their follies! Still, no matter what Edward Alleyn thinks of me, I admire him as a great actor," Will blurted out.

Jonson replied, "I see you are a big enough person to admire your enemies."

"But is he a big enough person to escape them?" I asked. Will laughed with a twinkle in his eyes.

"If I didn't admire my enemies, I would be a very lonely man. Here, with competing companies and patrons, everyone hates everyone else. A foul smell is in the air of playwriting. Each belch and fart of wisdom passes as perfume. Theatre in London is a blood sport, a complete replica of my history plays. Power. Power. Power. Power. Power!" Will pounded his fist upon the table. "But I must say that Edward Alleyn is an unusually gifted shadow in this theatre world. I like him much.

And if he hates me, so what? I shall be honored if my words have won a space inside his brain!"

All the playwrights, including Christopher Marlowe, try to live like gentlemen, but that is hard to do. London is expensive, and not everyone has saved money, as we did, before arriving. There are much drinking and promiscuity, promises of parts in plays that often fall through, and vows of patronage. One month a playwright is popular, and the next month he is dropped from his company. A patron can always drop his entire company because of lack of funds. Or the plague may appear from nowhere and close down the theatres. So far Will had been lucky, beyond our dreams. Will always saves most of the money he makes for future dealings in London and Stratford property.

Will belonged, first, to the Admiral's Men, whose patron had once been an admiral and had endless financial resources, so we didn't have to worry. Then he joined the more prestigious Lord Chamberlain's Men, a company he lifted from oblivion with his plays. We only worried when theatres were closed because of the plague. Thank God for our seven years of savings, and we made sure our new friend Marlowe never worried about money either. My husband was a penny pincher, but when it came to Marlowe he was always generous, always ready to lend Marlowe money whenever he needed it—which was quite often. Though Marlowe was queer and Will was not, I believe they bonded because all Marlowe's erotic affairs with men had ended so badly; he welcomed a platonic relationship with a fellow playwright whom he admired. Wit and language meant everything to both men, and they admired each other's outrageous talent.

Though Marlowe and Will were similar in many ways, they had different ways of looking at the world. Marlowe was an atheist, a Machiavellian, an epicurean, and a pederast. Will is a secret Catholic, posing as a Protestant from a well-to-do family; his mother was an Arden. Will believes strongly in God and is a family man who follows the motto of moderation. Will never allows himself to participate in drunken debauchery because he fears that too much alcohol may poison his brain, and he needs all his wits about him in competitive London. To protect himself, he never speaks of politics or religion.

He has always known there is much money to be made in the theatre as a popular playwright. His works command large sums from his patrons because they please the theatre-mad audiences. A playwright who can write quickly and brilliantly and satisfy the tastes of the time may become a rich man—if he lacks not discipline.

Only a few years past, wandering players were arrested as vagabonds; all were vagrants until Queen Elizabeth took up the throne. There was no such idea, before her, as commercial theatre. She loved poetry, great prose, and plays, which we would not have had under any Catholic king or queen. Although Will and I are secret Catholics, we realize that without the queen's Protestantism and the Anglican Church, we would not have a profession.

Will also owns a tenth of the Globe Theatre, having put up his money with that of nine other men when the Globe was removed on rollers from one location to another and rebuilt in Shoreditch. This makes Will not only an actor and a playwright, but a one-tenth sharer in the profits of the Globe.

"I cannot abide to be around noblemen because they know always what's in your pocket, but not what's in your brain," Marlowe once said. Will agreed. Marlowe continued, "I'd rather have a poet's crown of bay leaves than a castle."

"I can't see why we can't have both," Will said, always the businessman.

APRIL 23, 1601

To the tavern crowd, I was known only as Will's cousin Mr. Headington. Thank God my voice is naturally a bit masculine. Just as no one knows I am a woman—as in *As You Like It*—the other playwrights are unaware of my spending the better part of each day at the bookseller under St. Paul's Cathedral, researching for Will by poring over old plays, chronicles, Italian novels, or books on geography of the New World. There are no other playwrights who can enter a woman's mind like Will. Yes, he is not only gifted with a true insight—but he always consults me upon creating the mind and speech of a female character. Based on me, my outlandish freedom, my confessions, he creates these women from my ribs. Will, with his compassion and bawdy wit, is able to understand and love women, but I am the woman whispering in his ear. We are an "old couple" who understand each other without speaking.

APRIL 29, 1601

I was remembering, dear diary, only this morning, how we came to be introduced to Queen Elizabeth. Her Majesty is a most exclusive person and, to say the least, not easy to meet personally.

"Christopher!" Will asked in a fit of impetuousness, "I must meet the queen! How, my dear Chris? She the most elusive of them all."

It all seems so long ago. I recall that Marlowe was in a dark mood. He answered quietly, "Did you not meet her when you performed *Henry VI* at the court?"

"No! So many prattling courtiers and dizzy-eyed nobles packing the palace like prostitutes in Shoreditch that I had not the chance to be presented to her. I was simply another member of Lord Chamberlain's Men, standing there like a dewberry fool."

"But did not that hedge-pig, that Tilney, Master of the Revels, introduce you?"

"The contrary—she glanced my way a time or two, but Tilney directed her gaze always elsewhere."

Marlowe growled in displeasure.

"Tilney is a turd, but Tilney, I fear, is the only person who can present a playwright to the queen. You must bribe him with much money. Theatre is about nothing else," Marlowe said cynically. "But I know where you can find him, and in a... position of...vulnerability."

"We await with bated breath."

"There's a glorious woman who runs a brothel in Shoreditch, and she knows everyone from the queen's court. Ask her to arrange for an introduction to Tilney. He's there, I know, every night. She, the great whore of Shoreditch."

"A whore will lead me to the queen?" Will asked in amazement.

"Who else? We are all whores. Tilney above all," Marlowe muttered, and slapped Will's back before disappearing into his lusty and secretive corners of London. He was off to a male whorehouse called a molly-house.

We found Marlowe abrasively enchanting. He and Will were now brothers who played archery with wit and words, each trying to hit the bull's-eye of the target—which was the six thousand ears of the Globe.

MAY 20, 1601

Will felt it was important for his career that he be presented to Her Royal Highness, the queen, personally. One night we followed Marlowe's advice—a dangerous act—and went walking in the brothel section of Shoreditch, where the beggars, pickpockets, and murderers shadowed us. We passed strange-looking characters with dag pistols and knives in their belts, broken-down men with patches on their eyes, the scum of London.

The brothel Marlowe described to us was that of Doll Tearsheet, a large brick house on a dark street. Will knocked hard on the door—too hard, I thought; he was nervous—but no servant answered. Instead, the door swung open quickly, and there stood Doll Tearsheet herself, the great madam of London. She looked as a courtier with too much makeup, her rouged breasts spilling out of her corset, her dress hiked high above one knee. She offered her services to both of us. She stank of semen and perfume.

"It is another kind of service I require," Will said plainly. "I am a playwright, a friend of Marlowe, and I wish to observe a London brothel firsthand, as a writer."

"An artist's eye, eh? Yes, I bet. Look but not touch, you say?" She laughed, and I shivered. "We'll see how long that lasts."

We entered beneath a large chandelier as the sounds of the house enveloped us. We could hear heavy sighs, screams, and human cries of pleasure. I couldn't help but think that a whorehouse or a molly-house was a sexual zoo.

We ascended the stairs slowly as Doll looked over her shoulder. "It's the nice view, eh?" She laughed again, and by the stair's head, Will could contain himself no more. He began, as usual, to get down to business.

"In truth, I come for a favor."

"Of course, dearie! For a few pounds, why not? And for a few more pounds, anything is possible in Shoreditch."

Her perfume made me want to vomit. In her own way, Doll was pretending to be a great lady; though she spoke Cockney English she had snobbish airs. Her red hair curled about her cheeks and framed her face—a wig in the same style as the queen's. She had few signs of wrinkles, and her heavily applied makeup rendered it impossible to guess her age. Her silk dress was low cut—again, like the queen's. It showed her breasts and cleavage. She smelled of expensive musk oil mixed with body odor—and though she stank to high heaven, it seemed not to disturb her image of grandeur.

Doll was as fascinated by Will's profession as he was by hers. At her invitation, we soon climbed another stair to see her personal lodgings. Red-velvet curtains instead of doors blocked off various corners and nooks. We heard the sexual bellowing that came from behind the curtains. Doll ran a thriving business. Several well-dressed gentlemen sat politely on chairs, sipping sherry, smoking pipes, waiting their turn for the pleasure they had come to buy from the ladies and gentlemen of the night. There was an atmosphere of gaiety and almost innocent laughter amongst the patrons, who looked to me like the rich merchants in the banking systems that now flourished under Queen Elizabeth. A musician, dressed like a clown, played the lute in the background.

Will and I stood in fascination as we watched the female strumpets fluttering in and out of the curtains. Mostly they were long-legged young girls, parading around in scanty under-clothes, their huge breasts barely covered with wisps of black lace. They waited for the word from Doll—what and whom to do and where to go. The brothel also boasted a small group of dwarfs dressed in royal livery who handed out bonbons to the customers and the whores. A secret, erotic, and mad world we were observing. I took a bonbon and just listened to Doll's voice, a combination of low-life and highborn words thrown into the music of her lowly origins.

Doll bragged that she ran "as great a brothel as had ever been run in London." She went on to say, "Here, dearies, a gentleman will never feel rushed, cheated, disillusioned, or alone. That is our business. A good one at that."

The war between vice and virtue stopped at the brothel

entrance. The only difference between the Globe and Doll's whorehouse was that when the curtains of the stage were lifted, they revealed fantasy; when the curtains of the brothel were closed, they protected the privacy of a man's lust and desire. Doll led us to her private sitting room. A servant curtsied when she opened the door, as if Doll Tearsheet were the queen of England herself.

"Thank you, dearie," she said courteously to the servant, playing the lady.

We sat down on luxuriously comfortable red-velvet couches—more like beds, I thought—and Doll sat at her oak writing desk. A dwarf served us port. On Doll's desk a quill, an inkpot, and several sheets of paper sat at ready. She was a businesswoman, she said, who had learned how to read and write from a client who paid her in lessons rather than money.

A bit like my mother, I thought.

Doll, from a poor family in the South of London, found poverty so demeaning that it gave her the motivation to become a great madam. She was an entrepreneur of brothels. Her network of gentlemen, she boasted, was the finest in all of London; every highbrow married man in need of fornication or sexual sport was her client and "friend." She knew where their money was and how to exploit sex to gain it. In her house, her wisdom was apparent. She certainly was a bedroom philosopher-queen. A bawd and a shrew.

"Oh, I love humanity," she said, lapsing into East London Cockney. "Oy, love every man who crawls on his stomach for sex like a tortoise or an alligator."

"Your accomplishments are notable," Will managed to answer with tact. "But there is one talent I wonder if you have, and only one woman I wish for."

"I have many talents, and many whores," she bragged. Her breath stank of fish and sack.

"The queen," Will said, looking her directly in her eyes. "I

67

wish to meet the queen. Marlowe tells me you can use your influence to get me an introduction."

There was a silence, and she reached for a pipe on a small table. As she lit it, she answered sweetly, "I love Marlowe, such a gentleman. Although he ain't interested in ladies. He wants me to provide him with a beautiful young man, which I am happy to do. And you? Do you mean to tell me you wish to meet the queen?"

"Yes, the queen," Will said once more. "I wish to meet her personally. She has seen my last play, I know, and yet I have never spoken a word to her. Can you arrange this?"

"Of course I can, dearie. Her Master of the Revels, Mr. Tilney, is one of my favorite clients. It is he who brought your work to the queen's attention a while ago. Only because, of course, all London was talking of it, and he could not appear ignorant of the trends. As you may assume, there is no one of importance whom I do not know. Master of the Revels Tilney, in fact, is here now. If you know them well enough, you can recognize your customers' voices, their laughter, even their screams of pleasure."

She took a puff from her pipe and blew it out slowly. I could sense Will's urgency. Doll continued, "Tilney is one of those strange gentlemen who need to fornicate the way other men need to eat breakfast. I always have a very young girl to please him, and there is no favor he will deny me. I could persuade Tilney to arrange a personal introduction to the queen herself for a small fee. Say a bag filled with a hundred gold coins?" she said, making her price ridiculously high.

"In this world of entertainment," Will has told me more than once, "it's not what you do, what you write; it's whom you can afford to buy."

"I do not want to haggle. We can afford the price," Will said. He continued in an amused voice. "We shall pay it." And we did. As we walked down the stairs, we heard Doll shout after us, "I hope to see myself in your next great play, Master Shakespeare. Though I doubt anyone could capture me correctly."

"I doubt it indeed," Will whispered as the door slid shut tightly behind us.

That was the first step towards an introduction to Her Majesty Queen Elizabeth. In England, many great friendships begin in the gutter.

June 3, 1601

Today I thought back to the beginning of Will's career as a playwright. I remember the first performance of *Henry VI*. Will's history play was received with wild enthusiasm from the nobles and from the pit. After the success of this chronicle play, Marlowe insisted on celebrating Will's triumph at the Mermaid Tavern. In front of all the actors and playwrights, he applauded Will so loudly that Will's reputation from that day forward was made.

"Bravo, Will Shakespeare!" Marlowe screamed so everyone at the Mermaid stopped drinking and listened. "Bravo! We have found ourselves a poet-king, my lowly lads," he gestured to Will. "Henceforth, he needs no name. Only the Writer he shall be. For after this, there shall be none like him."

And I remember that Marlowe bought drinks for the whole tavern. Within a few weeks, Marlowe had written his own English chronicle, one that echoed Will's style. Now Marlowe and Will were competing with each other in English chronicle plays. And they became closer friends than ever. Though everyone at the Mermaid believed that Christopher and Will were fierce rivals, the opposite was true. Christopher and Will really loved each other.

In the weeks that followed, Marlowe and Will spent hours talking about the crafts of comedy and drama, with me listening in as the interested cousin. They were both theatrical visionaries. How can I forget those days? They were great days of awe and wonder.

I remember another moment with Marlowe.

"Where do you do your research?" Marlowe asked one night as we sat around our table, eating the oyster stew I cooked once a week for Will.

"My cousin, Mr. Headington, is my angel. As well as my cook!"

Will slapped my back.

"When Arthur does research he reminds me of a hungry dog digging for a bone, researching the world of the English past from the *Holinshed's Chronicles* or, even earlier, the chronicles of Edward Halle. You know of the place: the bookstalls of Richard Field, under Saint Paul's cathedral."

"We've known him years," I added. "He often comes for dinner at our home."

"Arthur's quill stays as busy as his mind, and he writes notes for me of fascinating bits and secrets that make my characters dance and leap up from the pages of the past. I mix such facts from dusty books with my own new-carved, new-spun words, my own flying, spirited imagination and ideas."

"Will is a magician," I added. "He conjures characters from out of the air."

Marlowe took us into his confidence. "As I am a cobbler's son, my parents had to scrape up every penny to send me to the university, but you, Will, avoided those ridiculous years, that jail of academic life. The pedantic world of Corpus Christi was a bore. You are lucky, Will, to have a smart cousin who does all your dirty work, you lazy dog!" He pounded Will's arm and stole his glass of ale.

"I am," Will said, not casting even a glance my way, to hide his pride in me, I think. "Arthur is my North Star. We playwrights are explorers who depend on the compass of imagination. I am sure that for many writers, education even impedes imagination." Will elaborated. "We playwrights are like little gods, creating people out of quill and ink, humans out of myth and language. And where is it written in Greek myths that gods went to university? Each prince, each king, each hero, each queen, each ditch digger, each merchant, each blackamoor, each soldier must speak differently from all others. They must breathe differently, they must move differently, each true to himself or herself. Each character's speech must suit him or her alone—that no two characters speak alike."

"Yes, no university can teach such talent. But you have learned to write so *well*! With such metaphors, such magnificent language that I am entranced by it—"

"As we were by *Tamburlaine*!"

"No! Far more than *Tamburlaine*! How did you learn to invent new words?" Marlowe was earnest, as he rarely was. And he pressed Will to answer.

"The ear. I was born with a curious ear. My anvil and cochlea are unique. It's not just the cock but the cochlear that counts," Will said, making one of his usual puns.

We all laughed because we loved Will's enthusiastic punning. Whenever he made a pun he was like a child, proud of himself.

"My craft is a mystery," Will continued. "Born of the universe and of many years of writing. And great reading has inspired me, but true inspiration comes first from other stars, from distance, a hidden place far away that I cannot trace back. It is a fever that runs down through my brain to my soul and then down my fingers and my veins into the quill. It is almost as if, Christopher, I have a burning fire inside of me, a fire with its own divine spirit, and when I write, this fire is puffed up by the bellows of my brain, and suddenly there is the enchantment of the magician, appearing in a puff of smoke."

Marlowe said, "Writing is the act of madmen, and the acts of madmen exceed the previsions of the sane."

"Will is a poet," I said, "and if you can write great poetry, you can write anything."

"The silent one speaks!" Marlowe remarked, laughing.

I blushed, I am sure. "Will began creating plays to imitate the people around him," I shyly said to Marlowe. "He would draw the characters from life, and he always had the ear of a poet."

"He flatters me all the time," Will said with a motion to me. "But flattery is the food of a writer. Without appreciation and flattery, a writer lies in his own hell. Flattery gives him the wings to heaven. The truth is, I have the courage to be totally inaccurate and not give a damn. That is the difference between an artist and an academic. The poet loves lies, loves ragged edges. The poet loves to cheat on history."

"Fantasy your mistress!" Marlowe applauded.

"I completely made up, for example, the irksome personality of Joan of Arc. Tell me this: who in the audience knows what Joan of Arc was really like? So I decided, as the playwright, to make up her personality and to hell with historical accuracy."

"Joan of Arc—or, as we say in France, La Pucelle—my favorite wench in history," Marlowe said with passion, affecting a strong French accent to impress us. "It took a bitchy provincial woman to be the best man for the job to save France. You fabricated her perfectly, Will."

We laughed. "I decided to make her into the same shrew that my landlady was when I stayed at an inn on my way to the north as a young tutor," Will said. "I got inside the hooks of my landlady's soul and her character. I then molded her into my Joan of Arc. What person at a university has the gumption to do that? What academic professor is a playwright? No, my dear Marlowe, no one can teach it, as no one can teach a frog to leap. An academic would suggest that she was an innocent maid. Which I, as a poet, consider ridiculous, and so I gave her the character of my landlady. Tough, strong."

Marlowe drank a toast to Will, surprised as he was by the honesty. Not often did I see the two so merry as that day.

"So, my friend, you must share your wealth. Lend me your cousin Mr. Headington to dig for me, to be my researcher!"

I am sure I did not jump, but my blood did. Our love for Chris was colored by my secret fear of him, his darkness that I only sometimes saw. He had been in prison, was always dueling, always drunk, and was known as a murderer as well as a spy for the queen. The last thing I wanted was to do laborious research for a raging maniac who was not my husband. I took a deep breath.

"Never, Christopher!" Will said laughing. "Find your own relatives to do your research!"

"But I have no literate relatives!" Marlowe complained in a loud voice. "I'm just a cobbler's son, and every man in my family is also a damn cobbler. None of them have any souls!" He laughed at himself.

"Well, you know where Richard Field, our friend the printer and bookseller, is, Christopher? Right beneath St. Paul's Street. You can go there, and if you mention my name, Mr. Field will do everything to help you," said Will.

I sighed with relief.

"Tell me, dearest Will. How do you get your army speeches to sound so natural? That is the hardest part of writing history chronicles for me."

"My cousin Arthur and I improvise the speeches before I write them. I've studied military history for years, Christopher, so I have the vocabulary down pat. We polish and rehearse the plays until I finish the first draft. Every word I need is on the tip of my tongue. Sometimes it takes me months to create a play, and I go back and read the speeches out loud to my cousin. I've developed an ear for military terms and make sure I've used the right vocabulary. My cousin is also my rhyming dictionary."

I could not help but feel amused at the way Will described my role. I knew he was proud of me, but he never let on that he and I were often the same voice.

Thinking back to the good times we had with Marlowe, I admit, we soon became a threesome. Marlowe always treated me kindly as Will's quiet sidekick, even though he often behaved as a barbarian. We tried to keep up with Marlowe as he crawled through the pubs and taverns, where he ate and drank and used foul language and got himself often into some kind of dispute with other playwrights. His self-destruction was always present, and he was often out of control when he was drunk. "Go fuck yourself!" he said to anyone and everyone, including, on occasion, to us, but what we loved about Marlowe was his satanic arrogance that often changed to the humility of an angel. It was through drink, fornication, and foul language that Marlowe sought purification through evil.

In order to get him out of his nearly perpetual and agitated state of complete drunkenness, we began to ask Marlowe to join us at our humble lodgings for dinner. He was glad to have a home-cooked meal. And over the table, his nervousness about death spilled out among the dishes.

He worried of enemies who would kill him. He tended to be dramatic—he knew many people despised him. But at our home, he relaxed, drank less than usual, laughed a lot, and dined on simple but healthy food, as I was a very good cook, and Will too. I remember Marlowe saying to me, "Do you want to see what human eyes have never seen? Look at the moon. Do you want to hear what ears have never heard? Listen to the birds cry. Do you want to touch what hands have never touched? Touch the earth, and when you do all these things, do them as if it were for the first time. The playwright must have no formula, writing everything down through the joy of doing things for the first time. He cannot be a man but a child, stripped naked and finally tied to the stake. He must raise his eyes, even as he is in the flames."

Marlowe was used to living with one parasitic male lover after another. He soon realized that we wanted nothing from him but good conversation. He loved us, and we him. Marlowe was silent about his childhood, since it had not been a happy one, but he kept us amused with stories of his adventures as a spy in France and Spain. Will always said that Christopher Marlowe had the best sense of humor in England. He was great company.

After Marlowe became our friend we often went horseback riding together in the suburbs, as both Marlowe and Will were spectacular horsemen. I had been riding all my life, so I was able to keep up with them. The three of us enjoyed galloping over the fields outside the city. Often we picnicked under an oak tree in an empty field. We would uncork some wine and spread out a white linen tablecloth, upon which we would place cheese and bread. We exchanged ideas about playwriting and read sonnets out loud. Marlowe's voice I still hear at times in my dreams.

Come live with me and be my love,
And we will all the pleasures prove,
That valleys, groves, hills, and fields,
Woods, or steepy mountain yields.

And we will sit upon the rocks,
Seeing the shepherds feed their flocks,
By shallow rivers, to whose falls
Melodious birds sing madrigals.

And I will make thee beds of roses,
And a thousand fragrant posies.
A cap of flowers and a kirtle
Embroider'd all with leaves of myrtle:

A gown made of the finest wool,
Which from our pretty lambs we pull;
Fair lined slippers for the cold,
With buckles of the purest gold:

A belt of straw and ivy buds,
With coral clasps and amber studs;
And if these pleasures may thee move,
Come live with me and be my love.

The shepherd swains shall dance and sing
For thy delight each May morning;
If these delights thy mind may move,
Then live with me and be my love.

Will loved Marlowe's poems as well as his plays. Marlowe exclaimed of Will's genius, as both a playwright and a poet, that what made his work so interesting is that his characters come alive as people. They seem to listen to themselves and are always changing.

"The *Henry VI* trilogy is not just about kings; it is about believable, ambitious men who are ruthless and hungry for power. It's better than my own history play," Marlowe said one day as we sat in the fields. He marveled, as he did with none other, over how Will had found a way to make each character a whole human being instead of the stickpin figures written by their colleagues. "I adore," said Marlowe, "the risks you take."

Will thanked him for this compliment. I heard Will tell Marlowe lovingly many times that Marlowe's poetry had inspired him. He encouraged Marlowe to keep writing history plays as well as tragedies. Marlowe's play *The Jew of Malta* later inspired Will's *Merchant of Venice*.

They say that common enemies make common friends, and Christopher Marlowe and Will agreed that they both despised Robert Greene. The playwright Greene, as everyone knew, was a man who cheated innkeepers by leaving unpaid tavern tabs. What was worse, before he came to London, he had run out on his wife and children, leaving them penniless and fending for themselves. Greene was often a person we made fun of.

Marlowe was aware that Greene was extremely jealous of Will, as he was of Marlowe. Greene went around London bad-mouthing both of them. Greene made money by turning out pamphlets introducing Londoners to reading about cheats, pickpockets, shifters, and vagabonds. He talked against every playwright. He wrote trash and gossip as well as novels and plays. Marlowe was particularly annoyed that Greene had sold the same play, *Orlando Furioso*, to two different companies, the Queen's Men and the Admiral's Men, without changing a word. Greene had become famous for his boasting, his jealousy of people with money, and his low-life companions.

"Let's not waste time talking of him. Greene is an insect that we should squash, not discuss," Marlowe would say, and then we went on to talk about better things.

Will loved to read his own sonnets to Marlowe, and Marlowe in turn read his verse to Will. The two often sat for hours sharing sonnets with each other. Will read one of my favorites, which he gave me as a wedding present:

When I consider every thing that grows
Holds in perfection but a little moment,
That this huge stage presenteth naught but shows
Whereon the stars in secret influence comment;
When I perceive that men as plants increase,
Cheered and checked even by the self-same sky,
Vaunt in their youthful sap, at height decrease,
And wear their brave state out of memory;
Then the conceit of this inconstant stay

Sets you most rich in youth before my sight,
Where wasteful Time debateth with Decay,
To change your day of youth to sullied night.
And all in war with Time for love of you,
As he takes from you, I engraft you new.

That day at the picnic, the talk turned from poetry to business.

"I wish I had sold *Tamburlaine* twice," said Marlowe. "The way Greene sold *Orlando Furioso*. I'm a lousy businessman and I'm a lousy conman, a terrible navigator of my own work. If it were not for the queen and her Master of the Revels prompting me for plays, my plays would never be written. I would rather eat, drink, and fornicate than write."

Indeed it was true. And it would be such that one night left him with a knife in his eye, dead on the dark streets of London, and leaving us without his laughter.

My Lifesinger
Thou speakest in a new way
Of love and work and play
Molding our language
So all can understand.
Thy goodness seems out
Of thy face to shine,
I drink thy words
As if they were wine
And in my mind
Thou are the only one,
My Lifesinger
Beloved.

Marlowe died by an accident, most strange. He would no longer laugh us to sleep. We wept for him, Will and I. It was ironic that soon after Marlowe died, Robert Greene, the pamphleteer, poet, and playwright, died also. He spoke of Marlowe and Shakespeare with a bitter attack. He called Will an "upstart crow, beautified with our feathers, that with his tiger's heart wrapped in a player's hyde he is all well able to bombast out a blank verse as the best of you," in his *Groats-Worth of Wit*, a short collection consisting of an unfinished novel and other scraps, put together for the press by Henry Chettle. In the same pamphlet he also referred to Marlowe as an "atheist." Thus, dear diary, two writers died. One loved Will. The other hated Will. Greene's base-minded words? Soon forgotten. Marlowe's words? To be remembered forever.

August 20, 1601

I remember how the first time Will met the queen, after Marlowe had sent us off with blessings, she pierced him with those dagger eyes.

"Thou art as Christopher Marlowe described you to me. A great poet and playwright."

"Thank you, Your Majesty."

"Thou speakest in a new way, with energy and life attending every phrase. Thou art a genius. Reachest thou into the past, for one purpose: to illuminate the present. History wakes for you; and for us it dost entertain when the words from your quill doest tell us. Nothing is better than poetry mixed with blood and gore and lust to entertain me."

Will bowed, his eyes not seeing how Tilney listened with the heart of a disappointed and rejected lover. Tilney's simple introduction—procured for a fortune—had undesired results. He had not intended for the queen to be totally besotted by the poet Greene called in his slanderous pamphlet "this upstart crow." I stared at Tilney, though he looked not at me. I saw his murderous eyes, as though projecting forth from them were images of heads hooded, feet shackled, and limbs trussed. My memory floated back to Marlowe. It was heartbreaking to think he was dead.

I remembered, so often, he drank to us—he drank to everything. "If whiskey were a woman, I'd be married for sure," he often said in his cups.

Will once tried to get Marlowe to give up drinking. I remember a conversation one evening after we had been singing songs. Will asked Marlowe, "How did a man of your education and genius happen to come to the London theatre?"

Marlowe thought for a moment and said, "I ask you, Will, if a man is intellectually refined and does not want to go into the boring world of law or the hypocritical world of the church, what else is there? The theatre, awful as it may be, is the only place for a poet or an intellectual to make any money in London these days. There's a market for plays now. Spying paid well and was exciting for a time, but it is not as glorious as people think. Spying is actually quite dull. I like adventure, trouble, power, fame, luxury, and beautiful young men. The theatre offers all these things if you are successful. Luckily I am, and you will be too, Will. Besides, I like the idea of imagining drama. I never knew whether Tamburlaine created me or I created Tamburlaine. He was an expression of the beast in me."

"You are not only a beast, though perhaps you know that beastly soul more than most. But you drink too much, Christopher. And we who love you wish to keep you around," Will said. "Your drink will poison your brain."

"My business is not your own! You'd drink too if you were constantly in danger, your life threatened by those who envy you," Marlowe snapped.

It was the only time I ever saw Christopher angry with Will, who had hit a nerve.

I had seen Marlowe quarreling and nasty in the tavern

with his lovers, but with Will, never. After that moment of Marlowe's bad temper, Will never brought up the subject of drinking again. It hurt Will to see Marlowe stumbling, slurring his words, falling-down drunk, always getting into brawls, and often wetting his pants in public.

"I must tell you of a theory I have," Marlowe said to us one night while we sat in our lodging, watching him as if he were a child and making sure he didn't fall down drunk as sometimes he did. "There is something I call 'creator envy.' It's a disease of malcontent and envy. To create is to be a god, and just as the devil envied God, people envy us, Will. We are creators, and those who do not have our ability to pull out of the thin air songs, plays, poems that I believe will stand the test of time, hate us. They know we are immortal and they are not. They will be forgotten because they created nothing and we created beautiful words and real people. The virility of creating, the energy, the magic, the imagination to make history come alive, to make people laugh, cry, to make them feel because we have the powers of words to express their repressed feelings. They envy us. Remember that. Creator envy is a disease like the plague, and everyone wants to kill the true creator, the true genius."

After telling us his theory of "creator envy" he fell on his face, and Will and I carried him home. Once there, Marlowe entered a street fight with an innkeeper's son named William Bradley. Marlowe's friend and fellow playwright Thomas Watson was also involved in the scuffle. The fight took place on Hog's Lane, between two playhouses: the Theatre and the Curtain. It ended with Watson sticking a sword into Bradley's chest, killing him. Watson and Marlowe were both arrested on suspicion of murder but were soon released without any charges on the grounds of self-defense. Marlowe carried a significant cachet because of his university degree and his spying work for Queen Elizabeth, which no doubt contributed to his easy treatment in the affair.

"It's nice to know the right people," Will joked. "If so, you might get away with murder."

Three months later Marlowe was dead. His body lay in a coffin, his face swollen and almost unrecognizable because of the wound to his eye. I saw Will weep for the first time weeks after Marlowe was buried. Everyone in the theatre was crazy, but Marlowe was crazier still, and yet perhaps the only sane soul we knew. Sane enough to write the greatest lines of poetry for *Tamburlaine*.

"'To march in glory through Persepolis.' That is the best line ever written for a tyrant," Will said. "I will always defer to Christopher's ear for iambic pentameter."

Marlowe's ghost has been at the parties of late, at each triumphant evening. He does not celebrate, I fear. But he watches with me. And he has seen for years what now others are only beginning to.

After our first meeting with the queen, as we prepared to leave, the courtier Fletcher, whom we knew, said to me in a whisper, "Tilney does not smile in earnest, Arthur. Perhaps you know this. He means, I believe, only ill to the Writer. I am sure of it."

The sly courtier walked away, and soon did we, with a ruined evening and an enemy in our midst. I remembered how Marlowe marveled that Will remained so trusting, talking always in rhymes and riddles, writing plays as easily as a pie-man makes pies. Will would not hear of my fears whenever I spoke to him about his enemies.

"Posh," he said sarcastically. It was his way of belittling my fears. "Fletcher wants only to seem of high import—he knows nothing and has the perceptions of a slug-eared clotpole. Of course Tilney is unhappy. He has no soul, I am sure. But he shall not take mine by means of hour-stealing worry."

Marlowe would not have agreed. But Will was as stubborn as he.

Looking at the queen I remembered that I once sang Will some of the love songs I wrote for him in my spare time, accompanying myself on the lute and lowering my voice, pretending to be a male troubadour:

One starry night when the world was asleep
I thought of a song that would be yours to keep
A song of love, a song so true, I give it to you.

       One starry night when the shops and bazaars
       Stood sleeping against the moon and the stars
         I wished for a love my whole life through
           I thought to give my love song to you.
As I lay in the dark with the language of trees
As if dreams could talk to you,
I thought of love that a boy gets to know
As he looks at the moon
On the smoke-colored snow.

       One starry sky—when the world was asleep

My love song was born and it's now yours to keep,
   Play it for your soul
   Sing it for your heart whenever we're apart

Will was pleased. He begged me to pen another, and I did so with pleasure.

I never had to ask for all the love you gave,
I never wore a mask—I never was afraid.
Thou art the silent one I cannot erase,
The rock and shadow of our life and all its space.

"Your songs are a revelation," Will told me when I had finished. "You are as talented as any poet in London."

I felt exhilarated. These memories ran through my mind as my eyes looked up and met the eyes of the queen. She returned my gaze with piercing eyes, as if she knew I was a woman, not a man. But I am imagining all this. She would never put up with her favorite poet deceiving her in any way. It was just my imagination. Or who knows?

I realized when we left the queen's presence what a superb actress she must be. She had not life in private, only the large stage of court on which she was forced to act her royal part by day and night. All London gossiped in private homes and public taverns about how the queen had just murdered the great love of her life, Lord Essex.

How could she have done so? I wonder. And how now must she feel? She must, in this evening hour, be lamenting his death by her own hand. This man, the only man perhaps, to have captured her heart, perhaps the only man to touch her hair, her breasts, that warm place between her legs, the only man she has lusted after.

And why? Had she killed Essex because as commander in chief in Ireland he had drained the treasury of English soldiers, left to rot on the battlefield, and met with disastrous defeat after having promised the queen he would be victorious? Everyone in court gossiped that the loss of the queen's money, the loss of prestige, the loss of loyalty led to his death. She had realized her beloved was now her enemy. But when Essex returned to London, in defeat, how did she see him? Had he still the charisma and charm that had attracted her in the first place? He remained a powerful man, even in defeat. Did she see him differently—as a threat? Or a lover? Realizing that he was no longer a hero, she must have known that he was still powerful. Whereas Essex had excelled in the art of sensuality, he could not excel as a great general. A great lover—yes. A good soldier—no.

84

And so she sent the Earl of Southampton to jail, arrested all of Lord Essex's male friends and followers, and had Essex executed immediately. That head she'd held, those lips she'd kissed—chopped off by the ax.

The queen was a born commander, and she broke any competitor, any rival. She knew no limits when it came to the energy and tactics needed to stay on the throne. She used any means at her disposal, no matter how distasteful. Her spies told her, rightly or wrongly, of Essex and his power, and she took no chances. If Essex had simply had a concubine, that would not have mattered to her. A strong woman overlooked such sexual transgressions to keep her power. But she could not overlook how this Essex had made her lose thousands of pounds and her reputation in Ireland as a victorious queen. She had gained a great reputation with Sir Francis Drake; she had defeated the Spanish Armada and gained the love and trust of her people. Now Essex spat on that love by showing himself, her most trusted and favorite commander, to be a weakling and a coward. The queen who defeated the Spanish Armada could not swallow such. She could not be made a fool. There was no forgiveness. She began to doubt Essex, to wonder if he had befriended her so long ago, had seduced her those many times, only to be her cohort, one day king. And so she ended his life. She lopped off his head to defeat his lust for power.

All of this was kept quietly hidden. Months passed before it was known that Essex was no longer in prison, but dead, buried, gone. If she did regret the act, this slaughter of her best friend, lover, and commander, she showed no trace of it. She was, as always, a secret soul. That was what it meant to be queen, head of church and kingdom.

I often reflect about the kind of woman she must be. A new woman, different from all, a woman with a lion's soul, ambitious, power-hungry. She possessed an inner whip that drove her— planted by her tutor when she was young, propelled by her loss and pain, by the necessity of control. Power replaced love and sensuality. She was a queen who preferred her crown to the pleasures of Eros.

No one could change her mind once it was sealed. From time to time she left decisions to others—to Tilney perhaps, or Lord Burleigh, whose estates and place in Parliament also gave him the queen's ear. But her only true advisor was herself. God's surrogate on earth, she believed herself. She had a sharp mind and sharp elbows for anyone who dared intimacy or tried influence. Her strategy was to rely on no one and present to the world an ambiguous picture of femininity. She fought like a man, spoke like a man. A brilliant rhetorician—no wonder Will admired her. Language, literacy—part of her arsenal. Masculine when the times called for it, and yet feminine when she needed be. She must not be too cold, too removed. Her people must fear her, yes. But they must love her too. Her throne depended on genealogy, not money, not power. No, her power depended on the show she could put on. The common people could overthrow royalty at any time, if ever they had unity and a leader. So she wooed them. Like an actor on a stage, till all went home with fond thought in their minds, with loyalty in their hearts. She knew history well—how the most powerful kings and queens of old had become mere footprints in the sand, replaced by the morrow's winds. And so the inner whip thrashed and burned and she continued. A queen and our patron saint. Will called her "the queen of curds and creams." He laughed whenever he said this. We were all beholden to the crown of a difficult businesswoman, familiar with every detail of the machinery of state. The only councilor to betray or desert her was the Earl of Essex, who was executed on February 25, 1601. He became her dead lover who could no longer make a fool of her at court or in the larger mirror of the world.

Ben Jonson told us, "Master Tilney would kill Will for his own interests."

"Why?"

"Tilney has money put in his purse from the wealthy families, the parents of playwrights. If their sons want to succeed, Tilney is the one who chooses the plays the queen will approve of. His patronage leads to the queen. How many families want their sons to be successful in the theatre? Many. That means money to Tilney.

"Will? He no longer has to bribe Tilney. Now he is a favorite of the queen. Don't you see? Will is now outside Tilney's power market. Thus, he is a dangerous man. Tilney took down Kyd. Should he not Will?"

I remember feeling a pain of truth in my stomach when I listened to Ben Jonson. He had a cloak-and-dagger sensibility. He saw evil and conspiracy everywhere. I trusted Ben and his malcontent, justified as I now felt it to be. Even Will always said the death of Christopher Marlowe, the stabbing at the house of the widow Eleanor Bull in Deptford in East London, was totally invented. It is said by some that Ingram Frizer, who stabbed Marlowe in the forehead, above the right eye, was an assassin, hired at the behest of one of the queen's agents jealous that Marlowe held the queen's ear. The death, the cover-up—all a conspiracy, according to Jonson and many others.

I remember one night with Ben at the Mermaid. His marvelous comedy *Every Man in His Humour*, which was revived at the Globe, had just triumphed.

Edward Alleyn had played the lead role. At that time I thought Edward Alleyn, with his great voice, even when he was not on the stage, and his impeccable manners was truly a great gentleman. Alleyn did not join us at the Mermaid Tavern. We all knew that after he married Henslowe's ugly stepdaughter she was very jealous of her new husband and never allowed him to stray far from her, insisting he come home after every performance. Since she was responsible for his recent great fortune, he did not dare, at least at this point of time, disobey her wishes. Thanks to his father-in-law, Alleyn, as everyone knew, had gone from an actor to an owner of theatres and many brothels, from an actor to a very wealthy man about town.

"The best way to achieve wealth is marry it. To hell with Alleyn!" Ben Jonson had said. "His rich wife, that goatish woman, Henslowe's daughter, should be in trousers and he in a skirt. Your wife, my dear Will, I'm sure knows the proper wardrobe and the proper place, making few demands on you, content to stay home in Stratford with her in-laws and the children."

Will answered, "Oh, yes, Ben. Of course." Will had a wicked smile, and neither of us could control our laughter. At that moment, for the first time, despite our pact, our swearing that we would never reveal the nature of our relationship, Will told no one the truth.

We sat at the tavern as Ben Jonson shared his misanthropic opinions about everything. "There is a conspiracy to murder Will. I am sure of it," he said, looking me in the eye.

"Why would anyone want to murder my cousin?" I asked in a whisper, choking on my rage.

But Will heard Ben's prediction. His smile slipped, only for a moment. Then he laughed heartily.

"I have so many enemies, I cannot now remember all their names. Bernard Miles hates me because he's an aging actor and I refuse to put him in my company or in my plays—he is one of the many jealous actors who feel that I, as head of the company, should favor him, whether he can act or not. I know that I am envied and hated by all. The poets Thomas Nashe, Gervase Markham, George Chapman, Barnabe Barnes since they all are vying for Southampton's patronage, which I have and they do not. They certainly despise me. And now the queen has appointed as Master of the Revels that Edmund Tilney, who has so much power; he tells her that Beaumont, my friend and former roommate, under torture, has accused me of being irreligious, intemperate, and of cruel heart. And I am only the first two!" Will let forth his full-throated laugh of a child. "Beaumont has also accused me of being a blasphemer and an atheist. When I was brought up before the Privy Council, I was released on a bond and ordered to stay within twelve miles of the royal court. If it were not for the queen's intervention I would have had my ears lopped off—or worse, my head."

Never far from violence himself, Will, like Hamlet, often feigned lunacy in order to avoid a brawl or a duel.

I try not to think of Ben's words. Instead, I want to dream of Will's triumph. But his success leads only to the recollections of Ben's prognostications: "The presiding genius is hated. Tilney took down Kyd then Marlowe. Should he not Will?"

I attempt to ignore what is obvious. That Master Tilney loathes my husband. That Dekker has moved his heart against him. We are in the shouting heart of London, singing the success of our years and our labors. And I fear the quiet and the dark. I fear the morning I wake up without him, when all the rest, as Hamlet said, is silence.

DECEMBER 23, 1601

"Eavesdropping is part of the craft of a playwright."

Will said that to me when we were young, when being in love makes everything art—breathing, seeing, touching. Even then, the act of eavesdropping was a special craft, and it remains my husband's favorite pastime. His ears are thieves. Sometimes we sit together in a tavern and he looks up as though staring aimlessly at the ceiling, disinterested in anything but the rafters. But his ears are working like spies. Listening, memorizing, and cataloguing the conversations of strangers. Unsuspecting commoners tip their glasses and spill their brains and hearts, ignorant that their words are being taken down in the memory of the man whose eyes are on the ceiling. Unknowing that their words may one day be shouted and sung from the stage.

"Eavesdropping is an art," he says, "a test of my ear and of my actor's memory. A discerning ear and an absorbent memory are two of my most important God-granted gifts. I spent my days listening to grave diggers chit-chat before I wrote the grave-digging scene in *Hamlet*." Will is now in a good mood every day.

"I know," I laughed. "I sat on a grave taking mental notes with you and almost caught my death of cold when it began raining, and do you remember my sitting with the madmen to get their words right?"

"I do."

Will and I once went to Bedlam to hear all the crazy people. If Will had not eavesdropped on the lunatics, he would never have been able to write the play within a play in *A Midsummer Night's Dream*. That was so daring of Will. He lifted the material straight from Bedlam.

Still, neither of us boasts ears like Ben's. He sees and hears as though all life were human drama. Yesterday, while he dined at the Golden Fish, while he pretended to stare at the huge ships with great white masts, at those great galleons that sail to the New World, he took down conversations.

BEAUMONT: We have trunks filled with plays, and they've never—not once!—been on the boards! You must let us pay you to make sure they are seen.

TILNEY: You can always take them on the road, my dear Beaumont. Tour them. You don't need my permission for that.

FLETCHER: Ridiculous. It pays nothing. I remind you that we are not a pair of provincial playwrights. We are two of the most important playwrights in London, but what is a playwright with plays in a trunk? A has-been fool.

TILNEY: Yes, yes, of course you are anxious to be on the boards, but before we continue this rather embarrassing, vulgar, and somewhat boring conversation, I must ask you two a very personal question. (*They lean in, anticipating.*) Why is it that both you highborn gentlemen dress exactly the same? It is a bit outlandish, yes?

BEAUMONT: Because it gets us noticed! You should know the value of such endeavors. And Fletcher and I used always to argue—constantly— about each other's attire. So we threw out all our clothes and started with new garments. We decided to dress the same, and that would end all our unpleasant tantrums. We went out and bought a new, handmade wardrobe. Now we buy everything in twos. Two pairs of shoes, two pairs of trousers, two ruffs, two codpieces.

FLETCHER: But his codpiece is always bigger than mine.

TILNEY: Thank you for your honest answer, but I didn't come here to discuss codpieces. Did I?

BEAUMONT: No. We came here to celebrate the wonderful, the admired Tilney, Master of the Revels, whose talent is larger than any codpiece. Tilney, whom the queen trusts to choose her plays. Who shapes the taste of the city, and who will soon give our plays their chance. Greene, Lodge, Nashe—all those twits and university wits have their plays in front of the queen, in royal performances no less! And Shakespeare? I hate him.

FLETCHER: I *loathe* him.

BEAUMONT: We *loathe* him. That provincial upstart seems to please the world with all his gaudy toys, his language games. It is time for our brilliant collaboration, *The Knight of the Burning Pestle*, to be plucked out of the rubbish pile, and to appear in front of the queen and on the boards of the Globe. Speak straight now: how much?

TILNEY: I speak no other way, unlike some here, and how much is quite a lot. Ten pounds in my purse, and the queen will see your plays by next week's end.

BEAUMONT: Ten pounds? That's a fortune!

FLETCHER: It used to be five pounds, Tilney. We were told—

TILNEY: Things are more expensive now. Many years ago the world was different, before Shakespeare was on the scene and whipped away every playwright.

FLETCHER: He's a shag-eared scoundrel! His puns are filthy, and he smirks as they fly, as though he's making love to the entire theatre at once.

TILNEY: He is. And they scream with pleasure every time he moves his tongue, every time he tickles them with his quill. And the queen—she is a bawdy broad, no more the Virgin Queen then that whore Doll Tearsheet. And it is that shag-eared scoundrel that these days warms her up.

FLETCHER: Since ten pounds is not in our pockets, we shall pay you five, and offer the rest in other ways. Surely there are many means. The two of us could make you quite happy, I am sure. We are a passionate team.

TILNEY: (*Laughing.*) Barter doesn't interest me. Money does! Do you have any idea how many actors and playwrights want to get the queen by offering me sexual favors? Sex is the lingua franca of the commercial theatre. I am not interested in erections. Put bread on my table if you want to see your plays performed.

BEAUMONT: Is there no way we can...tickle your fancy?

TILNEY: (*Stands.*) My fancy is tickled by money. Put money in my purse. But thank you for lunch, gentlemen. I'll have to skip dessert.

Ben Johnson wrote this all down and presented it to Will and me, as if it were one of his masques, in that playful, jolly voice that barely contains a smile. We chuckled together, but it was my own little masque that offered an amused chuckle. Unlike Will, I cannot smile at the hatred in the hearts of his rivals. It does not shock me, just as Tilney's greediness comes not as news. I have been in London long enough that I am no longer surprised by much at all.

Theatre, I see, is a dirty business. And yet Will remains optimistic about all things. Only Will, of all living playwrights, has a religion that might be summed up as "fulfillment." He has an insatiable zest for the varieties of men and women in the universe. The universe is man's stage, but man holds the center. It is a sign that Hamlet has lost his balance in the depths of despair when he finds that he can no longer appreciate humanity.

Will does appreciate humanity in his own life, and I have seen that. Will does not like to speculate, as Hamlet does, on the possibility of conspirators. Unlike the ghost in *Hamlet*, who has a gloomy picture of the next world, Will thinks only of the excitement of his next play and rejects the "quintessence of dust." At his most optimistic, Will's faith can be expressed in his own divine words: "There's a divinity that shapes our ends, / Rough hew them how we will."

APRIL 30, 1602

I am often surprised: no matter how dark my mood of night, the morning brings amnesia and possibility. Today was a beautiful day, and the triumph of *Hamlet* had put us both in a very good mood. We decided to take a walk in our neighborhood to buy some food at the nearby market. What a difference the city of London is from our town of Stratford-upon-Avon. In Stratford, around the home where Will was born, there are clusters of farmhouses on the very edge of the forest of Arden. In Stratford, children run around freely; there are handsome, great trees, buttercups, and daisies along the dirt streets. There are hens scratching about, and people are friendly. In London, millions of strangers roam the street.

Except for a neighbor or two, no one knows who we are. People on their way to market, faces grim, jostling each other and rarely stopping to say good day. But it could not stop us from enjoying the sunny, beautiful morning.

"Tell me, coz"—Will never calls me Anne in public—"why is there such a hatred and envy towards me?"

"Well, look at it this way, coz, in all your history plays, which are so magnificent, every scoundrel is fighting and

94

scheming for power because there can only be one king. The difference between the power of one who wears the crown and one who does not is the difference between night and day. Ambition is the nature of human beings. Power is sinister. Men kill for the sluttish spoils of opportunity. The same is true in the theatre. There was only one Marlowe; now there is only one Shakespeare."

"Ah," said Will, and suddenly he was far away. "Marlowe."

I tried to bring him back. "The fact that the queen bestows on you the Olympian gifts of money and fame, rewards that can only really be given to one playwright, makes many people outsiders. Those who loved you when you first came to London and were unknown are now insulted by your prominence, and they have become your warlike brothers. Many people, not only playwrights, are envious."

I continued, "What makes things worse, coz, is that you are a simple man who keeps your word and does not try to live ostentatiously. You are a patient man who does not swagger. There are many Iagos in London. The audience never knows why Iago hates Othello, and we will never know the reasons for all the hatred in the souls of these rascals, knaves, and filthy rogues who would like to break your neck and who scoff at the miracle of your success. You insult their drab lives. They are stale old mice that have to eat dried cheese, while your appetite is satisfied in poetry, in playwriting, and in business. But do not plunge thyself too far with anger. You have the privilege of the queen's love. Continue to create. I will help you. Remember, you are worthy of your success."

I was so proud that with all his genius, my husband was not a vain or conceited man. He is always humble. This sunny morning I wanted to sing to him, but held tongue and throat. As we walked I whispered a song, and he listened with pleasure. We had each other. He needed my love and I needed his, and so we were tied together. I sang to him quietly:

Thou art my hero, my lover
Thou taught me how to grow,
My hero, my lover
Thou changed my life so
　　　　My hero, my lover—thous't all that I know

Hero and adventurer are all I've really known
Without yon, my lover, I never would have grown
I never had to ask for all the love you gave
I never wore a mask—I never was afraid.

Thou art my hero, my lover
Thou taught me how to grow.
My hero, my lover
Thou changed my life so.
　　　　Thou art my hero, my lover
　　　　Thou taught me how to grow
　My hero, lover—thou art all that I know
Thou art my hero

"Thank you, Anne," Will said. "'Tis a beautiful song."

I gave him my love in song and words. That was all he ever wanted, as words always give him pleasure. Words were my magic of bounty.

"Of all the glib and sleepy creatures of the world, thou are all to me," Will said.

I answered him with a couplet from one of his sonnets that I love: "Then happy I that love and am beloved, / Where I may not remove nor be removed."

SEPTEMBER 15, 1602

This morning I heard a child laughing in the street beneath our window and I began to cry.

"What's wrong, my love?" Will asked.

"I cannot stop thinking about our children. I miss our daughters," I said, trying not to weep.

On some afternoons, the weight of years seems present. These past few years in London have been difficult. Will writes day and night, and I am always trimming the wicks on candles. I can't help but remember that before we came to London we had enjoyed seven marvelous years! They were the seven best years of both our lives. The children loved running around in the grass under the apple trees, looked after by a doting grandmother and grandfather. Years of mirth and laughter, children, music, books, and flowers. It was a perfect life for two poets in love.

I remember those precious days of being young, which will never come back to us. It seems it was yesterday afternoon— or another lifetime: I cannot tell rightly. Will and I sat in our luxurious little barn and discussed what we could do to increase our finances. Since no woman could take part in the London theatre, we envisioned that I would dress as a man and one day play the part of a servant or a distant cousin. We also agreed that we would wait until the children were at least six and seven years old before we left. We loved them dearly and wanted to have a chance to play with them and teach them how to read and write and play musical instruments before we followed our dreams and Will's career. Late into the night we discussed how we could make money in Stratford-upon-Avon while bringing up our children.

"Well, my lady," Will said with mock gentility, "one thing is certain: I will not work as a scribe for lawyers. Kill all the lawyers, as far as I'm concerned. I have a better idea. I will teach music, right here in our little barn. You know how lazy I am when it comes to anything but acting, writing, or reading. Now people will come to me and put money in my hand, and I won't even have to leave my house."

"What a practical idea," I said.

When we were first married at the little church in Shottery, how thrilled I was to have the title "Mrs. Shakespeare." How sad it is now that I have not been called it in many months. Will was a natural entrepreneur. Soon word spread all over Stratford and my hometown that the brilliant young Will Shakespeare was teaching the lute, the viol, songwriting, and singing. Suddenly the road to our house was filled with people, young and old, who wanted to learn how to sing or play instruments. They were hitching their horses to a huge pole that Will's father had set up outside our barn in order to help our first financial enterprise.

Students came on foot, on horseback, and in carriages—children, silversmiths, cobblers, tailors, tinkers, even some bored wives of the well-to-do merchants. Everyone wanted to raise his or her musical skills in Elizabethan England, as the queen had placed a premium on the art of playing an instrument. I often watched the joy on Will's face as he taught aging men how to use their voices, children how to play the rebec, and women how to compose songs. Will was a born teacher and a natural enchanter of people. He sang beautifully and inspired those whom he taught. He became a musical mentor, and money rolled in. He was a famous teacher in the very small world of Stratford-upon-Avon.

I wanted to teach village women to be literate, and I wanted to make money at the same time. I had long talks with my mother-in-law about setting up a classroom in the house to teach reading and writing to some of her friends. It was important now in the Protestant era to be literate. It was either that or be suspected, under the rules of Elizabeth, of not knowing how to be a good Protestant and a high member of the Church of England. If you did not read the *Book of Common Prayer* in church, it seemed as if you did not take the new religion of the state seriously and were suspected of being a recusant, a secret Catholic against the state.

The English language was replacing the Latin of holy Catholic mass. The monks were gone. The ritual of mystery plays was forbidden. Church paintings of the holy family were, in churches, whitewashed. And knowledge of the English language made you a good Christian and loyal subject to the queen. Thus I became a teacher of reading and writing English to curious women who did not have the privilege that men did of schooling.

I charged very little for my classes, but to my surprise women came in groups to learn to read and write. While their husbands worked in the fields or the stores or the markets, they dropped everything to learn their own language. I was a good teacher. My father-in-law set up dozens of stools in the large living room, and suddenly I found myself making money as I looked at the worn-out eyes of farmer women that now showed hope. They came to learn. They came with joy and money in their purses. They came to change their lives. They came as thirsty for words as their husbands were for ale.

I began by teaching the women of the village how to write out what they knew by heart. They came trouping into the house with haggard faces, hands that were rough from work, but with eyes eager to learn so they might be able to talk to their children, who were all in school. Under my guidance they learned the alphabet and how to write out the nursery rhymes they had taught their children to sing:

Fee fie foe fum
I smell the blood of an Englishman

Hickory dickory dock
The mouse ran up the clock

Jack be nimble, Jack be quick
Jack jump over the candlestick

Piggildy piggildy pill
The fox ran up the hill

'Tis true that everyone knew these nursery rhymes as well as old wives' tales. Later Will used nursery rhymes in *King Lear*. They were easy for the women to learn how to write. I showed them how to prepare a quill with a knife and how to make ink, the alphabet of their new lives. Old women with age spots on their hands and wrinkles on their faces were thrilled to see their own handwriting on paper. They were ecstatic to be able to read and write and raise themselves from the barnyard to the church. In their old age I helped these women become literate human beings, and young women with wonder on their faces came with their mothers to study with me.

Within two years, many village women went from being illiterates who could only sign papers with an *X* to being able to write their names, stories, essays, and little books. Some of the old women were naturally talented. Many women, young and old, began writing poetry and sonnets. The tradition of poetry was an oral one, and now poetry and songs could be handed down from woman to daughter or daughter-in-law by writing. Soon they were writing about practical things, such as cooking and physical remedies. They all learned quickly. They dressed for my classes as they dressed on Sunday for church, often clad in bonnets or hats.

I watched as caterpillars turned into butterflies. They wrote the epics of their lives. Their womanly stories were about giving birth, the miracle of saving lives, the grandeur of helping our children grow and our men to lead better lives. Now they had a legacy, language. They became upstart writers.

Their minds were opening, and they were heroic in their own right. I think I held the first literature classes in England for women that were not wellborn. I was able to give to others the gift my mother gave me: the gift of language, writing, and poetry. Where Will's teacher had taught him the alphabet with a hornbook or a parchment on a stick, I taught poor and not-so-poor women to sing the alphabet out loud and later to write. Many years later, when Will was writing *The Merchant of Venice* and studying Judaism, he told me that religious Jewish children learned to know their Bible and holy books by singing them out loud. I had stumbled on a technique used by Jews thousands of years ago. The singing of words became the trademark of these women who were being educated in the Shakespeare house. They sang their lessons out loud. Their voices were heard by Will and me with great pleasure.

"Since we are busy in the education of others," Will said, "why can't we now educate each other?"

"About what?" I asked.

"About everything in the world. Philosophy, human behavior, the sea, the universe, military battles, arms and armory, geography and science, botany, the Renaissance in Italy. All we need, my love, my beautiful Anne, is the time and the desire. That we have. And books. We must study what we don't know. We will borrow books. We will learn everything together. We will study the heavens and the universe."

He was excited at the thought of us teaching each other.

I said, "Reading will replace the university."

He added, "We are each other's lovers. Why not share our minds and be each other's tutors? We will go to a new poet's university of bodies in bliss and minds in exchange of information. The world? Our library."

Thus began our years of reading and sharing what we learned with each other, which seemed to go by so quickly. The three children were our measuring rods. Susanna went from being a crawling baby to a dark-haired tomboy always playing ball. The twins, Hamnet and Judith, grew quickly from toddlers into charming and funny child companions. Will and I spent a great deal of time playing with them, and we loved them dearly. We read to them as well as to each other. John and Mary Shakespeare loved us so much and approved of everything we said and did. As proud grandparents, they gave us their hearts as well as their hearth and home.

During this time we befriended Richard Field, a book printer who later went to London to apprentice with Thomas Vautrollier, the city's greatest printer. Field, our savior, generously let us borrow any books we wanted. We kept up our relationship with him all our lives. He was our walking and breathing researcher and university library. We didn't need Oxford. We had Richard Field, who gladly lent us his books and chronicles and helped us with research in Latin, Greek, French, Danish, and High Dutch. He filled our hunger for learning with his precious books. God bless him.

Once a week we went to Mr. Field's printing shop. Will's greatest pleasure was to open the wooden door of our dear friend's shop and breathe in the distinctive smell of ink, an odor Will loved all his life. He loved looking at Mr. Field's hired printers bending over the pages of manuscripts, reaching into the inky trays, pulling out the letters, and setting them into rows. The printer inking the frames in which the type was secured, and turning the huge screws that pressed the ink forms down onto the mechanical beds, where long sheets of paper were laid out—such sights were miraculous to my husband. He would stare at the printing presses for hours. With Richard Field's cooperation, we had books on every subject we explored. Just as Socrates had his school, where he sat and asked questions of his students, Will and I took turns playing Socrates for each other's delight and enlightenment at night, by candlelight.

I remember we studied everything to do with the sea, gathering practical shipping vocabulary. Will had never seen the sea, nor had I. Neither of us would have made good navigators or sailors, because the very thought of being on deck made us both seasick. Yet we knew that the poetic imagery of the sea would one day fit into the plays that Will dreamed of writing when we went to London. We taught ourselves many of the charting terms about steering systems, the vocabulary of collision reports, the whole history of ships, how the great Elizabethan barques with billowing sails went to the New World, and how they were made. We studied cargo capacity, letters of indemnity, and a depth of draft for ships until we actually felt we were in a maritime environment. We read out loud to each other every book on ships and the sea that Mr. Field could lend us—but also books about many other subjects as well. Of course we had no idea at the time that one day, when Will was writing his plays, hundreds of metaphors about the sea would find their way into his prose and poetry.

After a year devoted to studying the maritime world, we began our studies of the world's geography. We took a two-week trip by horse down to Oxford from Stratford to browse through the Oxford library and look at the Ortelius *Atlas*. Back at our barn, which was our own private university, we studied everything we could about Europe, creating homemade maps of Asia and the New World. Then we studied law. We tested each other on the vocabulary of law and memorized such new words as *torts* and *plaintiff* until we could jabber like lawyers. Will loved to invent "new words" that made fun of legal terms, and at night we traded legal puns and gibberish.

Another year was devoted to our study of military wars, armory, and Anglo-Saxon culture. Ancient history became my obsession, and I learned that Britain as a place was first mentioned by ancient Greek writers. Will also loved military history. At night, when our teaching was over and the children were in bed, we sat by candlelight and quizzed each other about military words until the sun came up.

"Give me five names for weapons that are used by soldiers," Will demanded.

"Fine," I said. "A partisan, a halberd, a bill, a pike, and a hunting spear. Those are five names of spears. Now you give me ten weapons that a soldier would carry."

Will thought for a moment and answered, "A beheading ax, a crossbow, a bird bow, an arquebus, a dag pistol, a mace, a dagger, a sword, a rapier, and a two-handed sword. What is another name for a soldier's helmet?" he asked.

"A burgonet!" I answered, proud of myself.

"Bravo!" Will said. "Soon we will be professors, not writers. When we go to London, Anne, we will dance the dance of wits, and with as much learning in our heads as the university boys have, we will spar with them and leave their brains bleeding! I can write of war as well as any military general."

How beloved were our long nights of chatter and lovemaking in our own little barn, sleeping together, dreaming together, and creating the private world of lovers who were man and wife and good companions.

One morning I was saddened by the sound of the church bells chiming for the death of a young Moorish servant whom I had befriended at the market in town. He had worked for a wealthy family and always used to laugh when he saw me. He was a charming and extremely sensitive young man. I imagined he must have been secretly lonely since there were no other dark-skinned young men in town for him to talk to. Children can be so cruel, and they discriminated against him because his face was a different color from their own. His ancestors had come from Northern Africa. He was an outsider. As a literate woman, so was I. We talked to each other and took walks in the damp morning grass. We made up songs that we sang to each other on our way to the markets. One day, my friend the Moor was found in the cellar of the wealthy family he served, hanging from a rope. I mourned him for weeks and wrote my own attempt at a sonnet for him. I very shyly showed it to Will:

I cried this morning
For the boy, now dead,
And thought I heard his voice
Inside death's bell,
Chiming to the world that
He has fled
Into a world
Where Moorish angels dwell.
The spirit of this boy will live two times,
Once in this world and later in my rhymes.
And if you think of him, remember not
His eyes filled with tears.
He loved life so. In early springtime he forgot
His servant's fate filled with chores and woe.
I speak in whispers now that he is gone.
It's glory how the dead can carry on.

"That's a charming verse but it's an awful sonnet," said Will. "The rhymes are wrong, and it should have fourteen lines, not sixteen, to give strength to the final couplet. But otherwise...I think your attempt is admirable."

The master spoke. I listened to his praise and comments in awe. He then showed me his own sonnet. I saw immediately that his was a masterpiece. I realized I knew nothing compared to my husband. But I was not ashamed. I had seen him so thirsty for knowledge, so eager for its source in anything. I now found in him my source. He was the great poet; I was just a beginner, an amateur sonneteer. If I couldn't be great, I could at least appreciate greatness when I heard it.

Let me not to the marriage of true minds
Admit impediments. Love is not love
Which alters when it alteration finds,
Or bends with the remover to remove:

O no; it is an ever-fixed mark,
That looks on tempests, and is never shaken;
It is the star to every wandering bark,
Whose worth's unknown, although his height be taken.
Love's not Time's fool, though rosy lips and cheeks
Within his bending sickle's compass come;
Love alters not with his brief hours and weeks,
But bears it out even to the edge of doom.
If this be error and upon me proved,
I never writ, nor no man ever loved.

"Will, you are the finest and most talented sonneteer in the English language," I said with shinning belief and awe. "I'll be your cousin, your assistant, your lover, your wife. I admire you with all the grace and love of a student. Let's leave for our new life now. We will tell our children and grandchildren about our journey one day. It's time for you to write in London, not in Stratford-upon-Avon."

One morning we woke and looked at one another, and we knew. It was time. Time to go.

"What are we waiting for?" I cried. "Greene and Nashe are famous for their linguistic beauty, Marlowe for his wit and intelligence, Raleigh for elegance. But to my mind, nobody can write as quickly and brilliantly as you, Will. Nobody can compare to you in the writing of the sonnet."

"True," Will answered, laughing at my high spirits.

"Let's go to London now. I guarantee you that nobody who ever went to Oxford knows as much as you do after poring over books, making lists of words, creating your own thesaurus, and keeping notebooks of rhymes and aphorisms. Life is our universe and our universality. You have so much humor and so much creativity. These past seven years have been blissful, but now…"

"It's time." He finished my thought.

We owed it to his talent—a gift from God—to try our luck in the biggest city in England. I knew with my feminine intuition that it was written in the stars that he would be a famous playwright as well as a poet. We would leave our children for a few years. Happy as they were in Stratford, knowing as we did that we would see them often with London a three-day ride. We also were certain they would thrive in the country air where the dirt of London is almost unknown and their grandparents were there to embrace them—still.

No. We agreed London was no place for children: we did the right thing by staying with them while they were young and needed our full attention and love. But then the twins were six, Susanna seven, and, mercifully, Will's parents lived for them. Most poets have parents who would be furious if their sons plunged into the literary scene of cutthroat commercial theatre in London. Luckily, Will's parents were so proud of his talent that they kept urging us to leave. We appreciated and were amused by their great enthusiasm. They believed in our wish to try our luck in that vast city, where the queen paid handsomely for wit and language and plays.

I remember the magical moment in Stratford when we decided to run off to London. We wanted to leave immediately, before we lost our courage and sank into the domestic life we loved. We had to make sure our children understood that we were not leaving or abandoning them, but were going off to seek our fortune and fulfill our destiny, which they would eventually share. We tried to explain to them our decision to leave and our need for money and a legacy of literature.

"Where are Father and Mother going?" asked Hamnet, who was the apple of Will's eye and the most curious of our three children. He saw us packing a leather bag to put on the horse's back.

"We are going to London, son," I replied. "I'm going to pretend to be your father's cousin so that I can help him in everything he does, just as I do at home. It's a great adventure for both of us." I held him in my arms and let him sit on my lap.

"And what will Father do?" Susanna wanted to know. She also wanted to sit on my lap.

"Act and write plays," I said. "And poems, too. In London, where the queen lives."

Womanish tears came out of my eyes at the thought of parting. I thought the children would be sad that we were to leave them, but amazingly they seemed to share in our excitement.

"Will you bring us back presents when you come home?" Judith inquired.

"Yes, yes," said Will. "Wonderful presents, jewelry and trinkets and musical instruments and swords. I'll wrap them up for each one of you so every time we come home will be a time of surprises."

They understood that our reunions would be happy times.

"I love surprises," said Judith, hugging her father and laughing.

My tears were now gone.

"And what will you write about?" Hamnet asked Will very seriously. He was a budding intellectual and poet. "Write? About what, Father?"

"The mythological worlds, about kings and queens and twins. I'm always going to write about twins because I love twins," Will said. And suddenly, "I love you, Hamnet."

"So do I," said Hamnet. "I love you, Father." He was a loving child and threw his chubby arms first around his twin sister and then around his older sister. Thank God we did not have to say a sad good-bye. The children knew we would be home soon. They knew.

We left with no tears, only laughter behind us. My mother-in-law helped put our clothes into leather bags that we attached to the saddles of our horses. We took very little with us. I had the clothes of another gender, and it was fun to dress for the first time as a man in breeches and pointed leather boots. I had even practiced lowering my voice a little bit when I spoke, so I was convincing in acting out my part of Will's cousin. I bound my breasts, and since they were small I congratulated myself that I did look like a man. I had decided to ride in glory into London as a young man, not a woman, with my husband Will Shakespeare at my side. Once upon a time, it was 1592. Will and I arrived unknown. Now, ten years later, he had so many people jealous of him that I wondered if we would have been better off as ordinary country people. Man and wife, not genius and cousin.

Our memories were sweet: when we first came to London, we were speechless with wonder. But now, Will said to me just recently, after a decade in the play business, "I am weary of the constancy of the competition. London be damned. I'm not willing to give two shillings for all the knaves therein. Isn't it strange how time can erase the patina of joy and ambition?"

September 20, 1602

One of the many good things about Will being part owner of the Globe is that we can give away tickets to whomever we please. Theatre is the saving grace of the common working people of London. Will belongs to the masses, as much as to the highborn, and they love him, especially our cleaning woman. This was how I began today.

"Good morning, Mr. 'Eadington," Margret greeted me as she entered our lodgings.

I loved her East Cockney accent.

"Good morning, Margret," I said. "Thank God you came to clean up this mess. Will has ink all over the table again, and when he smokes, his pipe ashes all over the place."

Margret is a heavy woman, blessed with strong hands and bright red cheeks. Though I paid her weekly wages, I put a gold coin in her hand, and she was grateful for the small gift.

"Aye, I would do anything for you and your cousin. He is a good man and it was so kind a' him to give me the best tickets to *The Merry Wives of Windsor*. Me husband and I would go without food to go to the Globe, ya know. A life without storytellin' is no life at all, is what I tell him. Tell me, Mr. 'Eadington, how did your cousin learn to write so well?"

She always speaks more to me when Will is not around, as she, like everyone else, is in awe of "the Writer."

"He learned his craft in the best school: theatre itself," I answered, helping her change the sheets.

"I swear by 'eaven, oy never knew of a better writer," she said, with great conviction. "What a character is Falstaff. I know 'im well."

"Which is your favorite play, Margret? Now that you have been working for us since we came to London, you've seen them all. Tell me honestly."

"'Onestly? *Julius Caesar*, Mr. 'Eadington. That Caesar is a very exciting man, ya know. The motives of bad soldiers are most interesting, and oy love the conspirators. I like blood and murders, and in the end Caesar wins. Oy like the cruelty of Rome. It's not so far from the cruelty of London then, is it?"

It is not.

"And Master Will has a way of sayin' things oy think but could never say. 'Let me be boiled to death by melancholy.' That's as good a description of anger as oy ever heard."

She laughed. She was my only woman friend in London. I loved her dearly. She might never know I wasn't a man.

"You always went to see plays? Even before my cousin and I gave you free tickets?" I asked.

"Oh, yes, sir. By the by, if I were you, I wouldn't leave them golden goblets around. Someone could come and steal 'em."

I looked at the goblets on a shelf. They were gleaming and always polished by Margret.

"The queen keeps sending them to us as gifts," I said. "My cousin doesn't really fancy gold. He prefers pewter things because he thinks his wine and sherry taste better in pewter than in gold. We couldn't refuse them, of course. But would you like one? We never use them." I grabbed a goblet from the shelf. "It's a gift from me to you."

I suddenly thought of how well she kept our house and that in a million years she would never be able to afford a golden goblet. I was in a generous mood. Why not give her a gift? She held the goblet in her arms as if it were a baby.

"Oh Mr. 'Eadington. 'Twould be the greatest present I ever had. 'Tis too kind of you. I couldn't accept such a treasure. You are too kind to me. I used to work for another playwright and he was never as nice to me as you and your cousin. You are the kindest men in the world," she said, weeping with gratitude.

She wrapped the golden goblet in her shawl and tucked it away in her bag.

"And who was that playwright?" I asked out of curiosity.

"You knew 'im. Master Greene. He was a mean man, he was. He was always in the debtor's prison and never paid me my wages, so I quit and came to you when Mr. Marlowe told me you were looking for a housekeeper. I miss Mr. Marlowe, I do. 'E loved me because oy always made 'im kippers for breakfast. It's a shame 'e was murdered by someone who didn't appreciate 'im. I never believed the story about the bill. Be sure a' that. Marlowe never argued about money. 'E let it flow through his fingers."

"I don't believe that he wasn't murdered," I said.

"It was conspirators," Margret said softly.

I felt a chill when Margret said the word *conspirators*. With all the lofty philosophy of Will, which was "live and let live," London was filled with dangerous men who held grievances against my husband, men who had "creator envy." Still, despite all my fears, I have to thank God for this beautiful day. Sunshine is everywhere, and the smell of burning leaves is drowning out the usual London stench. I love September, I do.

I wrote this song while in the Mermaid, drinking ale and waiting for Will to arrive. I knew it would amuse him, and for a moment, I was lifted by his laugh:

Writing a play is a gamble, a game,
That you play as an angel or sinner.
Writing a play is a gamble, a game,
But there's never a loser or winner.

"Anne, thou art my best friend and you have me always in good humor," he said.

'Twas one of the most enchanting compliments, and I treasure those kind words always.

SEPTEMBER 24, 1602

Today will be a very trying day, I'm afraid. Will is often very touchy about conversations with the queen.

"Don't be such a delicate flower," I said to him, laughing at his infrequent bad moods.

Today his melancholia shines like a dark shadow over our breakfast of hot tea and warm bread, but this morning, this beautiful, cool London morning, we must dress quickly in our finest clothes to ride to Whitehall and have a private luncheon with Queen Elizabeth. Will hates these "little luncheons." After *Othello* was presented in public at the Globe, it was presented for the first time at court. All this protocol is because the mayor of London does not want theatre to exist at all, nor do the Puritans. They feel that wherever a mob gathers it is possible that the plague can fester (and that the lustful urges of the human race will stir and spike!). The mayor forbids all theatre entertainments in the city, and so we trek, each day and night, to the playhouses in the suburbs of Shoreditch, where his ignorant arm does not reach. The queen, a great diplomat, who would rather lay diplomacy on a wound than a plaster, named the Globe Theatre presentations "rehearsals." After the public performances, the entertainments are presented for the mobs and the nobles who fill the hive of the theatre like bees taking to honey. When *Othello* was shown to the court last week, with the actor Burbage replacing Edward Alleyn as Othello, Queen Elizabeth was more than pleased. She was exhilarated. She wrote us a beautiful letter that said, "*Othello,* with the great Richard Burbage, was the finest tragedy ever to appear at my court."

Now, a week later, a messenger appeared on our doorstep. Will and I were summoned to lunch at Whitehall Palace. As we rode there this morning, in the queen's luxurious carriage, Will, usually in a good mood, was surly and pouting.

"Why do we have to go to her insipid luncheons?" he asked. "I know the queen has become a friend, as much of a friend as a monarch can be to a playwright, but why me all the time at her private luncheons? Why doesn't she pick on Jonson? He loves luncheons and tittle-tattle."

"She adores you, Will. You don't get drunk. You don't vomit all over her dinner table the way John Donne did last week. You are a gentleman. You are very witty. Besides, actors and playwrights have a reputation for loose living. Elizabeth admires that you are a moderate person and that, in spite of this, you are so creative. She adores your imagination. Remember that she used to write poetry herself? The queen, I am sure, gets bored with all the fops in the palace who aren't witty or intelligent to talk to. All the affairs of state annoy her—she's too cultured for their baseness. I'm sure you are her favorite companion, as she certainly can't talk to that fop Master Tilney."

I can imagine what Tilney whispers into the queen's ear. Tilney, I've heard from Ben Jonson, tells the queen that Will's history plays, which are often revived at the Globe, are not only about the past but also about the present—that Will is always seditious and has insulted the queen with her pomp and power.

I said to Will, "Ben believes that Tilney is—"

"Enough. One cannot know what is true and what is false," Will said, smoking a pipe and looking out the window of the queen's carriage at the blood, vomit, and garbage on the filthy streets of London.

He won't hear any talk that upsets him. The carriage ride through town today was dreadful with the stench of death.

"Ben Jonson is not a liar," I said, bringing up the subject of Ben's gossip. I was annoyed that Will paid no attention as we sat bumping along to court in the magnificent carriage with our darling Buckman holding the reins.

"I said nothing of his truthfulness; nor did I insult his tongue. I spoke of proof's absence only," he continued. "So, Dekker hates me. His *Shoemaker's Holiday*, when it was presented to the queen, fell so flat one could hear it break. And still he considers himself a far greater playwright than me, with his lecherous lines and sour-faced, dizzy-eyed pronouncements. So he would smile over my corpse. Jealousy is a terrible disease that breeds within this theatre. I doubt not that Dekker has the desire to poison me. He simply hasn't the fortitude."

Will's confidence in his own safety was convincing. But when I thought back to Tilney's smile, I doubted again the safety in which Will thought he dwelt. English is a harsh, uneven, and broken language—a hodgepodge—and thanks to Will's quill, it has grown from a rude and unpolished tongue into a more composed and perfect language. His power is one that shifts the earth on which we walk, the ground of language. Will's kind of power, the power of words, moves not lightly through a world. Everyone has praised *Othello* as a masterpiece. All London is filled with Iagos who are evil for no reason at all.

The carriage stopped. We'd arrived at Whitehall after passing the royal topiary. I was always amazed to see the green topiary hedges, clipped by the gardener's scissors to resemble balls and birds and swans. As we climbed the marble stairs of the palace, Will grumbled about lunch.

"I hope it's not another undercooked pheasant lying in a thick gravy so rich that for three days afterwards I'll be farting."

"Will, be careful!" I laughed. "The royal guards are listening to us. They aren't deaf."

"Alright. I promise not to use the word *fart* in front of the queen. Also, I promise I won't use the word *dildo,* and I won't talk about penises and sodomy, and clitorises and nightingales. I'll save all that for the double entendres in my plays that the queen, of course, being an old bawd herself, enjoys secretly and understands as well as anyone. All the groundlings in the pit know exactly what I'm talking about, and they laugh their heads off. I bet the queen gets her jollies from hearing about dildos, even though she sits on the throne as if she were an innocent virgin."

"Quiet, Will. Maybe one of these guards standing at attention is her secret lover and will be pleasuring the queen tonight, so keep your voice down."

We giggled as we climbed the royal marble stairs of the largest palace in all Europe. Whitehall is magnificent in its own sprawling way, sitting on so many acres of newly clipped green grass filled with rose gardens and magnificent statues. It outdoes every other palace in the world with its fountains, gardens, and topiary. From a distance, the architecture overwhelms. Inside, the details and delicacy make one marvel. The walls are covered with tapestries from Holland, France, and Belgium. Ben Jonson told me the palace has fifteen hundred rooms.

What does she do with them all, I wondered. Ben also told me that the palace had been extended over many acres of land, and that Henry VIII, Elizabeth's father, had expanded the main building and added a bowling green, tennis courts, and a pit for cockfighting, as well as a tiltyard for jousting. (Now the queen has gotten rid of the cockfighting arena because, it is said, she finds the sport disgusting.) Whitehall Palace was built to dazzle both friends and enemies.

We walked through her marble halls, passing hundreds of female courtiers dressed in white dresses.

"White is the color of our Virgin Queen," said Will sarcastically.

We stared at hundreds of handsome male courtiers richly dressed in colorful velvet doublets with padded shoulders, to protect that part of a man's anatomy during a sword fight. The male courtiers mingled with the female courtiers, whispering. Everyone seemed very jolly. It took a full half hour to walk past halls filled with drapes, mirrors, wood carvings, and statues to reach the queen. I noticed that many of the dresses of the female courtiers were so stiff they looked as if they could stand up on their own. The hoops in the skirts were outrageously large, and the bewigged women courtiers themselves reminded me of painted and overstuffed furniture. I looked at the boned stays of all the pretty women and wondered how they could breathe. For once I was glad I was dressed like a man, not a woman. A codpiece is nothing compared to a tight bodice, which presses so hard against the breast that a woman can barely breathe. The royal dressmakers have never heard of nipples.

A courtier announced us: "William Shakespeare and his cousin Arthur Headington."

The queen was already seated at a small table. A symbol. Only a very few of her favorites were ever allowed to lunch with her privately. We bowed to her. Tilney, at her side, did not even feign friendliness. He covered his viciousness with a half smile. She lifted her hand and said in a friendly voice, "Thou need not bow. Your punctuality is honor enough. Do take this offered seat. Sit down. Lunch is about to be served."

Her cutlery was golden, and her goblets also. The table-cloth was made of the finest handmade Belgian lace, and her plates were French porcelain, delicate, with patterns of flowers wrapped around the initials of Her Royal Highness. I looked in awe at the petit point of the tapestries of *The Unicorn in Captivity* and thought of poor Will, who was now a unicorn in captivity himself. I know that tapestries are a form of textile art, woven by hand on a vertical loom with weft-faced weaving, in which the warp threads are hidden in the completed work. I saw that many of the threads in some of the queen's tapestries were silken or golden, creating a magical effect on the walls. Several of the tapestries depicted large and magnificent unicorns being hunted and captured. The creatures, which stand for the life of Christ, looked out at us with such sad eyes. Other tapestries showed naked, pink girls dancing in fields. I always am impressed with the queen's taste, no matter how many times we are invited to visit the palace. Musicians play rebecs softly in the back of the sitting room, not so loudly as to drown out conversation.

I felt a tinge of excitement when I found out that there were to be only the three of us alone in the queen's small, private dining room. The queen began talking about tarot cards as we sat politely, eating our tiny lunch that consisted of dainty cucumber sandwiches, thank God, not the usual pheasant.

The queen said, "My tutor, a poet, did learn me in alchemy when still I was a girl. I early found a fascination in it, steeped in mystery as it is. These tarot cards are esoteric symbols holding the power to expand consciousness and connect the human soul to the divine."

"How very interesting," Will said courteously, though I could tell he was entirely bored.

The queen continued, "The alchemist tarot deck offers the human initiate a potent tool for personal growth. Western alchemy, as you must know, originated in Egypt. Originally alchemy dealt with the science of metals and was not meant as a spiritual path. Egyptian religion evolved out of a shamanistic and prehistoric path, developing various bodies of magic studies that were the beginnings of what we could call geology, metallurgy, and chemistry. Among those, I learned from my tutor, were techniques for separating gold, silver, lead, iron, and tin from ore. The Egyptians knew that bronze was made by combining copper and tin. After the Egyptians discovered bronze, it must have seemed like a type of miraculous gold made from base metal. This alchemy was used for dying, brewing, gilding, perfume-making, chemical recipes, and embalming the dead."

The queen was in love with her own voice; she was a little bit like an aging professor at her own alchemic university. She was obviously passionate about her tarot cards, an obsession neither Will nor I shared, but since it was not some old fortune-teller blabbing but rather the queen of England herself who talked to us so confidentially and with such enthusiasm, we sat listening to her lecture with the attention of good schoolchildren. And I began what would become an afternoon of suppressed laughter, watching Will wiggle beneath her soliloquy.

"The alchemical process was the most exciting learning of my young life. It led to my total reliance on the tarot deck, which I consult every morning. Now I wish to invite you both to my private tarot card room."

She rose. We stood and walked respectfully behind her. She spoke with true friendliness, and all I could think of was that Will considered this dubious honor of a private lunch a punishment, not a pleasure. He thought tarot cards were ridiculous, but being a true diplomat and gentleman, he acted the part of a grateful courtier.

"We are enchanted by your invitation, Your Majesty," he said, as he bowed his head to keep from laughing out loud.

The queen led us to an adjoining room, a large, red chamber housing a table, chairs, and tarot cards. Heavy red-velvet curtains and luxurious silk cushions added a theatrical air to the room. I desired nothing more than to pretend great interest. The queen picked out the priestess card from her tarot deck.

"The priestess is the card of creativity," she said. "I have many questions to ask of you about this. The priestess tells me that today I shall hear about all the secrets that make your great plays and poetry possible. Therefore, I wish to ask you, William Shakespeare, at this moment the reigning king of London's playwrights, about your writing. Being a writer myself, of course." Will tried not to laugh. "Tell me, what are your secrets for writing your amazing tragedies, such as *Othello*, which I love so dearly? Do you write from dreams? Do you write from intuition or from wisdom?"

She demanded an immediate answer. I could see that Will was trapped. He knew he was a poet for hire and had better be able to think on his feet.

"How are a whore and a poet similar?" Marlowe had once asked us in a riddle. "Both are paid to give immediate satisfaction." I thought of this joke.

"I have learned much from tarot cards," Will lied.

"Oh?" The queen moved forward. "Tell me what you've learned."

"I have many fools in my plays: jokers, just as in the tarot cards. As you know, Your Highness, I like to double actors. For example, in *The Merchant of Venice*, the actor, a shadow, who plays the fool changes costumes and then plays Portia. I love fools and I dislike lawyers. That is why the fool doubles for both parts."

"Go on," the queen said with excitement in her voice.

Will continued to improvise. "I read in *Rosarium Philoso-phorum* that fools who understand the sayings of the philosophers accurately, to the letter of the law, do not necessarily find out the truth. That is why there are the fools. There is no such thing as the letter of the law, and there are no ABCs of how to be a great writer, I'm afraid to say, Your Royal Highness. But I might say that as a playwright who often writes about kings and queens, I am a fool who understands the passions of power."

I hoped that this would end the audience and we could go home. The problem was that Will did not like to satisfy on demand. When annoyed, he had a tendency towards irony, paradox, and sarcasm. I was petrified he might satirize the queen to her face, or even worse, begin telling sexual puns that might offend her. Besides all that, Will often reverted to rudeness when faced with embarrassingly stupid questions, and the queen's inquiries were ridiculous. However, Will did not betray his annoyance. He looked delighted to be questioned by the queen.

Will was once asked by Ben Jonson, "How do you explain the universe, Mr. Shakespeare?"

He answered, "I don't," in a quiet voice.

This humbled Ben Jonson, who fancied himself able to explain anything.

Now the queen persisted: "What is the secret of your art?"

"Are you asking me what is my method of writing, or are you asking me how I write?" Will asked.

I was grateful he kept up the art of hypocrisy and gentility, unlike the time he snapped at Ben Jonson. There was no surliness or annoyance in his voice. He spoke sweetly.

"Either one," answered the queen. "Either one would be important for me to learn."

"Using my craft, I write from magic, Your Majesty. A playwright must have all the magic of his life in his head and then make all the elements of the play meld into a unity that is the play itself. Words, actors, scenery, wigs, costumes, special effects: they must all create a magic on an empty stage of floorboards. That is what I mean by *meld*."

"But why your unmatched popularity with the masses?" the queen asked eagerly.

"Originality, Your Majesty. The audiences of even the most uneducated playgoers, the groundlings, sniff out mediocrity, their eggs always at the ready. Neither as an actor nor as a playwright do I like yolk in my face!"

The queen smiled slightly. "Go on," she commanded, as if, like a little girl, she was playing a delightful game of creativity.

"The audience is as a wild animal. The masses in a moment can turn a bad playwright into a bear, waiting to be baited. The spectators want to be satisfied, and we poor playwrights and actors have to figure out what will make them laugh and what will make them cry and what will make them applaud. The playwright must be, above all, true to himself, and then he can be true to everyone."

I could see that Will was improvising on his feet, but being an actor, he was thrilling.

"What makes a great play?" the queen asked. She leaned forward in anticipation.

"Your Majesty, there must be a mythic story, because myths are fairy tales that are universal. There must also be exciting characters and amazing poetry, but then the way a play looks is as important to me as the lines I write for my actors. I am, after all, creating false history for the alchemy of writing."

"False history? I find myself enamored of that," the queen said. "Do tell me more. How do you write?" She now seemed insatiable.

"I consider for long days how to speak the words of the characters that I write, and I discuss them with my cousin. If it were not for my cousin, I might not be able to write myself. Two heads are better than one. I need my cousin to read aloud every word, every line, and every play so I can hear the music in my mind. Being a writer is very much like being a composer. There must be music! I write not only with my ears but also with my eyes. I am a strangely visual person, and I see each character distinctly made out of different elements of magic. Each character must speak differently in order to come alive. Each character must have his or her own voice. To give you an example, Portia must have a totally different vocabulary from Shylock, and Rosencrantz cannot speak like Hamlet. I know the story I want to tell, and then the characters come to me, and each character speaks differently. It is as if each of the characters were carved out of a different material. Once or twice I asked Fletcher to collaborate with me, but he was not to my fancy, and so my main collaborator is now my cousin."

"I understand what thou meanest. Thou hast said that each character possesses his own voice, but what do you mean by 'different materials'?"

"I visualize the element of my characters. Rosalind is made out of blown glass. Jaques is made out of pottery. Touchstone, the fool, is made out of stone in my imagination. That's why I called him Touchstone, of course. I write and rewrite so that I can change the language and polish what the characters are saying. I often daydream, and then in a great snit of concentrated bliss, I create magic. I admit I love sticking puns into my plays. Therefore my plays often take place on two levels, one on the poetic level and the other on the secretly bawdy level. The primary duty of any of my plays is to please myself. I am a prestidigitator. Occasionally I even feel giddy, as if I would soon float into the universe with fulfilled excitement."

He began to imitate a kite, dancing for the queen. I wanted so to laugh. It was one of Will's most masterful moments.

"I write neither slowly nor quickly. I don't care about time. I write, Your Majesty, in a universe of my own." Will continued to conjure up his method of creating.

"A universe of your own?"

"Yes, my own world. While writing, it is as if I am sitting at my desk, and a dark but brilliant meteor gushes against my brain, exploding into a million perfect words. I know this all sounds insane, but my wisdom is the magic of musical words. Some words are *viola da gambas*, some English guitars, some trumpets, some flutes, some comets, some horns, some bagpipes, some merely rebecs."

"Go on." The queen swallowed, and I saw her cheeks flush with color. "This is the most honest answer about the creative force, which is, after all, a kind of madness. I am taking mental notes on everything you say. I knew my tarot cards were pointing me in the right direction. Everything that you're telling me about writing could never be learned in a university."

"Your Royal Highness, what I am telling you is the secret art, mysterious secrets that I have revealed to no one but you."

"I am grateful," said the queen. "I request that you go on. Continue."

This was the closest I have ever seen the queen to begging.

"There are times when writing is almost an orgiastic fit. I don't worry about punctuation or historical accuracy. *Eros* or *agape*? Those Greek words have inspired me. I just let whatever inspires me come out of my body in a rough feeling. The joy of *eros* is the most important truth on earth, and somehow to relieve myself and to get rid of the *agape* in my brain, I write. I write to survive. As a man I cannot give birth. I write to achieve an inspired substance, which is to create poems, songs, and plays. A code is a game, and all writing is sort of a code we play against the gods, but codes can be, forgive me, ambiguous. That is why they are codes."

At that the queen laughed. Will laughed also at his own improvised cunning. The queen? She was having a jolly good time.

Will continued, "I learned much from my father."

"How did you learn from your father?" asked the queen, her eyes lighting up. I could now see she was more attuned to hearing about Will's personal life than about his theories of ambiguity. Had she not been the queen, I would have taken Will's arm and escorted him home.

"My late father, a successful glover in Stratford-upon-Avon, soaked deerskins in huge vats of urine and excrement in the old style of softening them, Your Majesty. Slowly the skins were marinated and softened, until they became, eventually, pure white chamois. I am a bit like my father. I soak all my characters in urine and excrement in the vats of my mind, especially the evil ones—Richard III, for example. I soaked him for a long time in filth and then hung him to dry in the sun of my imagination. The humpbacked Richard came out rather a shitty fellow, don't you think, Your Royal Highness?"

Will laughed like a child. He was talking nonsense, but she loved it.

"I've never heard anything such as this. I knew not that urine and excrement were what made gloves or great writing. Tell me, Will, how is it that you are so multitalented? You can write songs, sonnets, long poems, histories, tragedies, comedies, and all your lines fit the actors perfectly. You have no idea how I worship at the altar of your plays."

I could tell that my husband was doing his best to amuse the queen. This urine-and-excrement theory was a new one, something he had made up on the spot. On the other hand, Will never analyzed what he wrote; he just wrote. He was doing a wonderful job as an actor to convince the queen that he believed in things he didn't even know he believed in. Didn't she know that the art of genius is a mystery?

"A final question: what, in your own words, are your two greatest talents?" the queen asked.

She was like a madwoman who had escaped from Bedlam, trying to find her way back.

"Poems and plays that are really songs."

"Songs?" the queen asked.

"Yes, all writing begins with the earliest people on earth, singing songs to hear their own voices in the darkness. They were bewildered to be insignificant mortals in a vast universe so alien to human beings, but when they lifted their voices and sang they felt they were communicating with the gods."

"You break the rules, don't you? That is what makes you so great. You are giving me insight into the mind of a poet. It is so exciting to hear how a poet thinks."

"You see, when you write by the rules—and there are plenty of them, Your Majesty, for scribbling the well-made play—you never surprise yourself, and that is my point. My greatest talent is to surprise myself with my own writing Your Royal Highness, between you and me, life is so absurd, and people are often just fools."

The queen seemed pleased. I could see that Will knew that the queen, like everyone else, sometimes doubted her own sanity, and she enjoyed Will's humors and tone of voice. She liked to hear that "art" was enjoyable. Most playwrights complained and whined about writing being difficult, but not Will.

Will continued, "You want to shock yourself, and in that way you will shock your audience. As a playwright, well-made plays don't interest me, but clowning and the absurd do interest me. Is Romeo sane or is he irrational? Is there any reason for his love at first sight? I consider lovers lunatics. Anyone in love might as well get into his bed in the hospital in Bedlam for the mentally ill. Love, as I've pointed out in *A Midsummer Night's Dream*, is insanity. Would you say that Puck is evil or that Puck is divine? It is up to the audience to judge. That is why I usually steer away from motives."

"I'm enjoying this afternoon immensely," the queen remarked. "Tell me more. Please tell me more."

She had taken theatre off the clothesline of Catholicism and hung it out to dry, but she wasn't too sure what a play really was.

"Another secret?" Will asked. I could tell he was thinking on his feet. "My main secret is to make whatever I write seem new. Everything is new under the sun, including the sun itself. A poet has to have an interesting mind that is totally fearless. Also, between you and me, there are no mistakes. I live and die by that rule."

The queen was now satisfied. "I think my questions have opened the Pandora's box of your creativity. I, Queen Elizabeth, have little to say, except thank you. I assure you, Will, that I wish I could sit here for months hearing your thoughts about writing, but in the end, I agree with you: art seems to be elusive."

"Perhaps the only true mystery on earth," Will added.

"You, dear Will, are in the business of being brilliant, whereas I am just in the unfortunately dull but royal business of being queen, expanding my land and enforcing laws. That is why art, not history, is important to me. I need insight, not hindsight."

She paused. Then she changed the subject.

"What is your favorite of all the comedies, tragedies, and histories you have written? Which is your favorite play? I must know this, since I am interested in your opinion of your own work, not just my opinion."

"I must admit my favorite play is *A Midsummer Night's Dream*," Will answered.

"*A Midsummer Night's Dream*? Not *Hamlet*?" The queen was surprised.

She stopped. Master of the Revels Tilney had arrived like a snake and slid quietly into the royal tarot room.

"I love this play. Above all, the dream is a tragedy of vanity," Will continued. "And we are all vain. It is also a fairy tale."

The queen was silent for a moment. She then turned to Will and remarked, "How lucky you are to have a cousin who is such a bookish and valuable resource."

I bowed to the queen.

"Thank you, Your Highness," I said.

The queen turned her attention back to Will. I could see little beads of perspiration breaking out on his forehead. I knew he had no idea how he wrote, and all these ridiculous questions were getting on his nerves. Being an actor and a citizen who valued avoiding having his head lopped off for being rude to a queen, he smiled.

"There are rumors circulating around the palace that you had, from time to time, collaborators, such as Thomas Middleton, George Whetstone as an inspiration, even the late Christopher Marlowe," the queen whispered.

"Hogwash," Will replied. "Rumors are lies. All the gossip you hear is untrue, Your Majesty. These are just stories told by jealous individuals. If I say so myself, I have a unique voice. My only collaborator is Mr. Headington, and he insists on being anonymous. Playwrights, enemies—envious of my wit, success, and wealth—often say I do not write my plays. They say, 'How can a provincial know so much about the nature of human existence? He must have had a rich and educated collaborator.' They say all sorts of things," Will explained. "People ask, 'How could he write all those plays himself, a boob from the provinces?' It's all untrue, about provinces being a place for morons. Rumors also say I didn't write any of my plays because no one believes a man can write so quickly, and certainly not a man without a university education. Aristotle was his own university, and so am I. Rumors that I did not write my plays are all just pure jealousy and resentment over my talent." Will sighed a mock sigh. "My university was nature, and I have read over a thousand books."

"But where does such talent as yours come from?" the queen asked.

127

"Talent comes, you must understand, from dreams and inspiration."

"Oh, I do understand. You're a lucky man, Will, but I wish I had a Mr. Headington who could help me by listening to my writing as he listens to you. Perhaps you can loan him to me sometimes?"

I stood by quietly, nervous that Will might say no to the queen.

"I know I'm a lucky man to have such a valuable assistant."

"Will, thank you for letting me inquire into the alchemy of your writing. By the way, I'm putting together a secret collection of my early poems, and your cousin might prove helpful. I love to write, and if I weren't the queen, I'm sure I would be a poet. Which brings me to one more question."

"I am flattered to be your humble servant, Your Highness. Ask me anything, and it would be my greatest pleasure to reply." I could see that Will was exhausted, but constant diplomacy is part of his art. Never an angry word could escape his lips; otherwise good-bye career. Believe me, it wasn't just talent that accounted for Will's success. He was always kind and courteous. That was the part he played. Success is 10 percent talent and 90 percent courtesy, including having the courage to appear happy and courteous in public. He was growing agitated but had perfected self-control.

"Go on, Your Majesty. It is such a pleasure to enlighten you. What very little I know I am happy to share."

Diplomacy, now humility, but I was so proud of Will's performance. Everything was an act. He played himself so well, always the polite magician.

"Now tell me. she said, "which do you prefer, acting in or writing plays?"

"Neither. I prefer writing poems to acting or writing plays, but to tell you the truth, Your Majesty, if I wrote poems all the time I'd become as stale and dull as Sir Edmund Spenser, whose long poem, the *Faerie Queen*, lacks creative energy. Alternating poems, playwriting, acting, and producing—as you know, I'm a shareholder in the Globe and the Blackfriars theatres—that is what keeps my imagination fresh. Poetry gives me the gift of language, acting gives me the gift of understanding characters and playwriting, and producing allows me to be a businessman." Will started laughing. "Like a magician, the poet needs many cards up his sleeve."

He held the queen a total captive. She began to laugh, too. And at the height of it, Tilney interrupted.

"I'm sorry, Your Majesty. I have to end this conference," Tilney huffed. He sputtered with rage because we had taken up several hours of the queen's time.

Nobody had the power to hold her attention but Will. I knew that Tilney saw Will as a threat to his position. Will, being the linguistic magician that he was, had completely enchanted her. With that, the queen showed her temper for the first time to us.

"Leave us be, Tilney. We are having a bawdy and sublime discussion. Sublime, which thou may not comprehend as a man of no talent. We have traded sexual puns, have spoken of theatre, and have touched the stars of imagination. Too high we have floated for you, Master Tilney," she rebuked him.

"But this is my task, Your Highness. To keep you on schedule."

As I looked at Tilney, I observed that he was a most loathsome, self-opinionated, ass-licking scullion. An unpleasant class envy and aspirations of social climbing dominated his mind. The wheels in the chariot of his head constantly turned in an effort to speed him towards more royal power. Also, he smelled of the perspiration of greed. Greed emitted an odor, one I had smelled so often in London. With his stupid face and his stiff, fixed smile, Tilney pretended to everyone he met.

The queen composed herself and spoke with more power than the shouts of Burbage or Alleyn: "Beware, Tilney, or one day you shall wake to find I have made Master of the Revels another man. In front of me sits the greatest playwright who has ever existed in the English language. While you have only bribed and palmed your way into becoming the most powerful man in the English theatre—though you have only a power born of my own trust in your taste for the revels—after the rise comes the fall. You may find yourself one day, Tilney, in the position of Cardinal Wolsey, who, thou shalt recall, did meet with a callous end."

Tilney grew red, bowed lowly, and offered, "I am sorry, Your Royal Highness. I did not mean to offend."

He glared at Will as he slithered into the queen's good graces and exited, aware that the queen no longer wanted him near.

With that, Elizabeth turned to Will and remarked, "One day my age will be known as the age of Shakespeare, not the age of Elizabeth." As she left, Tilney ran after her, glowering at Will and me. I am sure he is a dangerous man. Dear diary, I have reason to be afraid for Will's life. A man like Tilney is an enemy. How many other enemies does my husband have?

The courtiers opened the heavy doors to the queen's tarot card room, and we exited to a fanfare of court musicians, who had waited patiently outside the doors. The queen loved pomp and golden horns and cacophony, and she reveled in the fanfare. It lightened her spirits and made her forget her loneliness.

Will and I soon met the fresh air, and our friend Mr. Buckman drove us to our lodgings. He heard us laughing at the queen and her often absurd questions, but pretended to know nothing of it.

Shortly after, we went for a drink at the Mermaid. Dekker was there, besotted with himself and feeling such envy towards Will that he could hardly smile at us. Will was rich while Dekker was drowning in debts. Will had just come from the queen's audience and received a new commission. Dekker had just come out of debtor's prison. Dekker's life was even more miserable now that he was partially impoverished. He drank ale and looked lost.

"Watch out for Dekker," Ben Jonson quipped as he passed through the door. I looked up to the bar, and Dekker had gone.

OCTOBER 3, 1602

Often I break loose of a dream
And often I am having the same nightmare
About someone killing Will.
This morning I woke in an icy sweat.
I realized last night I dreamt I was on a ship with Will,
Bound for Bermuda,
Will, like a captain, was all bright
Before the morning watch.
And then I saw him,
Face to face,
Dekker, the playwright,
With a razor-sharp dagger in his hand.
I felt so sad
To see Dekker, murderous and mad,
And in the sanity of self-deception
I knew
The hammering dream of Will's assassins
Might be true.

OCTOBER 4, 1602

I try, for distraction, to think of other things than those who conspire to kill my husband, but I think of the threat against him all the time. I try to be careful, but I find myself so full of secret melancholia these days. It burns in me and drags me to low places.

The man that I now most detest in London is William Cecil, first Baron of Burleigh. He is the chief advisor to Queen Elizabeth, twice secretary of state, and if I had to compare him to an animal it would be to a weasel. He struts around the palace, all bushy-tailed, squeaking orders to everyone and sipping whiskey out of his leather flask. It is because of Lord Burleigh that Elizabethan laws, especially against crime, are so harsh. He is in love with death, that final cure for all who are unlike him. He delights in the hangings that take place on the three-cornered gallows at Tyburn. He also delights in seeing women burned alive who have been found guilty of poisoning their husbands. Lord Burleigh makes sure these women, convicted of high treason, are condemned to be hung, drawn, and quartered, their innards thrown to the dogs in front of bloodthirsty mobs. He sees that all criminals are dragged through the city on hurdles pressing against their bones, to the place of execution, where after much speech making and some prayers by the minister, and often some pathetic wrangling, the condemned are made to mount the ladder, then, in the words of Lord Burleigh, they are "turned off." At Lord Burleigh's insistence, it happens before the poor condemned man is unconscious, while his eyes are still open and he cries and screams. The victim still flinching, he is cut down, his parts and entrails cut out and burned in a fire while his body is dismembered and dipped into burning tar. His head is displayed on a spike in one of various parts of the city, such as the bridge at the Tower of London. Lord Burleigh takes credit that so many traitors' heads are stuck on top of London Bridge. So many are hanged or pressed to death under the guise of "saving the queen." When we first rode into London, 'tis true, I threw up when I saw such disgusting heads on their spikes.

More than this, although Lord Burleigh pretends to be a gentleman and is always saying hypocritically sweet words to the queen, everyone knows he often takes credit for her speeches, when in fact she wrote them herself. She is so much smarter than he is. Will and I were once invited as special guests to Parliament to hear one of the queen's speeches. It was so brilliant that tears formed in my eyes that a woman could write so well and, moreover, deliver her words as well as any great actor in the Globe. I remember every word she said: "For as much as it is manifestly seen to all the world how it hath pleased Almighty God of His most singular favor to have taken this Our Realm into His spiritual protection these many years, even from the beginning of Our reign, in the midst of the troubled estate of all other kingdoms next adjoining, with a special preservation of Our own person, as next under his Almightiness, supreme Governor of the same."

When the queen concluded, she gave Will a copy of her speech, written on royal parchment paper. Will was, I must say, as impressed as I was by the speech, especially since he secretly believes her to be a fool in queen's clothing.

The next day, Lord Burleigh told everyone that he wrote her speech. What a liar! Every day the queen commends him as her minister, and he in turn flatters her with his little weasel face. She has no idea that he spends much of his time, like Master of the Revels Tilney, gossiping behind her back.

Yes, Burleigh is the evil power behind the queen, instigator of the *peine forte et dure*, death by crushing. This is the penalty for "standing dumb at the bar," or refusing to plead guilty or not guilty. Without a plea, the trial of the condemned man cannot proceed, and thus the prisoner avoids legal condemnation, which carries, without forfeiture, transfer of all his goods to the queen.

Burleigh is the devil himself, the monster who convinced the queen that beheading with the ax is a privilege reserved for noblemen and gentlemen of high standing. That, in fact, was how the queen's mother, Anne Boleyn, died. I often dream of seeing Lord Burleigh himself hanging from the scaffold or being beheaded, his head lopped from his neck and tumbling on the street. It makes me wonder what kind of man could be so interested in violent death?

It was only at the request of the queen that our beloved late friend, Christopher Marlowe, who was once involved in a fatal quarrel, was spared Lord Burleigh's punishment of the gallows. The queen pardoned Marlowe, but Lord Burleigh was furious. He hated Marlowe for being that worst combination of men, a homosexual and an atheist. But the queen, who makes all decisions, did not care what Burleigh wanted. To her, Marlowe was England's greatest playwright. She often had his *Tamburlaine* presented at the court for visitors. 'Tis said at court that the queen adored Marlowe almost as much as she adores Will.

Lord Burleigh is one of those lords in Parliament who, in his upper-crust voice and polished noble manners, demands that the city rid itself of vagabonds, minstrels, diseased homeless beggars, jugglers, peddlers, tinkers, and scholars from the university who plead for money. He is a little sadist. As a child, it is rumored that for sport he pierced the eyes out of birds. How horrible! Jonson, who is a great gossip, told me this.

Among the other distinctions of Lord Burleigh is that he was appointed the godfather of Henry Wriothesley, known as the Earl of Southampton, when Henry succeeded to his title at age seven. These were the events that led this cutthroat of a lord into our lives.

The disgusting and greedy Lord Burleigh proposed his own granddaughter as a suitable wife for Southampton. Naturally, Southampton took one look at Lord Burleigh's granddaughter and must have vomited. She was among the ugliest noblewomen in all of England, and even if Lord Burleigh was rich beyond most people's dreams, Southampton revolted at the thought of marrying her. Lord Burleigh's granddaughter had such underarm odor that nobody wanted to get even near her, especially Southampton, who could have any of the beautiful women in London. Lord Burleigh was as mad as a loon to think that the good-looking Lord Southampton, with his long, curling red locks, his huge green eyes, so rich, so educated, and so charming, would want marriage for money to anyone. Southampton is the greatest "catch" at court, and all the queen's ladies-in-waiting are in a tizzy about him. He is an amateur poet as well. When I initially met Lord Burleigh all I could think of was this nursery rhyme:

> Half a pound of tuppenny rice,
> Half a pound of treacle.
> That's the way the money goes,
> Pop! goes the weasel.

But what does this have to do with our meeting Lord Burleigh? Dear diary, Lord Burleigh, out of despair, came up with the brilliant idea of commissioning my husband to write eighteen sonnets in order to entice Southampton to give up his bachelor life and settle down with a wife, namely his grand-daughter. He wanted desperately that his granddaughter be married to one of the richest bachelors in London. I remember the day he called on us. Will thought it a godsend. The theatres were closed because of the plague.

"A huge commission of sonnets from Burleigh? A miracle of money," he said. We then had one of our rare arguments.

"Did Southampton not commission me to write several poems, and wasn't he very happy to see his name, the right honorable Henry Wriothesley, Earl of Southampton and Baron of Titchfield, on the dedication of both *Venus and Adonis* and the even more remarkable poem, if I do say so myself, *The Rape of Lucrece*? Commissions will make us rich, Anne."

"Nothing good will come of this," I said.

Will disagreed with me and pleaded his case jovially.

"Both of my long poems, thanks to Southampton, now are published, and their popularity drives them into many editions. Lord Burleigh knows this. He cannot reach Southampton; his influence does not extend that far. Only in poetry! And for us—this is a calculation undeniable—it all adds up to a big commission! I want to purchase property—in Stratford. An expansive estate that has just come on the market, which is really a bargain and needs some fixing up, can be ours. We shall call it New Place, and we shall have a home and gardens—beautiful gardens!—and our daughters shall marry there, and we shall live there when we are old!"

I was not at all convinced that money was worth tangling up our lives with Lord Burleigh. He wanted eighteen sonnets as if he were asking for eighteen scones.

"Writing poems is my work, Anne. It is by my poetry that I will leave my legacy and through which I hope to become immortal. No one is going to remember my plays."

"You are a genius and an idiot," I told him. "A thousand years from now people will remember all your pen ever scratched."

I told Will it was absurd to think that the Earl of Southampton, so handsome, rich, and desirable, would ever lie in the bed of Lord Burleigh's granddaughter. He had already refused to marry many of the prettiest young ladies at court.

Burleigh announced that he was visiting, and when Will told me to put on a good face because a fortune of money was involved, I did so. I do not know why. Perhaps it was simple. I wanted more of Will's sonnets, the packages in which he painted rhythms with words, like painting with colors, and of course I liked for him to be happy. Being paid for his beautiful sonnets made him happy indeed.

When I had first asked him how to write sonnets, he said, "Paint this rhythm, not this thing."

That was the first lesson I ever had from a genius. As usual, Will is opaque. When he wrote plays, he loved breaking the rules, but when he wrote sonnets, he enjoyed following a strict form and keeping to strict rules. Eighteen of Will's sonnets were now written in one week for the Earl of Southampton, not for love but for money. All his other sonnets were for me. Neither Raleigh, nor Marlowe, nor Thomas Wyatt, the greatest of all Tudor poets, could write as beautifully about love as my Will.

When I first met Will, when he was sixteen, he was teaching himself the form of the sonnet. He loved the idea of only fourteen lines of poetry, the last two lines a couplet. The last two lines were important to him, and they were the challenge. Will said to me, "If you put an entire lifetime into a couplet, Anne, then you know you're really a poet. The challenge is to create the perfect couplet. I often study Sir Thomas Wyatt, who took the sonnet form from Italian, in which Petrarch used it with such genius. Wyatt outdid Petrarch, in my opinion, by creating the sonnet form in English. Listen to this, Anne."

> *How oft have I, my dear and cruel foe,*
> *With my great pain to get some peace or truce,*
> *Given you my heart; but you do not use*
> *In so high things, to cast your mind so low.*
> *If any other look for it, as you trow,*
> *Their vain weak hope doth greatly them abuse:*
> *And that thus I disdain, that you refuse;*
> *It was once mine, it can no more be so.*
> *If you it chafe, that it in you can find,*
> *In this exile, no manner of comfort,*
> *Nor live alone, nor where he is called resort;*
> *He may wander from his natural kind.*
> *So shall it be great hurt unto us twain,*
> *And yours the loss, and mine the deadly pain.*

For William Shakespeare, genius at any form was an expression of the confusions of the human condition. Many sonnets were about love: love of life, love of sexuality, love of the paradox of youth and old age. Often he would tell me I was the "dark lady" of his sonnets because somewhere in his mind he was afraid I would leave him.

The more I read and reread the sonnets, the more I thought they would be immortal because they expressed, in musical form, many of the emotions Will never spoke about but kept to himself: dark emotions and fear of youth lost and tossed away. Some had disturbing thoughts of death. Since Will was a jolly fellow, most of the time I could see the true shadow of his thoughts under his sunny personality.

"Why don't we ever discuss all these feelings inside you?" I asked as a wife who really wanted to understand the sphinx inside her husband. One moment he was ribald and bawdy, and the next he was private and silent.

"I don't like to talk about my darker feelings, Anne. Besides, whatever I have to say I have said in my plays or poems, and that is why I am a writer. I let my characters speak for me. My poems express my fears as well as my joys. I consider it vulgar to talk about oneself."

For me, of course, life is different. I love to talk and be open about my feelings. Perhaps because I am a woman.

And so I suppose I did not argue further about Burleigh because I wanted to see my husband's soul. His sonnets are my looking glass.

I fear that soon the calamity I foresee will arrive, and the madman Burleigh will own his name, and his madness will spin round us. Madness and greed of a crazy lord in need. The very rich seem to always want more money in their purses.

OCTOBER 5, 1602

Sadness sticks in my throat. Our lucky days have ended. The pestilence of the plague that killed our son has

138

returned again to London. Many of the actors have gone on the road, touring to make money. The thousands of people who attended the theatre now stay behind closed shutters because it is believed that the plague is caused by people mingling together. The mayor of London has let it be known that the best way to avoid the plague is to avoid crowds. That is why he insisted that all brothels, theatres, and bearbaiting arenas be closed. The royals try to pretend nothing is wrong. Some of the merchants do business as usual, and royal dinners still take place at the court, but the theatres are all closed, and no one knows when they will open again, so the actors that remain in London band together in groups at the Mermaid Tavern and drink. During the plague, patrons stop giving huge sums of money to their companies. The Admiral's Men, Lord Strange's Men, and even the Lord Chamberlain's Men are all out of funds. Even the children's theatre is not performing plays. The playwright Lyly, who writes for the young boys' companies, has stopped writing. Everyone wonders if the plague will last or blow away so London life can be normal again.

While the plague rages through London, public executions continue on the streets, thanks to Lord Burleigh. When I woke this morning I began thinking about how the plague began. Its birth, they say, was in Africa; then it went to Central Asia, where it became entrenched amongst rats. It runs east and west along the Silk Route, carried by Mogul armies and traders. To travel that road is a journey of millions and millions of deaths.

The plague brings an array of horrible symptoms to those infected. The classic sign: the appearance of buboes in the groin, in the neck, and under the armpits. They soon ooze pus. They bleed. Victims show black spots or damage to underlying tissue until they are covered in dark blotches. Most victims, like our poor son Hamnet, die within a week of the infection.

Whenever the plague strikes, the English economy begins once more a vicious cycle in which the deaths from the disease reduce the productivity of laborers, causing poverty to deepen. The grain output suffers, causing grain prices to increase. Ancient English kings, such as Edward I, out of fear that the lords' high standard of living would decline with the plague, would, as soon as the buboes started to appear, impose fines and rents on their poor tenants—as if death weren't enough of a tragedy. The wooden shutters of London have slammed shut to avoid the death outside. It looks to me like black splotches of ink are once more thrown onto the faces and limbs of those with the disease.

Meanwhile, the quills and ink of the London playwrights have stopped scratching. Ink is now blood and pus. Death silences poetry and wit. Will himself always ignores the disease when it comes to London. "Since I do not have buboes on my groin, I intend to keep on writing," he said to me. "I also intend to keep making love to you, more than usual, as long as my groin lasts. While the plague is outside, we make love inside. This is our glorious rebellion!"

But of course, the ravages of the plague affect Will's mood as they change the mood of everyone. All food markets, including the fish and meat markets, shut down. No carriages roll along the streets, and the familiar clip-clop of horses, which usually forms an enjoyable cadence outside our bedroom window, is silenced. As the city of London is slowly depopulated by the plague, we see men in black hoods carrying stretchers through the streets with white sheets draped over the bodies of the dead. Will despises the plague doctors.

"There is but one difference between these doctors and lawyers: doctors bury their mistakes," Will complained. "I can just see them now, London's great plague doctors visiting the poor victims of the disease. They visit as many people as possible, if they have been affected or not. I hate the doctors who make their fortune from disaster. I see them scurry around in great tall hats and masks with beaks, looking like overstuffed chickens—the beaks filled with spices and herbs to purify the air the doctors breathe. I see them in my mind's eye, pushing away with their wooden sticks anyone who gets too close to them and putting on their white chamois gloves to protect their hands."

Will says to me this morning, "If I were not a poet, I would go into the glove-making business during this epidemic and make a killing. Thousands of gloves are needed; they are worn once and thrown away. The plague doctors wax their clothing as a preventative against droplets of spit latching onto them. They cure no one, Anne, and stuff their own pockets. A plague on the plague doctors. A pox on them and their white masks, white gloves, and waxed clothes."

I can write no more now. There is crying in the streets.

November 1, 1602

Miraculously, the Black Death has left town as quickly and mysteriously as it arrived. It evaporated into the smoky sky.

I lay with Will on the bed today. The window was open as he read to me, and my eyes became heavy.

Shall I compare thee to a summer's day?
Thou art more lovely and more temperate.
Rough winds do shake the darling buds of May,
And summer's lease hath all too short a date.
Sometime too hot the eye of heaven shines,
And often is his gold complexion dimmed.
And every fair from fair sometime declines,
By chance or nature's changing course untrimmed.
But thy eternal summer shall not fade,
Nor lose possession of that fair thou owest,

Nor shall Death brag thou wander'st in his shade
When in eternal lines to time thou grow'st.
So long as men can breathe, or eyes can see,
So long lives, and this gives life to thee.

I wept when he finished. I do not know why. It is beautiful, yes. No verse on earth more beautiful.

The heavy doors of the theatres have reopened. The Globe, the Rose, and the Blackfriars are once more in business. Londoners rush now, with all their hysterical obsession for drama and comedy, to see life on the stage—a way to heal themselves from the real life from which they run. The bubonic plague has presented every person with the possibility of death, and Will Shakespeare now uses poems and plays to heal our wounds.

Burleigh came to pick up his sonnets for the Earl of Southampton. I care not for Southampton. While Will is a modest person, the handsome and conceited young Southampton is a show-off and throws his fortune around, sending Will expensive presents and bragging that Will was writing poems just for him. In his vanity, he thought Will was inspired by him. I told Will I didn't fancy the Earl of Southampton any more than I fancied Lord Burleigh, but Will tried to change my mind about our youngest and richest patron. To me, Southampton was a royal pain in the ass. To Will, he was a financial godsend.

Lord Burleigh was not the type of lord to make small talk. He came to our home and got right to the point before we even clinked glasses and had a sip of sherry.

"As you know, the Earl of Southampton will become a very rich man when he is twenty-one," Burleigh said. "It is his father's wish that by that time he should be married. Otherwise he will have to pay a very high penalty of thousands of pounds to me. I am not interested in the penalty, though. That is chicken feed, if I may be so blunt, compared to his entire fortune coming into my family. As is the law, his father's enormous fortune was left to him because he is the only son. Recently I had a splendid idea. I told him he should marry my granddaughter. He actually laughed in my face."

I would have as well.

"Will, only you, with your sonnets, can change his mind about remaining single. You, with your sonnets and couplets will convince him. At least he will read them. This is why I am here. My ward admires you. He is in awe of your poetry and all your plays."

"That's very kind of you to say, but it's untrue," Will said modestly. Will was the ultimate diplomat when it came to paying respect to patrons and playing the part of the humble poet, which of course was all an act. Will knew the value of his own writing and didn't doubt for a moment that his poetry was worth a fortune.

"Now, I want to make a deal with you, Will," Lord Burleigh said in a conspiratorial tone of voice. "This is just between you and me and your cousin. Now is when I need your services, and I am prepared to pay you a large sum of money."

"At your service," Will said.

"I need you to convince the Earl of Southampton that he should immediately get married. I can't convince him. Perhaps poetry can."

This scene, taking place in front of me, was a little like Hamlet trying to catch the conscience of the king with a play. Only Lord Burleigh wanted a series of poems, not a play.

"These will work much magic," Will said with confidence.

I knew Will would say yes. He was a charming salesman of his own words.

"You have come to the right poet," Will continued. "My poems will do the trick, I assure you. I will have eighteen magnificent sonnets to sway your ward towards your needs by the weekend."

"So soon?"

Lord Burleigh was amazed. No poet in London, not even the facile Sir Walter Raleigh, could write as quickly as William Shakespeare. I was interested in what Will would charge Lord Burleigh for these sonnets that he wanted written in such a hurry.

"Eighteen sonnets will command a lot of money," Will said. "I don't write poems by the yard so I'll have to think of a fee. It will be due when I give them to you. If you are not satisfied, Lord Burleigh, with my poetic arguments, there will be no charge."

Lord Burleigh was more than grateful and patted my husband on the back.

"You are a wonderful and honest fellow, Will. Make sure all your sonnets are very convincing," he said, and with that he left our home to dream of great, great wealth.

Once the door was closed, I asked my husband why he had not named his price.

"It is not good business, Anne, for a poet to look too hungry or too greedy. The rich only like the rich. No one rich respects a desperate poet. I have to make it appear as if money is the last thing that interests me when, of course, in this case, it is the first thing that interests me. I shall calculate exactly what our new home, New Place, will cost. I will include renovations, the planting of several orchards, and what it costs to buy the expensive lot of land behind our house, which I think we should also purchase because it's only going to make our home more valuable and assure us of privacy. Whatever that figure adds up to is exactly what I will ask for."

JANUARY 23, 1603

I am tired of begging, and Will won't listen.

The Earl of Southampton is married. We heard of it today from Ben Jonson.

But he did not marry Lord Burleigh's granddaughter. He married Mistress Elizabeth Vernon, with whom he fell madly in love, and she with him. Perhaps it is her beauty that convinced him to marry, or perhaps it is that Elizabeth Vernon is as shy as he is outgoing. He has married the wrong woman. He never even read the sonnets.

Guess what? Lord Burleigh came back to us today and asked for his money back.

"I never gave a guarantee," Will told him. "I only promised that the sonnets would convince Southampton to bring his fortune into your family if he read them. He never saw them. That was not the agreement."

"If you do not return me the money I gave you, I will kill you," Lord Burleigh said.

He threw the sonnets in the air. The pages flew like huge, white swan feathers and then fluttered to the floor. I picked up a sonnet and held it to my heart. Thank God I make copies of everything Will writes, I thought to myself, otherwise that sonnet would be lost forever.

"I will no longer be a laughingstock!" Lord Burleigh exclaimed. "No longer will I be held beneath the writer, the lowly, bad-bred bard! I shall end this now and be remembered as the one with the courage to take down the hated Shakespeare!"

He pulled out his rapier. I was also wearing a rapier and reached for mine; I surprised him. We started to fence.

"*En garde!*" he shouted.

He parried. I danced around him; he danced around me. Our rapiers made the sound of scissors. I saw Will's amazed face. Burleigh is a swordsman, but I was light on my feet. He was no match for me. Locking rapiers, we danced, each of us intent to kill the other. Suddenly my rapier was at Burleigh's throat. He dropped his sword and fell to the ground. He lay under me and I put my foot on him. I stuck my rapier in his arm and he began to bleed.

145

"You're lucky it is your arm and not your throat," I said, looking down at him. "Let me teach you a lesson, my dear lord: poets never give money back. I am so glad that Southampton ran away with Elizabeth Vernon, rather than being in your family, you pig. You're just lucky you're alive. Now get up and get out."

He slowly picked himself up from the floor, holding his bleeding arm. He limped to the door, leaving a trail of blood. I grabbed the handle of the door and opened it. I then kicked him in the ass so he fell on his face outside the door. I threw his rapier at him. He held his arm and looked back, as an animal wounded.

I slammed the door and listened to Lord Burleigh dragging himself down the steps. I secretly blessed my older brother for teaching me to fence when once, many lives ago, I was just a farmer's daughter in Shottery.

February 11, 1603

"I recommend you disappear for a season."

It was Ben Jonson's suggestion. The biggest gossip in London, he knows more than most can guess. And he believes that a secret conspiracy exists to kill the Writer.

"Why?" I asked, trying not to betray my fear.

"Very powerful men are envious of Will's business success and his extraordinary talent. Poets are to be altruistic and stupid, but Will is exceptionally good at keeping money in his pockets and filling theatres. He must take precautions," Ben said. My skin prickled with a sudden cold sweat. "You must disappear for a while."

"But that's impossible," I answered in a whisper. "Will is revising *Troilus and Cressida*, and it is going to appear again at the queen's court, as it is one of the queen's favorite tragedies. I'm afraid Elizabeth identifies with Cressida. Will and I can't just disappear. The queen now spends many mornings talking to him in her private chamber. Since she is ill and Will is her favorite confidant, we can't leave London."

Jonson looked me in the eye and whispered, "You must leave."

"Who are these enemies?" I asked.

"From my seat in the center of London, the conspirators are three, none of which will surprise you, save one. Tilney, Lord Burleigh, and Alleyn."

"Of course…but Alleyn?" said I. It was my turn to flush bright orange.

"All of London knows that Tilney is jealous of Will because he has taken away his power as the most important advisor to the queen," Jonson said. "Lord Burleigh feels he was cheated by Will out of money for the sonnets he commissioned to convince Lord Southampton to marry his granddaughter, sonnets that failed to do the trick. But why the great Edward Alleyn would hate Will is a mystery to me. He and Will, I thought, were friends. Will always admits Alleyn is a much greater actor then he will ever be. Why should he be jealous of Will? Do you have any ideas?"

"I do not," said I.

I felt guilty because I was lying to Ben. I had never told a lie before in my life, but this lie was so painful that I could barely think of what I was covering up. An event had occurred years ago—how many now?—just before *A Midsummer Night's Dream* had captivated all of London. I often think of it—not in longing, but in regret. I experienced my own midsummer's nightmare.

Will had been asked to make a journey with the company, and we had accepted. But at the last minute Will asked if I would stay in London by myself. He had never asked such a thing before. He wanted me to copy and edit *Troilus and Cressida*, which needed some dialogue before it was shown at the Globe. Will would never let anyone see his work, let alone edit it, except for me.

Reluctantly, I agreed to stay in London. It was the first time we had been separated since our marriage, and I missed him terribly and felt lonely. Why hadn't he taken me with him? I was angry at him without realizing it. But it was my fault. Why didn't I find it in my heart to tell him he couldn't leave me alone because I was so miserable without him? London was only bearable because I helped Will in his life and art. Why didn't I tell him that? The answer, I know, was simple: I am so devoted to him as both a great writer and as my husband that I never say no to him, especially about anything related to his writing. When we kissed good-bye, I promised that all the editing he gave me to do would be finished when he returned, as well as the accounting of the ticket sales from the Globe. I wanted to play the strong woman.

On that scorching hot and muggy Sunday after Will left, I sat in the largest room in our modest lodgings, which we used as our writing room. I missed him so badly that I was sadder than I have ever been in my life. Some women want solitude, but I want intimacy. The sun streamed in through the windows, and it was relatively quiet on the usually noisy streets beneath us. Before Will left, we had discussed the first version of *King Lear*, which we were now rehearsing. Will told me that with *Hamlet* he had discovered a new technique in playwriting that he called "inwardness" that could sew his fantasy and dialogue into new ways of expressional insight and psychology. This inwardness could make the female character of Cordelia more vulnerable and therefore more human. Will had become a psychological genius as far as I was concerned. He understood the demented thought of a king who is aging without wanting to age, of what it meant to lose your mind.

"Inwardness sheds light on the soul," Will said, "whereas soliloquy sheds light on the brain."

Will, as a genius, could now, with his craft and art, enter people's brains and souls. At Will's request I was helping him edit his two magnificent and future plays. It hadn't bothered me that I had neglected my own writing. However, after Will left, I decided to dedicate a day to rewriting one of my own new poems. Why not? I know that writing poetry is my only way of defeating the deathly feeling of being unloved and alone.

> Give up perfection now and learn to call
> Old sounds false, and new sounds beautiful.
> We are the summit of the hills we see.
> Two wings of sunset beat inside our minds
> And we become the sunset and the sun
> Also, pine tree, bending in the earth
> Like dancers tipped upon a stage,
> Become the silent dancers who are part
> Of everything we listened for and thought.
> We are the summit of the hills we see—
> Matrix of that falcon sun and all
> Things renewed inside the eye's cold whirl.

What was I trying to say? That we had to accept life as it was, not as we dreamed it should be? Was love just an illusion? Will often compared lovers to lunatics. I had no idea what I meant by that poem, but it pleased my ear. When Will was away I was a secret troubadour with an ear pressed to the clouds. Another poem came to me in a dream, and I wrote it down as if it had mysteriously written itself. These poems, I admit, were God-given gifts, as if formed in a heavenly mind and then dictated to my human mind. I was sure I was inspired by the creative aura of my husband's genius, where thoughts became things and things became words of my poetry. All this new poetry was my secret code that I showed only to Will because he loved to listen to my secrets and always delighted in things I created from dreams.

That afternoon
In an Egyptian dream
Two swans arrived. Silently
I watched them float.
Feathers of one swan were changed
Into the scales of copperheads.
I saw the slanted eyes of swans
Open into serpent tongues
Until the eyes of swans become
Slanted eyes of poison snakes.

White swans into white serpents changed.

Will loved that poem when I read it to him later. He laughed at the idea of swans becoming snakes. He found the poem erotic since *snake* was another word for the male organ. Often I wrote erotic poems that seemed to come out of nowhere. The last poem had come to me because I had been doing a great deal of research about Egypt in preparation to help Will write *Antony and Cleopatra*, a tragedy he had in mind for the future. While Will was gone, I thought of how much I loved going to rehearsals and watching him work his craft. He was brilliant in everything he did; no one in England could write like him, and few actors were as naturally talented. He was a great character actor, excellent at becoming the character, excellent in imitation of accents, able to fence and to move easily from farce to tragedy. He had been recently taking pratfall and juggling lessons from Kempe, and he excelled at mime and cartwheels, so he could even play clown parts. Will loved these lessons. He could now juggle oranges, apples, and balls, and he practiced all the time, while I, his witness and audience, sat on a wooden stool in the kitchen and laughed until tears ran down my eyes.

I smiled when I thought how my darling Will was taking "clown lessons" from our old friend Kempe. As I was thinking about Will doing his tumbling and learning somersaults, I heard an unexpected loud knock on the door. I wondered who it was. We were very secretive, and no one but the late Marlowe, the queen, and Kempe had ever been given the address of our lodgings.

I became oddly frightened. No one is safe in Elizabeth's England.

"Who is it?" I cried.

"Edward Alleyn. I've come to return a book," a deep, familiar voice called out. I sighed relief. Something in the way he said it reminded me of his performance in *Tamburlaine the Great* and *Dr. Faustus*. I remember Will having been thrilled by Edward Alleyn's speech as Tamburlaine, and the two shadows had swiftly become good friends. Will had said, without jealousy, but with a touch of sadness, that Alleyn put him to shame as an actor.

Alleyn has a magnificent chest, which I saw because his shirt was open without buttons. He is very tall and was physically made to play heroes. He had a halo of light blond hair, a thrilling and natural charismatic presence. He also had what Will called "an actor's instrument," as his voice is able to conjure fear, joy, or sadness and project to the last rows of the Globe. Everyone at the taverns in London talked about how Alleyn had recently married into great wealth.

"What a male whore," Jonson said to me. "Alleyn has sold his soul to the devil."

Alleyn's wife was rumored to be short, fat, and uncomely. Henslowe owned three theatres and many brothels and was the wealthiest impresario in the London theatre world. Alleyn had stopped acting for a while to run his father-in-law's theatres, bear pits, and brothel houses. Elizabethan audiences and even the queen were sorry he was no longer acting. He had thousands of fans, and you could say he was the first real star of London's exciting theatrical world. What did he want? Why was he at our door? Why was returning a book so important?

"Come in," I said, wondering why Will had given him our secret address. As I opened the door, I realized I was not in my male "cousin's" costume. I was wearing a blue-silk shirt of Will's that showed my breasts. I actually blushed as I ran into the other room to change. Like the giant that he was, Alleyn strode into my bedroom after me, laughing at my modesty. His head almost reached the ceiling.

"Don't worry, Anne. You didn't fool me for a moment," he said in a soft and charming voice. "Marlowe told me the truth. I bought him many glasses before it spilled out that Headington is Anne Shakespeare."

I blushed. He laughed at my modesty. I had changed into Will's green-velvet bathrobe; it was thick and masculine, but of course now my secret was out. He had seen me half naked.

"I can sniff a woman a mile away. Once I saw your armpits when you were helping to hang up costumes at the Globe. I knew immediately they were the armpits of a beautiful woman because they had soft black hair on very delicate, white, ivory skin, but your secret is safe with me, my lady."

I began feeling slightly fearful of this blond giant. He walked up to me, nothing between us but an inch of air, then his hand. Suddenly he pulled off my robe and started kissing my neck so passionately that I could hardly stop him. His mouth was all over my body, my navel, and then down to my thighs, and he held me so tightly I could hardly pull away. Ashamed of my nakedness, I quickly put back on my robe, but I had to admit to myself that I had been surprised by his kisses and felt a warm sexual arousal. I was also shocked by his behavior because Alleyn is supposedly a secret Catholic and a happily married man—although sad that he has no children. He spoke to me in an intimate, husky voice, which made me remember that I am a passionate woman.

Wait a minute, I thought, why would I be suddenly aroused sexually by another man? Was it because wearing men's clothes and working night and day with Will made me lose my femininity? Had Will been so very busy writing that we seldom made love as passionately as we had when we were first married? Had lacking any other man in my life but Will made me curious about what it would be like to be with a body other than his? I suddenly realized that Will had paid almost no attention to me as his sexual partner recently. Yes, 'tis true, he cared about sex in the beginning of those first exciting days in London, but his ambition to be king in the playwright's circle of the Elizabethan world had caused him to write day and night.

He is always thinking of his old age and how he needs to have money stored away for himself, for me, and for our children. But it isn't only money he thinks of. He is determined to be famous, to be immortal. Doesn't he constantly write about immortality in his sonnets, and isn't this insane desire for success and perfection driving him to forget about us? Our relationship? Hasn't he forgotten, like so many men do, that a woman is a flower? If you do not water her with affection, attention, constant reassurance, and, yes, romance, then she dries up and dies?

And I know that as a woman, I need not just sexual passion, but words. Words. Words of love. All the *I love you*'s went into his character's mouths, not my ear. Did he ever have any idea that I felt I was just his writing partner, instead of the woman he once lusted after? Did he realize that men and women have different brains? Different needs? Different ways of feeling loved? Yes, I gave Will my understanding of how important his writing is to him. I had helped him become a very important man in London, loved by the queen herself as well as by thousands of spectators. Had he forgotten that I need not only his gratitude but his passion and affection as well? I am not a character in a play he invented. I am flesh, blood, heart, and soul.

He always said, "You are all woman to me, Anne." But were those just the words of a fancy talker, a glib poet? Even a genius needs to remember that his wife is only human. Was this a case of a genius pouring all his passion into his work and little into his marriage?

When Will wrote, "Let me not to the marriage of true minds admit impediments," did he think that he and I were the marriage of "true minds" instead of the marriage of two bodies, two humans? What had happened to our feelings of wonder upon seeing each other naked? Is Will afraid of getting old? Is that why all the sonnets talk about his love for youth? Does it ever occur to me that Will is perhaps attracted to someone young and beautiful, someone to whom he could tell his true feelings?

And what is happening to the Anne I used to be? Has becoming a mother and a helpmate made me lose my sexuality in Will's eyes? Is love to man a thing apart and to woman her whole existence? Did all men take their wives for granted? I know Will believes in marriage as a good Catholic man, and that he has inherited very conventional moral values that are important to him, but he is also utterly ambitious to rise in the social classes of the rigid English society. Being granted a crest has meant so much to him. He is now officially a gentleman, not just a playwright. The crest his father had always wanted has now been given to him by the queen, bought with the money his father didn't have. All his sisters and brothers look up to him in awe as the star of the family, but does he feel his success entitles him to stop paying attention to me as his "great love" and wife?

I have never questioned my love for William Shakespeare. I consider being at his side and sharing his bed and table a great honor. But what about me? Do I need to create my own life? Have I fallen into the trap of not wanting to be the wife of a genius but to be a poet in my own right? I know I am nothing as a poet compared to Will. He is a meteor god sent to earth, and I am only a small star twinkling in his universe, but being the wife of a godlike man is starting to get on my nerves. He is too good-looking, too talented, too brilliant, too smart. Perhaps too smart to love me anymore? Does he ever think of me anymore as Anne, the poet who helps him? Or does he think of me merely as his old wife? Will I ever be more than the woman who gave birth to his children and helped give birth to his plays?

I often wonder about these things. If Will had been less of a strange person, perhaps I would understand him more. He is passing strange. At one moment his mind is floating in the cosmos as he composes the most beautiful lines ever written, but I am not a spectator of his plays. I am his bedmate. Does he know I need more from him than just the occasional "Good work, Anne" or hug of affection? When he wrote the sonnets to the "dark lady," I wondered if he had another love besides me. I was, I admit, suspicious of another.

"Don't be ridiculous, Anne. You are my dark lady," he told me.

"Oh really?" I protested. "My skin isn't dark."

"It's poetic license," he had said laughing. "You are my dark lady. You are my Juliet. You are my everything. Do I have to tell you all the time how marvelous you are?"

I feel like an addendum to his genius, but at other times I am so proud of him. I am the luckiest woman on earth to have such a man. Why am I constantly feeling unsexed?

I remember once at the Mermaid Tavern, Marlowe said to me, "Oh, so the silent one speaks."

Little does Will know I am getting bored and tired of being the "silent one."

I came back to reality. Alleyn was saying, "I am in love with you." He was standing in front of me. "I've desired you, Anne, since the moment I saw you. Of course, I know that you are Anne Shakespeare. There is a huge myth that you, his wife, are still living in Stratford-upon-Avon with your in-laws and children, but Marlowe, who loved me dearly, confided in me, and I was sworn to secrecy by Marlowe that the myth is a lie. I didn't need Marlowe to tell me that a beautiful woman walks in the trousers of Will's cousin. Ever since we exchanged eyes for the first time, I have loved you. Your face is one of the most interesting faces I have ever seen, Anne. Your skin is so white your eyes are without peer in England, so deep blue that I could swim in them forever. Your lips are full and desirable, and I want to touch you whenever I am near you. Your Arthur Headington disguise has never fooled me. I smell who you are, and it is the smell now of a sexually aroused woman."

Before I could even find the words to tell him to leave me alone, he had carried me and thrown me on my bed. He kissed my body, and as he did, my ship of ecstasy very nearly sailed into a tempest. His strong arms were around me, then his legs. Damn you, Puck! And then the wind through the window blew. The sunlight fell warm. And realization came. No matter how difficult it was to control my passion, I did not have the nerve to actually consummate our mutual desire. If I did, it would mean that my marriage oath of fidelity was a lie. I could not do that and lie to either Will, my children, or myself. I could not go through the hell of actually deceiving Will.

I said, "No more," though I only half meant it.

He heard me and looked into my eyes.

"I cannot," I said.

"You cannot stop now. Why—"

"I am the Writer's. And his alone."

Alleyn jumped up from the bed, and his countenance was utter confusion, sadness, anger, then resignation. Oh my God—what was I doing? Everything I prized—our domestic life, our writing together, our life with our children—would be over. I was a married woman, not a whore. What was I doing? Alleyn could tell what I was thinking. Was I actually playing out the role of Titania, who, in a dream, falls in love with a donkey?

"Like all great actors, I am a psychic," he said. "I know you are afraid that your husband will find out about our passion and all hell will break lose. But your marriage is over. Anne, my darling, marriage is like the moving spheres; it is never constant. What is perfect in the beginning becomes burnt out, a dead star, and yet what you and I have just now experienced, Anne, is heat and rebirth of a new universe, the birth of us. We have the kind of heat that only the perfect bliss of two well-matched lovers can provide. You were made for my body, mind, and spirit, and I was made for yours. I want to divorce and marry you."

He was tempting me, and I was amazed that I was experiencing the temptation as a great pleasure, not as a sin. He was suggesting not subterfuge, but a life with him forever. What would happen? Since I knew that Will was gone for several days I luxuriated in the thought, just for a moment, that I had a whole week to spend with this new lover. I was completely thrown off guard by how changed I felt after being kissed by him. It was such a relief to be a woman and not have to pretend I was a man. With Edward Alleyn, I could speak in my feminine voice.

"You must go," I told him.

"I love you, Anne," Alleyn said, stroking my face, which was filled with tears.

His voice was low and gentle, an excellent thing in a man. We were now experiencing the lovers' high that comes from passion. I was throwing away all reason, but it didn't bother me for the moment that I was behaving in an insane way. Insane? Yes, I had lost all reason and become someone else. I was no longer Anne.

"Anne," Alleyn continued, desperate to consummate our passion. "You work so hard for your husband. You need someone to take care of you. Everyone knows you run the Globe. Will is in charge of keeping the accounts, but it is you who does all the work. Come run off with me. You can live like a woman, not an accountant. I know you write great and original poetry; Marlowe told me. I want to publish your poetry. I now have a printing press of my own and I could publish your work. With me behind you, you will be known as the first great woman poet in London, Anne. Your work will come down through the ages, and one day your poems will be read by every schoolgirl and schoolboy who studies the poetry of our time. You will be the only woman poet of the Elizabethan Age."

Where was Puck? He was now tempting me. In my secret mind, that had been one of my many dreams as a young girl, to publish my poems. But no one was interested in anything I wrote, because I was a woman. Now, with Edward Alleyn's money and influence, and his desire to win me over, could he really change all that? After all, there were a few women poets who have their poems in pamphlets. No, I was insane to listen to this. As a married man, Alleyn would lie and promise me anything to achieve what he desired. No, I had to be Mrs. Shakespeare and bask in the glory of my husband, but I couldn't help my fantasy. If I were to run off with Alleyn and he published my poetry, it would be a scandal, but it would only make my poetry books more popular. It was almost as if Edward Alleyn were the devil, tempting me in a dream. I listened to all this in a haze of fantasies.

"What are you thinking of?" Alleyn asked.

"I'm thinking of how enchanting it would be to have my poetry actually printed in a pamphlet with my real name on it, Anne Hathaway of Shottery," I replied dreamily, not of course connecting the publication of my poetry with sexual favors.

I felt young and beautiful again. I felt hopeful that I could actually be a known poet. What had come over me?

I pushed Alleyn away from me, but without much conviction.

He said, "You have given up who you really are, Anne, to be William Shakespeare's wife. I will give you a new life. You and I will run off to France and to our new universe. I will divorce. You know I am a very rich man. We will live like a king with his beautiful poet queen in another country. In France there are many women poets and intellectuals who can become your friends, unlike in London. To hell with London; we can start our life in Paris, you and me. You will divorce. We will marry."

"Will cannot manage without me," I said dreamily. I felt confused.

"You were born to be a poet and my wife, not to be the good wife of William Shakespeare."

He was holding my hand so tightly, but my eyes fell on my gold wedding band. Was all this real? I took off my ring and hid it in a drawer so I wouldn't feel guilty. I jumped up and put my clothes on. Edward dressed also.

"Let's flee at once," he said.

In a moment we were out the door of Will's and my damp lodgings and on our beloved street, running over the hot mud and the familiar cobblestones I always walked with Will.

"I'm afraid the neighbors will see us together and talk," I said, fearing that gossip could ruin Will's career.

"Once you are with me they won't be your neighbors anymore." He laughed and looked at me with such affection that I felt warm, flushed, and giddy.

Alleyn had planned to own me and take me away from London. He had it all mapped out. He had arranged for a small boat with sails and a captain at the wheel; it waited for us on the Thames. Once in the boat, we floated down the Thames while the sails billowed in the wind. I saw the Tower of London on one side of the boat and the Houses of Parliament and Westminster

Abbey on the other, as if in a dream. I closed my eyes; if it was a dream it was a beautiful one. The entire city of London seemed now like scenery, a backdrop to my midsummer's erotic escapade. I heard the voice of Alleyn, who kept talking in his low and seductive actor's voice, and I closed my mind to the past and listened.

"Let me tell you all about myself, Anne. You don't really know who I am. It was always my childhood dream to be an actor," he said.

"Tell me."

"The dream began when I was a small boy, an only child, living in a slum."

"Go on," I said, fascinated by his past.

"You might call it a house of hell, in the south of London. My crippled mother died when I was three, and I spent almost all my time with my hardworking father, who once made his living as a collier in the coal mines of the north. Later, he was an unsuccessful cobbler in London. I'll tell you this: my father was a decent man who loved me, but he was a drinker and impoverished and could hardly make a living. Often we had nothing to eat."

"Oh how terrible, Edward. It is amazing you pulled yourself up by your bootstraps. Please forgive the pun because your father was a cobbler."

We both laughed. We were having a wonderful time.

"For my sixteenth birthday, with the few pennies he had saved, my father took me to see a group of actors; I think they were the Admiral's Men. I knew they all wrote plays together, acted together, and traveled in a troupe performing around the country and in the great theatres of London."

"Oh, is that what changed your life?"

"Yes. There were men playing women; they all seemed to be reveling in acting and having a forbidden good time. It seemed that in this bawdy make-believe world there was a chance for me to one day escape my existence of poverty and hunger. I made up my mind. I would join the actors, who were going to London; being one of them would be my escape, my way out of poverty. I met an old actor, a man whom I paid, and he taught me to project my voice with perfect diction. Then, when I knew the craft of speaking, when I was just seventeen, I disappeared with a group of writers and players. I wrote to my father a letter explaining that I was born to live out my dream of being a great actor. Miraculously, he understood and never came after me. I soon arranged to send him money every month, and now that I am very rich he lives in great style from the money I give him. You see, because he loved me, I now send him a fortune. I can afford to. I lifted myself up from the fate of being a coal miner or a failed cobbler, like he was, to being London's greatest actor."

Alleyn was telling me the story of his life. But what was I doing with him? Puck now appeared. I came to my senses, thank God. I was not Titania and Alleyn was not Oberon. This wasn't a play. It was becoming a nightmare. Suddenly this love affair made no sense. I didn't want to be with him. I didn't care if I published a book. I wanted to go home. As tall, blond, and handsome as he was, I knew I could never love him the way I loved Will. Underneath all his fancy diction and fine clothes, I realized Alleyn was only a conceited actor. Yes, he was very handsome. Yes, he tempted me with promises to publish my book of poems. But he wasn't a genius. He wasn't my beloved Will. I saw that he was a narcissist who was only a great and famous actor, a fortune hunter, and now a scoundrel, running off with his good friend's wife. But I was a scoundrel too. I was about to cuckold my husband.

We were on the Thames; my head was spinning. I wanted to go home. I wanted handsome Edward Alleyn to disappear. I could never put horns on Will. I wanted to run away from Alleyn, but I was afraid of making him angry. He had no idea that for me, this was just a fantasy, a momentary madness. He continued talking, but now it seemed to me he was braying like a donkey. I pretended to listen as he continued to talk about himself. Puck be damned.

"Old man Henslowe, who was the smartest theatre owner in London—and still is, I assume—took a liking to me because all the plays in which I appeared were financially successful. I had developed a huge following from the thousands of theatre-going Londoners who loved to have an actor to worship. Henslowe introduced me to his very unattractive stepdaughter, Joan, during a great royal feast. Joan fell madly in love with me, and Henslowe offered me a fortune as a dowry. He didn't have any sons, and he wanted me to help him run his theatres, brothels, and bear pits. What came next, Anne my darling, are the two worst years I have ever lived through. My wife is an illiterate and mean woman. Although I once found her bearable, she and I have now nothing in common, and we secretly hate each other. She cannot bear children, she talks incessantly, and when she prattles on about shopping for expensive garments and recites all the court gossip, it makes me dislike her even more.

"Being with a woman for me is much more than sex. I must be able to communicate and talk with a woman who has not only charm and physical beauty but also a great imaginative mind. Someone who is witty and interesting—like you, Anne. As the leading actor of London, I can assure you that ladies have always thrown themselves at me, and even married ladies and noblewomen send me notes and invite me for trysts all the time, but they don't interest me. For me, a woman must be educated and intelligent, as well as beautiful. Anne, you are my ideal woman, and I have been worshiping you with my eyes, sending spies to find out the day when your husband would leave town so that I could call on you on the pretext of returning a book. I see you are the woman I have always dreamt about."

He grabbed my hand—the hand that once wore a wedding band on its fourth finger—and kissed it. Then he put his hand on my breasts. I pulled away from him. When was this madness going to end? Tell me, Puck. When?

"Now I must tell you the truth. I want to take you away from the foul air of London, Anne, and have you with me as my wife forever in the wholesome air of France. I have plenty of money, we have no children, and Joan can carry on very well without me. Anne, Paris is the most beautiful city in Europe. I don't see why my life has to be a tragedy with the wrong woman. Together we could live a merry and loving existence. My spies have observed you working like a little slave for Will—carrying books, spending endless hours at the printers, copying musty chronicles. You are always, I am told, cuing Will to learn his lines when he is acting, and lately keeping the accounts for the Globe, where he is a shareholder. With him, as his so-called cousin Arthur, you live a life you were not meant for.

"With me, Anne, you can live the rest of your life as a queen; you will read your poems to me every night. I will make love with you every night and every morning. I have a beautiful, large country castle in Normandy, and we can live there in luxury as well as in Paris. Since I speak French and have an international reputation, if I wished to I could appear in plays in France from time to time. I have offers to be paid a fortune in France to act in the *Comédie-Française*.

"We will be happy there together, Anne, my beloved; we can live only for each other. You have no idea how delightful and cultured the city of Paris can be if you have a fortune to spend, and we do. We would live in exile, but we would soon have many artistic and refined friends, all of them Catholic and nobles, thank God, and you can have a literary salon. Who wants to live in a Protestant country? Nobody in their right mind. I know you have children you love, but we can send for them. Their father is too busy writing plays to give them any attention anyway, but I have no children and would even adopt both your daughters as my own."

Edward was using his great performance voice. I was confused. Puck was applauding.

"You are tempting me," I said.

He continued, "Imagine the elegance you can enjoy living in Paris with your children and with me. Writing books that are published. There are many women writers in France, unlike England. And to hell with that old bitch the queen. She has destroyed all the old ways of worship and sacred traditions of belief and civility. You must admit the London playwrights don't have a carefree life. Everyone fears the queen. One day she loves you and the next she kills you. She had Thomas Kyd, once her best friend, who wrote *The Spanish Tragedy*, tortured and put to death. She put to death Essex, known as a good man, and Marlowe died mysteriously. You never know when she will turn against Will in the same way. You're not safe in London. You will be safe living with me. You don't need all the unrewarding problems of the stupid London theatre world."

He kissed me passionately as if I were already his wife. I wrangled out of his arms and pulled myself away, trying not to look disgusted. I could listen no more. My mind went back to when I had met Will. We had loved each other then, and we loved each other still. How could the paradox of this inequity of emotions be happening? Memory is a powerful drug. The past came back to me. I felt suddenly sick to death and guilty.

Unaware of my emotions, Alleyn continued, "I know Will is a moody fellow, and it is part of your job to pick him up from his melancholies when he cannot write. I, on the other hand, have a character that is always cheerful and never melancholy, and with me, darling Anne, you would have a life that is carefree and happy. Run away with me. I promise you'll be happy with me. Will won't even notice you're gone. He's too busy writing and sucking up to the queen."

I felt suddenly dizzy and wanted to lie down alone on the boat's deck and think. What was I doing? Had I spent too much time in the sun? Oh darling Puck, deliver me from evil and lust.

I had to run away. Suddenly I woke up from this midsummer's madness. I was under a false power, as Titania was in *A Midsummer Night's Dream*. Once the love juice wore off, Titania saw the truth. Isn't it amazing how love juice can suddenly turn into tears? Regret? Just as in the play, Alleyn turned into the donkey, the ass he really was.

I was Mrs. Shakespeare, not Titania, and I loved Will. I returned, slowly, as if from a dream, to the truth of my own life. I adored the brilliance of Will's wit and mind. We had so much in common; we had children, a family. We shared a stage life that we both loved, and I knew through Will's poems that he would be immortal. My discontent was foolish. Was I throwing all this away because I was besotted for one moment with a tall, handsome actor? I threw myself at the man in front of me, who now seemed blurry. I was dizzy with regret.

"Edward, my love, please, I beg of you to forget this event! This never happened. Please, I want you to lie and lie to yourself. Pretend you do not know me. I want you to just contract this event." I cried again, "This never happened!"

Unfortunately Edward Alleyn was convinced I didn't mean what I said. He only laughed at me. I jumped off the boat and onto a mossy landing. I began to run. Edward Alleyn ran after me. Puck, of course, was running with him.

"What do you mean?" Alleyn screamed as he ran behind me, as if he were too dense to understand that I would rather kill myself than ever have my husband find out I had dallied with another man. "What do you mean, forget this event?" He ran after me, thinking I was only teasing him.

I was a fast runner and now sprinted for my life. Was he stupid? Didn't he realize my sexual desire had totally disappeared and I wanted to be rid of him? Oh God, he was an idiot. How could I have ever found this man interesting or even attractive? Now I understood why Will created the character of Puck. Women who felt lonely could become mad and with the love juice of their imagination fall under a spell. Well the dream was over.

I turned around and yelled at him. "By *the event* I mean forget *this* ever happened to us, Edward. The way drunkards do not remember what they said or did when they are in their cups and their mind turns off memory. I want you to forget you ever visited me today. Please, I beg of you, forget me! Tell no one."

It was now dark, but we were near my street. I was out of breath from running. He caught up with me in front of my lodgings.

"So you don't want to run off with me, Anne, my beautiful poet?" he asked, sincerely wondering if he had done something to offend me.

"No, I want to pretend I never met you. I want to forget what happened today, to completely block it out that we ever had this idea of running away. I don't want you to speak of this to anyone. Please! Not to any of your friends, not to any of the playwrights. I do not want to ruin my life and Will's as well. And I love him. I beg of you to forget me!"

"Why?" he demanded.

Now he seemed angry. He thought he had found a new love, and he realized he was doomed to going back to his ugly, shrewish wife. I was not going to be his mistress, his future wife, or ever make love with him.

"Please don't follow me!" I pleaded. "I can't explain more. This was all a midsummer's mistake."

"Anything you say now you'll one day regret," he said.

He was furious. So was Puck.

"Please don't ever come to see me again. Go away. I have nothing to say except this is all a bad dream. Please leave me alone."

And take that Puck with you, I added in my mind. Thank God I was home. I ran up the stairs and bolted our door. I had run home in my bare feet, and I tried to get rid of the blood that was dripping all over the floor from my feet, to remove the stains of my mistake. To calm down I washed myself in our large tub with warm water and soap and changed into my kitchen clothes. I began doing ordinary things, as if nothing had happened. I made blackberry jam and stewed fruit and roasted peppers. Cooking seemed to calm my frayed nerves. How could I have doubted Will's love?

I thought to myself what a fool I was—a woman who had almost cast away her husband. It would ruin Will's life if he knew about this. I stripped the sheets from our bed and began washing them. I sprayed lavender cologne and lemon perfume all over the house, hoping to get rid of the smell of Alleyn's body. What if Will smelled another man in the bed? He would kill me. I had to forget that I had done this. I had to rub a cloth of amnesia over the part of my mind that remembered Edward Alleyn kissing me. What if Alleyn blackmails me and threatens to tell Will? Oh God, I tried not to even think of that. I was so grateful for my beautiful life, and in one second it could be ruined. What was wrong with me? Thank God we had never consummated this crazy passion. Yes, I would forget the event. I would never speak about it to anyone, especially not to Will, and it would go away. It would all be nothing but a secret afternoon in the midst of summer. Oh, dear diary. I am so happy I resisted the temptation to bed another man just because I was lonely.

I came back to the present; Ben Jonson still stood before me. Out of spite, jealousy, anger, and vengeance, Edward Alleyn had become a conspirator against my husband. My rejecting him made him an enemy. Standing there, listening to Jonson, the terror for a moment became rational. Of course Alleyn had his reasons, too close, too terribly intimate to be understood by anyone looking in from without. It was I who had made him hate, who had churned his lust until it became anger, his envy until it became rage. But he would not—not Alleyn—consider murderous action as a means of alleviation. That was someone else's prompt, and Alleyn, always eager to please, is now playing the role of conspirator, as though handed a sheet offstage and asked to enter with a scraggy whisper and darting eyes. He would not kill for me. He would kill for having lost a battle his opponent did not know he was playing—a loss more painful because it played itself out on a psychic plane, apart from any real action, aggression, violence, or show of skill or wit. I was Will's. The simple fact of it must have enraged him. I thought of nothing but Alleyn's anger.

Jonson had first uttered it, the word I now write here, the word that keeps me from sleeping and drives me to this ink and quill. *Conspiracy*. It is a word Will hears none of. He refuses to listen to me. Will is so humble that he refuses to think someone would desire his blood spilled. He refuses to believe he warrants the trouble.

"No one really wants to kill a scribbler. Marlowe was murdered because he was a spy and an atheist. I am neither. Why would anyone want to kill me?"

"Because genius inspires malice," I said.

"Oh stop it, Anne. You're imagining things. I'm not that much of a genius. You exaggerate."

I prayed to my mother in heaven tonight. It was she who was my best friend. Without her I have felt the loneliness descend. My fear has no one with which to commiserate. No one but these pages now. They turn from white to black, from open, empty space to cluttered, swirling imitations of my mind. And still, at page's end, nothing remains but the same thoughts in my head, now within and without. Now everywhere. *Conspiracy*.

MARCH 24, 1603

The queen is dead. The bells of all the churches are ringing still; they have been sounding all day the terrible toll of death at the highest mount in London. We mourn the queen; we weep for the London she built, and for the London she leaves behind. We did all of us today wander aimless as children, hungry for sup, but without anyone to call them home and to the table.

MARCH 25, 1603

I remember that before she died, the queen had called us to her bedside.

"I am the queen of England, but you are the king of writers," she joked to Will in her soft voice, surrounded by her huge, gold-framed Venetian mirrors, which held the reflection of all who came in her bedroom and also reflected her magnificent tapestries.

Will joked that she must be losing her mind in her old age, and that she was sounding ridiculous. Only he could have navigated a compliment like that, which in the mouths of lesser prophets would have sounded too real for the false artifice of humor.

But she laughed, as he knew she would, and as she knew he expected.

For all his rambunctiousness, all his charm, his poetic temperament, Will is not an overly emotional man. His tears are late in coming. But when she spoke—God in Highest

Heaven, I can hear her voice in my mind, the only place I shall ever hear it—when she spoke, I saw his tears. I have not seen them often. But they were there, more than a sheen across the eye, but not so much to pool and spill upon the cheek. Before she died, the queen asked Will to leave the room but to leave his cousin behind. Will looked at me and without hesitating obeyed the dying monarch.

"I know thou art his wife," the queen said. "Women must keep other women's secrets."

"Why have you said nothing?" I asked.

"I like not to upset a genius," she said. She added, "Take care of him; his life is in danger."

A day later she was dead. Her eyes were closed by a priest, and the bells of every church in England soon tolled the news.

Part Two

James

June 3, 1604

The King's Men. It has a fine ring to it, though I miss the rhythm of "Lord Chamberlain's Men," the way the syllables strung themselves along, the early rise, the later fall. Now with His Highness as our patron, all has been condensed into a single syllable: *King's*. The players are his now, and how busy we all have been.

I confess a boredom born of his dinners. Happily, he has kept Will busy writing plays, but the social calendar is now as dense as the Forest of Arden, where once I sat on the lemongrass writing my songs and poems on summer days. We have traveled home to Stratford-upon-Avon every few weeks—as often as possible. Without Will's father, only Mary Shakespeare cares daily for our grown-up daughters, who live with her. Time has flown, on fast wings. Will yearns to reunite with our daughters. I know this.

Will has bought the most magnificent house I've ever seen. Burleigh's sonnet payment is now wood and stone and large rooms, our New Place. We have added huge glass windows and installed beams of mahogany on the brick ceiling. The reconstruction of the house has been a long process, and now when I see it rising from the land I feel it is the architectural proof of Will's success, as our children were proof of our desire. Now Will imagines himself to someday be a gardener on his own land. In his mind he is already planting imaginary flowers.

I think often of Elizabeth, and how the theatre she invented seems to ache for her intensity and constant attention. She saw *Othello* just before her death, with Burbage playing Othello to perfection and Iago pleasing the crowd. How the queen pondered over his evil, and how Will delighted in never having revealed the source of Iago's hatred for Othello, his motives all muddy and deep. And so the imaginations of all who watch leap forward and back to build a second story of his motives in their own minds.

King James has called for *Macbeth* to be performed at his court many times, when ambassadors arrive from France or Spain. He believes it shows off the glory of Scotland and the English theatre, and I do not disagree. I am haunted by it still. It is a tragedy of power that, in the end, fails and will lead to King James on the throne. No wonder the king watches this tragedy over and over. It validates his reign.

I am told that one of James's first acts was to commission the tragedy that would become *Macbeth*, as though he had been waiting for the throne for this single reason. The story plays to his pleasure: gore drips from it, and witches populate it, and the king is a deep believer in such magic. And he's a deep believer in his right to rule; Will was less than subtle in this affirmation, writing the ending that gives the king all confidence that, though he fears assassination, his reign is prophesied to continue after the death of Banquo, his forefather. Holinshed again was our source, but as I told Will, "You have moved a long way from *Henry V*," his last chronicle play. *Macbeth* always calms the king's nerves. It predicts that the heirs of

Banquo will continue in glory, and King James is an heir of Banquo.

It has been twelve years since Will last wrote a chronicle with a villain as a hero, *Richard III*. The two plays look at one another and acknowledge their kinship: ghosts, prophecies, spirits, ambitious villains, long soliloquies, and glorious, brooding fate. The passage between Macbeth and Lady Macbeth, after the murder, is one of the finest examples of atmosphere ever created. I read it and sense the dampness of the walls. I am proud to have written it with him, proud of the imagery that was born of our collaboration: the play is splashed with blood, while water and darkness predominate. Once the murder has been committed, the blood of Duncan flows slowly down the stairs until it is splashed over Macbeth's whole universe, until eventually he stands alone in a universal sea of blood that cannot be moved by Lady Macbeth. Even Neptune's ocean will never make them clean! Darkness can be so deep, that deep. Macbeth speaks of it in that moment that can be written, I think, only with the genius that the Writer has at the tip of his quill.

Life's but a walking shadow, a poor player
That struts and frets his hour upon the stage
And then is heard no more. It is a tale
Told by an idiot, full of sound and fury.
Signifying nothing.

The king confided in me his belief that this speech was among the most powerful words ever written in a tragedy, and I felt at that moment the shadow of Elizabeth. The king is now as much an admirer of my husband as the queen was, though I sense the love is of a different kind. He grows so pleased by Will's flattery—the future reign, the witches laughing—but though a friendship seems to be present, privately Will confesses his dislike for King James. The king is also a slob. Stains from his meals always linger on his dirty clothes.

The constancy of James's request for *Macbeth*, and for Will himself, is a great annoyance to Master Tilney; he once chose the plays, but now the king rarely consults him. James saw the queen's increasing reliance on and affection for Will and simply extended it to the habit of his reign. The many plays that go on the boards every day at various theatres—the Rose, the Globe, the Blackfriars—are written by Dekker, Middleton, Jonson, Beaumont, Fletcher, Nashe, and my Will, the Writer, he who earns the definitive applause for his histories, tragedies, and comedies. The public has favored *Twelfth Night*, *Macbeth*, *Antony and Cleopatra*, *Hamlet*, and *Romeo and Juliet*. The king's taste is akin to theirs, and he is also eager to see the history plays repeatedly performed at his court. We see little of Tilney now, and it is a grace. My worry is a vague distress: without his pompous gait about the theatre, I am left to wonder where he walks, and who along his side. At court there is very little difference between a friend and an enemy.

As for myself, I now trust no one.

Every day I consider the idea of conspiracy—Jonson's story never leaves my mind for long, nor the thought that it may come to pass one day soon. When I suggest to Will that the Writer has enemies, that care must be taken, he replies always with the same dismissal: "We all live at the mercy of a falling tile, Anne!"

Whatever that means. Without Marlowe, there is no one to whisper in his ear, to cultivate a healthy sense of distrust, to watch with him for betrayal. Marlowe had warned Will about treachery. When Will wrote *Titus Andronicus* in 1593, a few months after Marlowe's murder, when he was trying to rival Kyd's *Spanish Tragedy*, he wrote a testament of that specimen of gory revenge as gruesome as any Greek tragedy. *Titus* became so popular in London that it was revived for many years. Will wrote of treachery so well, but now I fear life shall imitate art, his art.

JUNE 10, 1604

It's typical of Will to laugh so loudly at his own material that one would think him mad with drink. He sometimes cannot stop, caught up in his own bawdy puns. His puns are everywhere—scarcely can I even find them all. He builds them like puzzles, overlapping double entendres in his plays. Although Queen Elizabeth never quite understood many of them, I am sure King James grasps most, especially the puns and references to love between men.

Despite his pretense to adore Queen Anne, James has several male favorites, so many it is difficult to keep up with them. Of course, everyone in the theatre world was excited when King James ascended the throne because it was well known that he had developed a love of theatre from his mother, Mary Queen of Scots, who had taken him to the theatres in France when he was a child.

When he was first crowned king, I remember how the populace in London turned out to greet him upon his entrance, although that entrance was delayed by the plague. I remember how many commoners lined up to welcome him. Men threw their caps in the air, and even common women curtsied and cheered. His entrance into England was made even grander by masques, which were performed for him in Whitehall Palace. They were written especially for him by Ben Jonson and Thomas Dekker. Will laughed at them and the pitiful courtiers who performed them. He refused to write any masques himself, although he was begged by Ben Jonson to do so. Will never liked the form of the masque, and it disgusted him that the masques are merely amateur theatre, acted by overdressed courtiers who know nothing about language, cadence, or drama. He hates masques.

I remember how the king was crowned with great fanfare and ceremonies, and he immediately sent a message to our lodging, a flowery note, telling us how much he admired Will's poetry and plays and how he longed to meet him in person. The note was ignored, so then there was the gift: six golden dinner plates with his royal crest emblazed on each. Our breath was caught between a gasp of wonderment and a sigh of relief. Professionally, our reign was extended, in a sense; James had inherited us from the queen, and it appeared he planned to embrace us as she did. The plates were followed by many other gifts: food from the New World, jewels, furniture from Venice, which Will adored although the carved chairs inlaid with gold looked ridiculous in our humble lodgings.

"Kings were created by God, and therefore they do not have to obey laws created by man." James wrote this in Scotland when he was young. He apparently has always been arrogant— he is despised in Parliament. Why? Parliament does not believe in "rights of kings." Though he is pompous and self-promoting, with no respect for Parliament, even so he remains the person who commissions the King's Men, so the Writer is forced to respect him.

James continues to use the horrible Lord Burleigh to make many political decisions at court, so most of Elizabeth's policies of torturing Catholics remain intact. There is no less blood now than there was with our beloved, bloodied Elizabeth. Only more arrogance: his combining the governments of Scotland and England was a product of his pride. Neither the Scots nor the English cared to spit at one another, much less share an island and a government. The two are joined geographically, yes, but that is all. The cultures sit at a great distance and stare at each other in hatred.

The winter weather of craggy Edinburgh is freezing, while the weather of London is milder. Scotland does not have great theatre as London does. Scotland has no Globe Theatre, no Shakespeare, no Jonson, no Dekker, no Middleton, no Webster. The Writer was not born among them. A bagpipe is not a viol, a kilt is not a pair of trousers, and a Scot is not an Englishman. A King James is not a Queen Elizabeth, and he is having trouble uniting his kingdom. A Londoner cannot abide the habits, speech, food, and clothes of Scotland.

Everyone at the Mermaid Tavern gossips about the king. Ben Jonson loves to point out, when he is in his cups, the irony that James, the child of Elizabeth's executed rival, Mary Queen of Scots, is now the grown-up child who rules England, Scotland, and Ireland, not to mention colonies in the New World. Like Queen Elizabeth, James has severely suffered from a monstrous childhood. His father was assassinated, he stuttered as a child and was beaten by his tutor, and then when he was twenty, his mother, Mary Queen of Scots, was beheaded by Elizabeth. That he lent his tacit approval—since Mary stood in the way of Elizabeth's power and James knew that he was next in line for the throne, after Elizabeth—is not doubted, but one wonders what lies behind the eyes of one who can give his mother up to the ax and chopping block. He must have felt terrible pangs of guilt, but it expresses itself not in tears but in a constant crisis of nerves, as if his own existence proves the inhuman capabilities of those with tortured childhoods. Loyalty is mere sentiment in his mind that can change with the wind to hatred. And so he is suspicious of all. Will believes him to be mentally askew—and so do all the other playwrights, who laugh often at his twitching. Whenever we see him, standing flanked by servants, wearing his soiled royal robes, his eyes dart around the room. Quick movements distress him, and when there is dancing, he remains far to the side. He is always fearful that some gunpowder is going to blow off his wig and his head under the wig.

If only Will possessed some of the king's suspicions. If only the king would watch for Will as well. The king of the playwrights Will is, but he is as innocent as Othello of how many are his enemies; he believes he is in his own world, protected by the constant chattering of characters in his own brain.

"The mind of a thoroughly informed man is a dreadful thing," he told me once at the Tavern. "To know too much is to lack the ability to laugh at anything, especially oneself. Our dear king knows all, and thus has no sense of humor."

"But thou?"

"Me? I laugh deeply and loudly! I sing my life and dance wherever I go! I think not of falling tiles, or stabbing knives in the dark, but of falling words, and iambic pangs of desire. I think of lovemaking! I am a child, a fool, a wandering life singer! I know nothing—nothing! And that is why I laugh like a madman and sleep as soundly as a child. I am a fool in the forest of my own beautiful life," Will said.

As we toasted to each other with ale, I couldn't help, dear diary, but think there is a devastating irony in the fact that Will felt his life was beautiful while men are secretly trying to find a way to end it. Darkness and devils. I pray to my mother to keep the degenerate knaves away from my husband.

August 3, 1605

The king loves Will. I'm afraid that love is not returned.

"I'd find a better king in Bedlam," Will said in disgust one morning to me as we walked to the market. "He is intellectually pretentious."

Will does not really like to chat with King James. But the feeling is not mutual.

When King James had just arrived in London, many actors and many of our fellow playwrights, such as Ben, pretended to love him—even wrote poems to honor him. Will will cater as he needs, but he cannot laud. Will and I both agree that James is not a kind or ethical man. He enjoys bearbaiting and killing animals for fun, an act that Will, who loves animals as do I, cannot endure. "Seeing the king riding with his hounds," Will said after a long two days in the country, "is to experience the unspeakable in chase of the uneatable." And King James openly humiliates his wife, Queen Anne of Denmark, with his fops, by kissing and hugging his favorite young male courtiers even when he is in public—his own wife and children are forced to look on this disgusting behavior with a smile because he is the king. Will sees only the emotion, the secret anger and sadness of a spouse spurned. It makes me nearly weep to think of Will's loyalty to a king he cannot admire.

Unlike Queen Elizabeth, King James is a cheapskate. He spends his time counting gold in his counting house, like the nursery rhyme we all learned as children. Will once remarked, "Getting a shilling out of King James is as easy as getting a bear to bait a man. He doesn't spend money on anyone but himself and his favorites."

The king, there is no doubt, is somewhat dense. He inquires of Tilney all that Will means by his work. Ben tells us, like any good snitch, what he hears, and he writes his news in the form of a play. Ben is constantly eavesdropping at the palace, pretending to be writing a masque, but actually reporting to us what he has overheard.

KING: I have called you to my royal chambers because I saw *Othello* last week, Tilney, and there were an astounding number of puns about unfair treatment of women by men that I am not sure I understood completely.

TILNEY: At your service, Your Majesty. Nobody catches the dirty puns or double meanings of Shakespeare more than I do! For example, Emilia, in that play, asks why it is acceptable for men to be sexually unfaithful, while women don't have the right to be. In a really filthy speech, Emilia tells the audience that the idea that all women should be confined to home like domestic drudges is ridiculous.

KING: So what is it, Tilney, that Emilia says that is so juicy? Because I am not sure I caught all her sexual innuendos.

TILNEY: Emilia talks about the secrets of women, that women get turned on by the smell of sex and like to taste both sweet and sour. When Emilia talks about ills, she means to discuss women's unfaithfulness, and when she talks about affections, she means women's sexual desires and temptations. When she says, "It is their husband's fault / If wives do fall: say that they slack their duties, / And pour our treasures into foreign laps," what she means, my dear king, is that the husband bears some responsibility if the wife strays, especially if the husband seeks the vaginas of other women.

And then Tilney would sit and the others would laugh. Ben claims the routine is very old, and Tilney quite a bad impersonator, even of himself.

The theatre is not what it was. Unlike Queen Elizabeth, King James refuses to spend a fortune on costumes and scenery. He likes to spend his time in his private molly-house, which he created to give himself pleasure when his favorite, the Duke of Buckingham, or the queen isn't looking.

"He is a spoiled child in a man's body," Will once remarked. "And in the end, all children learn their lesson."

NOVEMBER 6, 1605

I read my last entry and marvel at Will's prophetic nature. The king has reason to tremble. He has learned a terrible lesson: enemies are out to get him. The Gunpowder Plot!

The plot to kill the king would have been the greatest catastrophe in the history of London. Thank God it was foiled—and by the king himself, no less. Sometimes paranoia pays off. Yesterday when the king was to appear in person to open a new session of Parliament, an anonymous letter was delivered to one of his lords, advising the fellow not to attend the ceremony. He handed it to the king, and within minutes Guy Fawkes was discovered in the cellar. The king always acts quickly. His royal guards apprehended Fawkes, who had stuffed the cellar full of gunpowder and iron bars concealed by lumber and coal. This is the greatest act of terror England has ever faced. Carrying a fuse, Fawkes intended to put into execution a desperate plot to blow up the entire Parliament, as well as the king, his wife, his children. The Gunpowder Plot, as they're calling it, was conceived by Roman Catholic conspirators angered by what they perceive as King James's persecution of Catholics. Under torture, Fawkes gave up the names of his coconspirators. We suspect all will be hung, cut down while still choking and barely alive, split open, hewn into quarters, and dragged through the streets of London for the crowds to jeer at.

Now the king appears a hero, having saved Parliament and his own head. Ironic, of course, as there is nothing heroic about James I. Being suspicious and desperately selfish does not a hero make. And yet, his superstitious nature saved him, his family, and all the members of Parliament.

Among those arrested is Father Garnett, the leader of the Jesuit mission in England and a close friend of ours. I cannot believe he was involved. He had supped at our table many times, and as Will and I dined tonight I did pray for his soul. The plot has simply made it too convenient for James to go after those he hates. In London, you need only such license, and blood fills the streets. I am grateful God saved the king—or, more accurately, that the king, by apprehending the letter of Guy Fawkes, saved himself. But Father Garnett is innocent. I pray he will be released from prison. Will and I plan to plead on his behalf with the king. A lot of good that will do. I already see poor Father Garnett's head lopped off and rolling in the street, with his eyes staring at Will and me, asking, "Why didn't you save me?"

JANUARY 5, 1606

Will and I had a Yuletide of great cheer at home in Stratford. Our grown daughters adore us, and Will's mother is dizzy-eyed in her magnificent new home, proud to say it was bought by her son's success. Although my husband has the same prestigious place under the new king's reign that he held under Elizabeth's, I have heard him recently for the first time begin to brood about retirement. He still feels he has a lot of plays inside him, but pleasing the king is beginning to get on his nerves. Will also finds himself missing his mother and the girls, and wishes to spend more time with them. The girls are growing up fast, and both of them will soon be married.

I have not allowed myself to think of Will's retirement very often, as it is too happy a thought to entertain, for fear it will remain only in thoughts and speech and not in deed. But when I allow myself to consider it, I am happier than I knew I would be. In truth, I do wish so to be back in Stratford, where I can look into the faces of those around me without fear that the smiles and false civility hide anger and deception. Will has never had a true sense of how dangerous it is to be in his position. But when I think of leaving London, I think only of how miraculous it will be that he remained alive to walk away.

Will's younger brother Edmund arrived in London five years ago to find work hanging on Will's coattails. Will is so kind and generous that he shows his brother, who has no talent, only his concern and love. Forgive me for thinking Edmund an idiot. He is an aspiring actor, and I fear I will go mad listening to him. Edmund has always suffered in Will's shadow, and now Will finds him parts in every play. Will is determined to help Edmund in a career for which, I feel, he is ill suited. Will admits his brother has no feeling for the stage, yet we must give him parts. I fear people will throw eggs and rotten vegetables at Edmund when he acts in the longer parts Will has promised him, which will not be good for Will's state of nerves. Having to spend time with Edmund, out of respect for Will's mother, has become very distracting for us both, as Edmund wants to be sure that Will is writing a large part for him in his new play.

"It's worth moving back to Stratford to stop being pestered by Edmund. It's hard to make a silk purse out of a pig's ear. Especially when the ear is your brother," I told Will, but he pretended not to hear me.

For him family is everything. Yes, Will is slowly becoming fed up with all the aggravation and problems in the London theatre. On one hand, he longs to retire; on the other, he dreads it as an admission of old age, or a concession that his talent has run out. He knows what the city will say. He is beginning to feel old—his knees and back ache often, which makes him feel vulnerable. I tell him that he shouldn't spend the whole day sitting in a chair and that we should take more walks, which are good for his back, but he is writing more plays, one after the other, faster than ever. He feels, I think, that he must say all he can before he can say no more. He dreads silence.

There are those who wish he had been silenced long ago. Murder is everywhere in the theatre world. Every enemy is your friend and every friend your enemy. Since Elizabeth there has been money in the theatre, and now James has paid fifty pounds for *Timon of Athens* because it has lots of slaughter in it. The king pretends an attitude of jollity and gayness, yet I have heard that he asks his lovers to whip him. He loves to laugh but he also loves gore. Will, a quill for hire, offers what the king requests, but he has—I can see it—become disenchanted with the king's patronage and stupid literary suggestions. He retreats into his mind and does not see what I do: the stares of Tilney and Alleyn, and the murmurs of those close to Burleigh. The sooner we go home the better, so that my husband may ride to glory in a carriage, not a coffin.

MARCH 3, 1606

My nights have been sleepless because of the nightmares. In my dreams, Marlowe comes to our home. He warns me to take care of Will, tells me to beware of fire and water, to watch for ropes and stones. I know not half of what he means. But I know how I feel when I wake: that there is an invisible and creeping jealousy against the Writer, and that it grows in London by day and frightens me by night. My only consolation is Ben, who now loves Will dearly, and has proven so devoted that I look to him for information of whatever kind he finds. If a plan is being hatched, Ben's spies will hear and tell.

MARCH 11, 1606

I confess here what outside I cannot say: I hate Dekker. I always have. But now I feel it so deeply, I cannot act as though I do not. Ben tells me Dekker has been speaking with Tilney and Alleyn, probably Burleigh too, and Ben runs after them to know their whereabouts. By the time Will wrote *Hamlet* his name was a tourist attraction for all those who came to see theatre in London, while Dekker's career had slipped into the grave of nothingness. His extreme jealousy is barely contained. To Will's face Dekker once said that *The Two Gentlemen of Verona* was a great achievement—but behind Will's back he called the work tedious and the puns and comedy uninteresting.

186

Will knows fully what bad luck does to a playwright, and to Dekker the pain has been hard and unending. Dekker was part of Will's company very early on—until Jonson called Dekker a hack, a "dresser of plays about town." He soon left the company. And all he's done since has been, to quote Will, "fasten his head on the spike of my reputation."

Dekker, I am told by Ben Jonson, has also had a lifelong problem with debt, and was once imprisoned for a debt of forty pounds to the father of a fellow playwright. Dekker finds himself in the poorhouse because he cannot imagine a new play.

"All he cares about is money and twat," Ben says.

Tilney's anger is fueled by jealousy, Burleigh's by greed, Alleyn's by pride, but Dekker's is fueled by poverty. I feel that the last of these may be the most powerful, as there are few more angry than the gifted poor. A frustrated playwright wants revenge.

Last night, we were invited to another dinner at the king's palace, but the king was not in attendance, having given his regrets that he was ill. Nashe sat to the left of Will, while Queen Anne took the head of the table. Ben Jonson was seated to my left, telling me how boring were the comedies that now flowed from the pen of Middleton. I could not listen to him. Though I sat in the company of actors, jesters, and playwrights, I felt as if I were in the company of petty villains. I felt overheated and kept wishing someone would extinguish the brilliant candles dripping wax from crystal chandeliers. I excused myself from the queen's table and wandered down the long halls of the palace, the wide spaces looming, the marble cool beneath my feet. I admired the tapestries.

Suddenly, I heard voices within a room near the western gallery, and I followed them slowly. The tension within the dialogue was deep, and it took me a moment to understand the owners of the shouts. It was the king and Dekker, and I listened silently to their argument.

"My dear James, who is your secret lover? It is not the Writer! It is I! And yet you put money into the purse of the bloody bard while knowing I am still in debt. You constantly choose his plays to be seen before mine, though you know his plays are not as good. You seem to think him a genius and me a novice."

"Must I love your plays because I love you?"

"Yes, you must!" Dekker screamed. "Will is manipulative, cunning. He steals from his patrons—he weaseled money from Burleigh, you know—and deposits it in ownerships of theatres and houses. He bought the largest house in all of Stratford, and where do I live? In a rat hole! Recently he bought a townhouse in London."

I could hear the king getting angry.

"Why are your debts my responsibility? Remember, you're not Shakespeare, Dekker." He continued, "Can you bear the truth? That his lines stay in my head for weeks!"

Then the king recited:

Fillet of a fenny snake,
In the cauldron boil and bake.
Eye of newt and toe of frog,
Wool of bat and tongue of dog,
Adder's fork and blind-worm's sting,
Lizard's leg and owlet's wing,——
For a charm of powerful trouble,
Like a hell-broth boil and bubble.

"Stop!" shouted Dekker. "The witches were put there just to entice money out of you. Everyone knows you wrote an epistle about witchcraft. Any schoolboy could have written those lines. I loathe William Shakespeare and his plays within plays. Like his mad characters, I will have my revenge."

"Do you mean to cause a scandal?" the king asked in an infuriated voice. "Haven't there been enough scandals in the theatre already? Calm down, my love. You haven't the heart for a scandal. Come here...."

They stopped speaking, and from all the thumping I heard, I assumed they were pleasuring each other. I began to shake. I returned swiftly to the table and I took a seat beside Inigo Jones, who is designing scenery for King James.

"I hate Dekker," I said to Will when we went to bed.

"A plague upon my enemies and a kiss upon my wife. Why don't you write poems again? Sing me one of your songs in the morning."

I began to cry, and Will wiped away my tears with a kiss.

"Aren't you getting tired of your disguise?" he asked. "You are probably fed up with playing the part of cousin."

"Yes I am. But I am getting even more tired of pretending we are safe in London."

"How can we go home?" Will asked. "You know I am intent on writing *King Lear*, a tragedy of a king with a disordered mind. I prefer writing this play, even to *Hamlet*. It will be my greatest tragedy, filled with pageantry."

"I prefer the pageantry of the vegetable market in Stratford to all the jostling of the theatre. You have your crest and your money, your fame, your fortune. What more is there?"

JUNE 16, 1606

The conspiracy is happening. And I fear once it has begun it will not be stopped.

The blood is still on the stage.

Will was to play the ghost again tonight in *Hamlet*, which is being revived for the hundredth time at the Globe for many foreign visitors. But the absence of Burbage, who is suffering from a temporary illness, forced him to step in and play Hamlet himself. He pulled in Bernard Miles, an older gentleman with a weak voice but a strong sense of character, to play the ghost.

"Whither wilt thou lead me? Speak. I'll go no further," says Hamlet.

And then it came, falling, just as the ghost said, "My hour is almost come." A huge brick from the roof's support toppled, smashing into Bernard and killing him instantly. I had looked away, down at my hands, where I held some of Will's sides from the play. I heard the thud of the brick breaking wood and the gasp of the audience. And then I saw him, sprawled upon the stage and bleeding from his head, all the audience aghast. Will was so much taken aback from the accident that he kept speaking his lines. Suddenly a roar went up in the theatre, and two physicians rushed to Bernard. I was down to the stage in a matter of seconds, pushing through the crowd and dragging Will to the back of the curtain. They placed a sheet over Bernard; the announcement of postponement did not go over well with the crowd. Bernard was carried home, where he still lies at this moment, a corpse, covered lovingly in a sheet, awaiting the ground. We have just heard that the king has ordered all the theatres of London closed, in memory of Bernard Miles, felled by a brick. I am sure the brick fell not by accident but by design. It was meant to fall, meant to kill, but not meant for Miles. It was meant for the ghost. It was meant for Will.

Tilney was sitting on the pillows on the stage, reserved as the most expensive seats, next to Lord Burleigh. On the other side of the stage was Edward Alleyn with his pathetically ugly wife. Dekker I had seen nearby, in a seat I'm sure the king himself must have paid for, as he could never afford to sit with the rich and noble. They appeared distraught, and Tilney actually more upset than usual. The crowd exited slowly from the theatre, many of them laughing and drinking ale as if they had seen a cockfight instead of an actor killed.

"We all are at the mercy of a falling tile," Will had said.

Yes. He was laughing to himself and at his favorite expression actually coming true.

After we left Miles's home we rode to our lodgings in the carriage provided to us, as always, by the king. Darkness and devils have been outwitted by some angel in heaven that is protecting my darling Will. Will has not spoken since we returned. I dare not tell him what I know he now must know himself. We must get back to Stratford—not for the sake of the children, or Will's aching back, or any other reason. Now for the sake of the life of the Writer.

July 4, 1606

In the whirligig of time, strange things happen. Evil is afoot. Ben Jonson barged into our home, triumphant. Will was at the theatre, and Ben had a story to tell, which he recounted as if he were reciting a comedic masque.

He told me of a meeting that took place yesterday in a private room at an inn in Shoreditch. Ben had seen three of the four attendees and recognized the voice of the fourth. He saw Tilney, Burleigh, and Dekker, the last of these limping. Alleyn's voice he heard—most in London would know it anywhere, as it has spoken across the crowds so many times; in many ways it is the voice of the Globe.

"The four of them gathered there portends a single thing," Ben said.

Lord Burleigh was furious at the other three. The meeting broke up as soon as they saw Jonson. They suspected him of snitching, and of course they were right. There is nothing now to do. Will refuses to leave, his head all day wrapped round *King Lear*, which he considers his greatest yoking of tragedy and comedy. His ambition to finish it consumes him, as though it is his statement against the fates that he will not grow old. And it is his statement against the conspirators he refuses to acknowledge, that they cannot drive him from the land he rules. I have only two hopes: that he finish *King Lear* quickly, and that we leave at earliest chance. Or that he lose the mind to write that I may convince him we can both write better if we are back home in Stratford. The foulness of the conspiracy has given me a fearful heart. I must struggle in my attempt to convince Will of the danger he is in. Courage, Anne. Courage.

July 27, 1606

The king's boring dinner tonight, in honor of one of his great loves, the Duke of Buckingham, was interminable. Four hours it lasted, mainly because of all the court dances. Will danced with a beautiful, young, dark-skinned woman, who stared at him in a way that made it apparent he could have whatever he wanted. Nashe kept elbowing me and nodding in their direction, as if I would be happy that my cousin would likely later be fucking in a closet in the palace. The final time he nudged me I slapped away his elbow and left the table. Jealousy is not in my nature. I was actually relieved to see Will having a good time.

The bookseller Richard Field was also invited to the dinner by the king. I had a great deal of amusement and gaiety chatting with him about books. Many of the gentlemen wore velvet doublets and carried swords and daggers; a few carried dag pistols on belts around their waists. I am always suspicious of guns as they have no purpose and no art but to kill.

The court gossip around the table was all very bawdy, as usual. Everybody uses double entendres, the way Will does in his plays. Nashe was talking about "noble" things, which is a pun on *penis*. The word *threshold* was used often, which of course is a pun upon *prick*. The king quoted the line "We have been down together in my sleep," which, we all know, means we have fucked each other. There were many prick songs as well as a lot of puns on homosexuality. I listened and blushed while Middleton talked to Ben Jonson about his "ragging tooth," which means "throbbing cock." Jonson, in turn, talked about whores that he had slept with in Shoreditch. They were both very merry. Middleton was chatting on and on about Iago's "thighs," which of course is a word for the sexual pleasure of the backside. Talking about sex obliquely is what King James enjoys after his first course of oysters. Dirty talk pleases him to no end. Oh, that's a pun! What a difference his dinner table is from Queen Elizabeth's, where the guests talked not about sex, erections, and fucking, but about literature, geography, and the wonders of commerce in the New World. She, at least, had some tact. Thank God the evening finally ended.

"I need a drink," Will said with heaviness. He drinks little at the king's palace. We decided to stop at the Mermaid Tavern.

Having seen too much that evening of Edward Alleyn, I needed a whiskey myself. Holding secrets has never been an easy task for me. And with Will, it hurts to hold truth in darkness.

Will and I ordered two whiskeys, and whom should we see coming towards us but a man both Will and I had grown to love in all our years in London—Inigo Jones, the greatest set designer in London. It was Inigo who created trapdoors, smoke, and all the inventive machinery that gives special effects to Will's tragedies and comedies. His sets made a visual miracle out of *A Midsummer Night's Dream*. His innovative scenery has also graced *Othello* and most recently *Macbeth*. In *Macbeth* he created a castle that was dark, damp, and dangerous. The set allowed Will to place his tragedy against smoke, fire, and brimstone that brought the play to life in a magical yet realistic way. Costumes and sets are now part of the spectacle audiences love, but I shall always prefer an empty stage, where people listen to the language and use their imagination for all the rest. But don't tell that to Inigo. That would put him out of business.

Inigo has a jolly temperament. He always wears workman's clothes and often is mistaken for a carpenter. Indeed, like Peter

Sharp, the great carpenter who built the new Globe Theatre after it was moved to Shoreditch, Inigo isn't just a set designer. He constructs a world of make-believe that allows Will's plays to exist not only in leafy green language but also in beautiful castles and woods. Although Will and I often say, "All people in the theatre are crazy, including ourselves," Inigo Jones is the one sane person in this industry that resembles, at best, a madhouse. We have overheard Inigo speaking with the comic Robert Armin about the death of Edmund Spenser. Elizabethan England's most celebrated poet apart from Will, Spenser was murdered in 1599, and the stories of conspiracy have only grown these past years. He had been Inigo's close friend.

"May I join Mr. Shakespeare and Mr. Headington for a drink?" Inigo Jones asked in mock reverence.

"Sit down and join us. A great pleasure to see you!" Will replied. "We adore your company." He is always especially polite to Inigo.

"I assume you have just come from the king's evening of showing off his poets and playwrights," Inigo said quietly. We knew he shared our contempt for King James. "I was invited but…I was unable to attend," he said with loathing in his voice.

"It was quite an awful evening," I said. "I could tell how bored Will was. He hates being a performing monkey. You didn't miss anything but dancing and trivial gossip and lousy food."

"I'm fed up with the king," Inigo said. "Fed up with him and his town and the tragic theatre scene, where men are reduced to battling like animals in a pit. The theatre is not what it was. King James is a vulgar fool, not a patron of the scenic arts."

"You shall have no argument from us." Will raised a glass.

"To tell the truth, I'm tiring of hammering away at sets that now cost me a fortune. Labor and materials have become so expensive in London. They are four times what they cost when we were young. And the king? Getting a pound out of his purse is becoming more and more difficult, since he only spends money on his lovers."

"And you're not his type," said Will, laughing. We joined him. "Besides, Tilney is advising him on costs, taking bribes, and marking up everything," Will mumbled.

"The king is constantly calling me into his private chambers and trying to find a cheaper way of building sets for your plays. I keep telling him there is no cheaper way. If he wants all kinds of machinery, walls, palaces, golden forests, silver brambles, columns of gold leaf groves, smoke effects, all sorts of new devices, the best of everything, he has to be prepared to part with a lot of money."

Inigo continued, "England, thanks to Elizabeth, now has the greatest theatre in the world. You are a genius. I am a genius. But genius costs money. Tragedies are expensive. A scaled-down *Macbeth* is worthless. Everything has to be larger than life. If you have a cauldron, it has to bubble and have smoke. If you have an army, you need to have a war with something other than plywood. Guns, spears, curtains, floors—all these things cost a fortune." He was no longer jolly. "Now the royal fortune is going on costumes, but not on scenery. The king likes the most expensive costumes that a tailor ever made. All he cares about are clothes. He's a costume freak. Silk has to be embroidered and velvet has to be crushed. Slippers and stockings have to be made in Paris, and all that leaves very little money for sets. I'm thinking of retiring. I don't like doing grand-scale sets on a budget.

"The queen used to say, 'Master Jones, give me the best sets that ever were created, and I will gladly pay for them.' Remember that? Now King James haggles with me for every piece of wood and every penny. All Scottish kings are the same. They want to cheat the artist, especially the set designer. I would have been better going into my father's banking business, but no, I had to go into theatre. Now all I can do is build one more set and retire."

"Yes, dreamers have always been foolish." Will smiled weakly. "And I. I now listen to a new muse: the King of Idiots, His Highness James. Queen Elizabeth would have never dared to tell me to change a word. She was a grateful audience, not a pompous dilettante."

Will usually tried to be cheerful and merry, filled with the zest and enthusiasm that made him so successful and made everyone love him, including me, when we first arrived in London. But now he became bitter and sarcastic. The evening was winding down. We were all a little drunk.

Will said, "Last week, the king, scratching his crotch, watching the courtiers bend over backwards to flatter him, asked me why I named Macbeth Macbeth. Can you imagine? I wanted to say, 'What should I have named him? Pierre?' But I held my tongue. 'Would you prefer Macheath?' I asked the king sarcastically. Do you know what he said?"

"He said, 'No, I'd prefer MacFuck,'" said Inigo.

Will smiled but did not break delivery. "He said, 'We'll keep it Macbeth for now.' He was giggling with one of his little fops as if the fop were his lapdog. 'But frankly, Will, I do think Macheath sounds better,' he told me, quite seriously. Suddenly the king's not only a Bible translator; he's a playwright."

"And a set designer," Inigo said. "He constantly tells me what to build and how to design it."

"Remember the old days?" Will asked wistfully.

"And yet Will is writing better than ever," I threw in. "We are starting to write a first draft of *King Lear*, and I believe it will be a poetic masterpiece when it's finished."

"Oh no," said Will. "My cousin is always flattering me." We exchanged glances.

"Come over and let me show you act one of *King Lear* tomorrow," Will said to Inigo. "At least I have a first draft ready."

"Don't mind if I do," Inigo said, picking up the check. "Don't even think of paying. It is an honor to be with both of you."

"Oh no," Will said. He reached for his purse.

Inigo grabbed the check.

"I'm not a cheapskate like King James. How many times have you and your cousin invited me to dinner at your home? It's the least I can do for a great poet."

Will and Inigo embraced. I saw them as two frustrated servants of the king, miserable in a London that had changed before their eyes. We were all fed up with the theatre; the make-believe world of the stage was becoming so competitive and expensive that Will talked constantly about going back home to deal in real estate, not make-believe estate. I am already packed.

AUGUST 8, 1606

This morning Will awoke and began juggling oranges. Four of them at once, before they all came tumbling down. He was in a jolly mood, feeling the nearing of the end of *King Lear*. I am not.

We are, alas, always juggling our moods. London is a very promiscuous place—it is all about sex and class, genitals and gentility—and the most promiscuous man in the whole kingdom is King James himself. The second most promiscuous man is his public lover, the Duke of Buckingham, one of the most powerful men in England. As Will says, "He has the king's ear and the king's rear." He attends every one of the Writer's plays, but since the plays must come to the king, and the king only sees plays at his court, the king does not come with the duke to the theatre. Thus Buckingham often comes alone. He sits on the stage as a royal member of the audience. I notice that he laughs at all the filthy jokes Will weaves into his sublime poetry. These puns and double entendres seem to titillate the duke, who, it is said, particularly loves sexual innuendos. We must juggle our moods and appear to admire the duke since he is the king's confidant.

Will wrote, in *Henry V*, that Sir John Falstaff dies having sex. The audience knows that Falstaff dies while having an orgasm, just as his prick starts to go limp. Will, with his sense of bawdy humor, created Falstaff to spend his life in a brothel. The audience, who knows that sex is part of everyone's life, from the common man to the merchant to the king, laughs when the character of the hostess, describing Falstaff's death, talks about the "finer end," the completed orgasm. When she says "between twelve and one," she means that Falstaff's erection pointed towards twelve, as in a sundial, and is just about to go down. This evokes the image of the male lying down with his penis pointing up. The audience loves such bawdy humor.

When the hostess talks about the "turning o'the tide," she means, as everyone in the audience knows, the penis as it turns from erection towards rest. When she uses the word "fumble," she means he was playing with himself. When she talks about Falstaff's "play[ing] with flowers," she means he toyed with his own cock. To "smile upon his finger's end" means to finger fuck. His "nose" really means his prick. When she talks about his "pen," she means his penis. When she says Falstaff "told of green fields," she means, of course, the female genitals, as in the women's fields, sown by the male seed. When she feels his knees and finds that they are "cold as any stone," she means cold as any testicle. Falstaff is a very bawdy character, so is there any wonder that he was the favorite of Queen Elizabeth, may she rest in peace, who was quite bawdy herself? The queen insisted, after Will killed old Falstaff, that he appear again. For this reason, Will wrote *The Merry Wives of Windsor*.

The Duke of Buckingham, who is probably always horny, came five times—Will would have liked that one!—to the Globe to see *A Midsummer Night's Dream*. When Puck speaks about being "merry" he is talking also about being horny. The duke almost fell off the stage laughing at Puck, the jester to Oberon and Titania, king and queen of the fairies. Puck is a sly dealer in filth and sex. He thinks that human beings and their stupid love games are a joke: "Lord, what fools these mortals be." Puck takes a fiendish delight in the squabbles and arguments of lovers, and he laughs at their pain and distress. When Puck turns to the audience, he tells them:

> I am that merry wanderer of the night.
> I jest to Oberon, and make him smile....
> And sometime lurk I in a gossip's bowl
> In very likeness of a roasted crab,
> And when she drinks, against her lips I bob
> And on her withered dewlap pour the ale.

The Duke of Bedford once accompanied the Duke of Buckingham to the Globe to see our dream play, and both dukes were so excited about the character of Puck that I thought they were going to perform oral sex upon each other before they left the theatre. Of course their high royal positions made them adhere to protocol, but I saw the lewd look of delight on both dukes' faces. Puck amused them to no end.

When King James fell in love with the Duke of Buckingham, he was so besotted that he wrote love letters to the duke, according to Ben Jonson. Jonson quoted the letters to Will and me one night at the Mermaid Tavern, and they were almost as romantic, but not as beautiful, as the love sonnets Will had written to me.

Jonson said he signed such a love note with a royal red-wax seal, so that no one would read it, but of course Jonson has spies amongst the servants of the king, and thus he knows of everything. Another bit of gossip Jonson threw out is that Queen Anne wrote a letter to the Duke of Buckingham, saying she would be "most happy" to know that he would be "most gentle" with the king because the king is in a foul mood when he does not see the duke. I am sure that people behave the same promiscuous way in Stratford, but when I was young it would never cross my mind that a wife would welcome her husband to have a male lover. I know I would not. Although Will and I are secret Catholics, and we may have been seen drunk, nobody ever dared create a scandal in the family. After all, we are family people. What kind of family man is the king, and how can Anne not spit in the face of the duke? I wish I could for her. I feel sad for the queen.

The Duke of Buckingham came to visit us yesterday, pretending to be literary, talking with Will about music and poetry. He gave Will a compliment as if from one artist to another. He said, "My dear Will, you compose and imagine in cadences. Your head is filled with cadences waiting to be born."

What flattery that impressed no one! As I acted out my part as the kind cousin, I put out the tea and some cakes, knowing that the Duke has a fondness for food that is very sweet, like most people in England. I noticed, as soon as he sat down at our humble table, in our modest lodgings on Silver Street, that he immediately took off his royal gloves. They were made of expensive white chamois and were soft and perfumed and garnished with embroidery and delicate gold lace. (I wondered if they could have been made by John Shakespeare himself, who liked to brag that he was a dresser of white leather gloves for royalty. His gloves certainly were not made for the farmers, shepherds, or yeoman in our hometown.) He also wore trousers and a jacket made of the softest brown crushed velvet and red shoes that even the pope would envy. Of course, he wore many gold rings, one of which featured a huge red ruby. It is said the king gave him that ring when they first met.

"What I admire most about you, Will, is your profound sense of ambiguity," the duke said, seated comfortably on our kitchen stool. "Your plots and subplots are always variations on the same subject. In almost all your plays, they mirror each other. The bond that exists between Hamlet and his father, for example, is mirrored in the relationship between Laertes and Polonius and in the kinship between Fortinbras and his father. I observe, with great delight, that certain characters, generally one from a high and one from a low estate, seem deliberately to parody one another and that they are paired as doubles, visually and scenically. Almost all your plays, Will, open in medias res, as if a conversation is taking place and the audience has just been allowed to join. No one else ever thought of that."

Will smiled in gratitude at the duke and thanked him for his kind remarks. For Will, the duke's comments on his plays were as welcome as cold bread pudding covered with mustard. But a playwright has to put up with all the inane and stupid comments of patrons, and so Will gave the duke his usual smile.

"Where do you find all your fabulous stories?" the duke asked.

Will tried not to yawn. He finds the duke so tiresome and always plays the sphinx, mysterious. If I borrow books from Richard Field, our friend the bookseller, for research, Will insists that I return them immediately. Will does not want anyone to know where his stories or ideas come from. He likes drinking ale with the other playwrights and me, but we always leave early. We socialize very little, and never does he speak of his work. Today we are hosts to the Duke of Buckingham, so we had to show courtesy and civility and listen to his terrible, raspy voice, but Will reveals nothing.

"I admire you, William Shakespeare. You are the greatest playwright alive and yet you live in such modest lodgings. Why is that?" The Duke never occupied a humble house in his whole royal life.

"My cousin Will saves all his money for his wife and children, Your Lord. He has purchased a huge estate called New Place that is by far the finest in all Stratford-upon-Avon.

He also invests in property and has several thousand tithes of property in Stratford. Recently he bought a townhouse to rent out in London, next to the Blackfriars Theatre," I said proudly.

"You are then a very rich man?" the duke said, thinking me just a servant.

I could see he was amazed that a mere scribbler could be wealthy from words. Like most very rich people I have observed, the duke is only impressed with money.

He blurted out to Will, "I have a favor to ask of you."

He had overly perfumed himself, and he looked like an aging actor who had put on a wig and makeup. He still smelled of rotting teeth to me, even if he was the king's lover and a royal duke.

"Certainly," Will said.

"My dearest friend in the world, outside the king of course, is the painter Rubens. You've heard of him?"

"Of course. Everyone in London knows Rubens." Will spoke in his usual amused voice.

"I would like him to paint your portrait, Will. He has painted mine, and it hangs in the palace in the dining room of the king. I would like to commission Peter Paul Rubens to paint your portrait since the king treasures you so much. He says you are the crown jewel in his life, and I know he is proud that all the Western world admires your plays. The portrait will hang next to mine."

"I must decline your generous offer!" Will said with the quiet voice I know so well, as if the duke had made a joke. Will always uses humor, I noticed, to diffuse confrontation. Only he can get away with it.

"Why is that?" the duke inquired, trying to be affable.

The Duke of Buckingham held the world in his often-gloved hand. He was the essence of royal entitlement. No one dared refuse him anything, not even the unattractive, paunchy, and foppish King James, who ruled all of Britain. Now Will was saying no?

"Your Lordship, I had a portrait painted of me when I was a younger man than I am now. It was painted by John Taylor, and I had a gold ring in my ear. I looked half bald and so serious that I do not think it flattered me. I looked ugly. Until I saw that portrait I considered myself a handsome man, but when I saw the image of my balding head, I felt that nasty feeling which told me I'm not as handsome as I think I am. So no more portraits please." Will laughed again.

"As you like," the duke said, rising to leave us.

He was miffed. I wondered what the real reason for the visit was. Could it have been simply to chat? I remember when Will joined the group of players of Lord Strange, the Fifth Earl of Derby, in 1587. Will adored Strange. One day Lord Strange, a crypto-Catholic nobleman, dropped dead mysteriously. Will suspected, as did I, that he was poisoned. But only friends of his had seen him the day he died. Only friends. What was the real motive for this visit from Buckingham? Was it to poison my husband while he wasn't looking?

My imagination, which has prompted my poetry and set me to writing, now terrifies me. I am carried away by it. A duke stops by to say hello, and all I think of is that he has a secret motive that is evil. God forgive me for those thoughts. It's time to go back to the oxlips of Shottery, the fields of daisies and hollyhocks, where I will be happy to write poetry again. Not for anyone's eyes but mine—and beloved Will's.

August 10, 1606

Will's entire attention is now focused on completing *King Lear* for the Christmas holidays. He talks only to his characters, or from their mouths. I do not know at any given moment whom I am addressing. In his secret mind, I know he is preoccupied with our daughters. With both of them fully grown, Will has grown suddenly guilt-heavy that he has not been more of a father. His new tragedy is about fathers and daughters, a king and his children. Will has no time to do anything but live in the moment of creation. He is in pain from a bad toothache, and he also complains that he cannot move gracefully with his knees hurting him as they do, but when he writes he is in ecstasy and forgets his knees, his teeth, everything—including his age.

Will asks me to help him with *King Lear*. I often feed him words when he needs new cadences. I am always there to be his researcher, his personal poet, and his muse. When not, I am distressing myself with dark thoughts.

Why was Bernard Miles the ghost that day and not Will? Is God's protection on the Writer? I secretly believe that Will talks to God when he writes and that God is his real collaborator. How else could he be so brilliant? Will tells me that the reason he writes so well is that he likes to surprise himself and, like a magician, to conjure up the people he is creating out of thin air. He also loves music—there is always music accompanying his plays—and now he is combining three things at once: music, tragedy, and comedy. *King Lear* is such a masterpiece of poetry that it may be his final play, I dare not think or say.

Jonson's spies sat in London's most fashionable tavern last night and saw the king and the Duke of Buckingham dining privately. The duke was overheard saying to the king that he suspected the king had another lover—a playwright. Of course I know, from my own experience, that Dekker is the king's secret lover. In any event, the duke has become insanely jealous (he's definitely an English Othello). Or as Jonson would tell it:

DUKE: My spies tell me you entered an inn in one of the unfashionable streets of Shoreditch. You were with another man. You were holding his hand. You kissed his neck. Who was it, James?

KING: If I must kiss a neck it will be yours, but I would rather kiss your long prick than your short neck, my darling Buckingham.

DUKE: Who was that man? My spies told me he was a well-known playwright. Who was he? Who? Tell me!

KING: So I have spies in my life now? Perhaps since I spy on no one, I am a totally innocent person, but you, who spy, are the one putting horns on my crown. Why do you need spies? You know I love you.

DUKE: Who was that man? Was he William Shakespeare? The poet to whose every tune you dance? Memory kills for a moment. In the past you have had others. Now you betray me for William Shakespeare? Why? Because he is smarter than me? Do you find him more interesting than me? Do you? Admit to me everything!

KING: Admit what? This is all fool's talk, my darling.

DUKE: Is it he? The miserable shadow? That scribbler? That cocksman with his cock for sale?

KING: Stop it. Will is a family man. Every fourth weekend he goes home with his cousin, who is his devoted servant, to fuck his wife and see his children. He isn't light in the wrist like we are. What nonsense.

DUKE: So you do not deny that it is he?

KING: I'm not saying no, nor yes. I adore you. Stop this foolishness at once. Next you will accuse me of fucking my wife.

DUKE: It is William Shakespeare, isn't it?

That was all Jonson told me, but it was enough to make me realize that the duke, as I suspected, is another man jealous of my husband's good looks, money, and talent. I am going to tell Will, as soon as *King Lear* has been presented to the king and is on the boards at the Globe, that we are going home. Theatre or no theatre, this is the end of us remaining in this insane business. Thousands of admirers mob Will when he leaves the theatre, so he has to wear a wig and disguise himself as he sneaks out a backdoor. Every day, women send him perfumed notes, begging for trysts with the great William Shakespeare. His brother Edmund is even bothered by actors and playwrights who want to use his influence to get to Will. William Shakespeare is now the most powerful writer in the kingdom. The king pays so much money for his new plays that all the other playwrights, who are practically starving, envy and hate him. His mother sends us letters telling us that she wants him back home. Our daughters miss their father as well as their mother. Our short monthly visits don't suffice. Even though our daughters, Susanna and Judith, love all that Will's fortune can buy, they would rather have us home. And I—how I long for our new and stately country home! How I yearn for the area of Stratford-upon-Avon! I am told that many visitors now congregate in Will's hometown—imagine that! As for myself, I miss the swans floating on the Avon and would do almost anything to return to them, to bring glad tidings that the Shakespeares have returned to Stratford for good. There is no evil there.

August 13, 1606

Will and I are now packing up our few embroidered vests, leggings, doublets, our papers and quills, precious inkpots, our simple dishes, and our boots and other shoes. We are off to Ben Jonson's house, where we shall live until we depart London, which I pray shall be soon.

Finally, Will has understood the gravity of the deceptively light whispers that have reached our ears on the wind of Ben's reports. The danger, he now sees, is real.

After the murder of Bernard Miles, finally Will has become protective of his own life. He now believes, beyond a reasonable doubt, that there is a conspiracy. He has stopped making fun of Jonson and his "foolish" conspiracy theory. Will knows that all the conspirators are jealous of him. He hates the actor Edward Alleyn as much as I do. For him Tilney has always been a fool. Will especially hates Dekker. After Dekker's release from debtor's prison, the tavern gossip has been that Dekker considers himself the best poet in London. Will says that Dekker's pamphlets, written entirely in rhymed couplets, are the work of a hack. Dekker, along with Jonson and Middleton, composed pageants for King James's entrance to London before his coronation. Dekker was insulted when Shakespeare refused to collaborate with them. Dekker wants to be what Will was born to be: a genius. Unfortunately Dekker is a very bitter playwright whose long imprisonment for debt has made him mentally unstable. He is a journeyman, not an artist.

Will speaks of the four collaborators as four blinking idiots. Last week, Will authorized one of King James's palace guards to spy on these enemies and to keep them constantly in his sight. He put a great deal of money in the guard's purse to do so. Will often talks about our early days in London, before he was a famous playwright and began being treated with all the pomp and circumstance of a god. Snobbery, greed, and jealousy are the main emotions of the conspirators. They hate that Will isn't only London's greatest playwright but also a gentleman with a royal crest.

Yesterday Will and I received a report from our spy, the king's guard, about a clandestine meeting of the conspirators. They were at a tavern, where they sat drinking whiskey and speaking in loud voices, unaware that a spy sat at the next table. They felt there was no reason to be discreet, as they would never suspect a man in the king's uniform to be a spy in the employment of William Shakespeare.

Lord Burleigh spoke first. "We must kill William Shakespeare this week. A pox on him."

Thomas Dekker interrupted him. "Two poxes on him. One pox is not enough. Do you know what I hate about Will Shakespeare? He steals from everyone else's plays. Greene was right when he wrote that Will is 'beautified by our feathers.' Will Shakespeare thinks that from his own life experience, he knows more than any other playwright about ambition, intrigue, love, and suffering. Shakespeare brags that he did not have to go to university, like all of us, because everything he knows he learned from life experience. Ha! I came from a wealthy family, and yet I have not been able to make money in the playwriting game. But he, whose father was a glover, believes he knows more than anybody and, on top of that, believes that with his crest he is a gentleman."

Master Tilney butted in. "That's why he is so friendly with Ben Jonson, whose father was a bricklayer. Jonson puts on airs as if his father were a duke. Both Jonson and Shakespeare should be removed. When I think of them a fever shakes me. They have ruined my influence in court."

Edward Alleyn spoke up, articulating his words as if he were in a play. "Can you imagine that Shakespeare considers himself a better actor than I am? I know he watched me when I played Faustus, and he copies many of my secrets of acting that took me years to perfect. Of course I swear he's a Catholic. He pretends to be so stable and a family man. He brags that he rarely brawls or drinks. As an actor he is a journeyman.

As a playwright he is so ambitious that he seeks to have the power of a king. He considers himself a dramatist, with a great literary reputation. I think he is a fool, posing as a genius. I don't like him or his stupid plays."

Lord Burleigh spoke in his snobbish voice. "Another thing I detest about Shakespeare is that he writes so many plays about women, as if he knows women better than any man in London. Many of his comedies are about the unfair treatment of women by men. I think he wants to portray women as though they are as important as men. Many of his women wear masculine clothes and demonstrate a dangerous independence. His plays are insidious. I'm tired also of his pathetically childish sexual puns. If I hear one more pun from William Shakespeare about testicles, I'm going to vomit."

Thomas Dekker spoke up, his voice seething with jealousy. "Let's get to the point. How are we going to murder him? We must use great imagination to destroy him."

"I'm all for slipping poison into his wine," Lord Burleigh said excitedly.

"I would like to see him die of something more painful," Alleyn replied in quiet anger. "I have in mind arson, setting his house on fire. That will kill him and his arrogant cousin at the same time. Once he is dead I'll dance on his grave to celebrate."

"Fire is a very good idea." Master Tilney spoke with hatred. "For a few pounds we can hire an arsonist to slip into his house late in the evening, so the house will go up in flames while he is sleeping. He will die quickly and without air. When he's gone, I'll have my prestige again in court."

Dekker asked, "When shall we do this deed?"

Lord Burleigh said, "It would be better if it were done tomorrow. I must say I have a tyrannous heart. I would be glad to set his house aflame myself. Then I will know the deed is done. Dekker, let's promise not to speak of this to anyone. We will wait, and Will will die by fire."

"Are you sure fire is better than a knife?" Dekker asked. "We can hire someone to simply put a knife in his heart, and then the peevish playwright will be dead and soon forgotten, and all of London will see my plays on the boards, not his."

Tilney said, "No, the idea of fire is less suspicious. No one will suspect conspiracy."

"Let us thrust virtue out of our hearts and be done with this thing. Shakespeare is a bastard, always seeming so gracious and modest," Lord Burleigh said. "I am happy to bestow on him a poet's crown of bay leaves after his death."

Lastly Alleyn spoke: "Shakespeare will be crushed by fire tomorrow night. I prefer not to hire anyone. I will do this deed myself. I want to see the man in ashes."

Even the spy was shocked when he reported all of this. Now we are getting ready to flee. We packed our belongings immediately. Ben Jonson has offered to take us, this afternoon, into his house. He has so much affection for Will that he has assured us we can stay in his home as long as we are in London. Thank God for people who really love us. I always knew that Jonson's kindness was the greatest gift we could have.

Will believes there's no point in reporting this conspiracy to the king. Tilney, as Master of the Revels, has too much power for us to go against him. Alleyn is beloved by everyone in London, especially the common people; still, there are not enough oaths in my mouth to spit at him. Lord Burleigh pretends to be a virtuous man as he sucks up to the king. Dekker? It would give me such pleasure to cut Dekker's throat myself. But Will says we do not possess enough evidence to have the conspirators arrested.

The best thing we could do to these scoundrels is to foil them, but we should ready ourselves to go home to Stratford. London has become too dangerous, but Will and I will have the last laugh when the house burns down and we are not there. It is now my job to warn the other tenants of what's going to happen, so they can leave as well. Will intends to give them one hundred pounds each to relocate, which I'm sure will make them very happy, as this house is a dump anyway.

The conspiracy has killed Bernard Miles, but the murders will end there. What is the point of being exceedingly rich and famous if it only brings you enemies who want to kill you? Who ever thought that being a playwright in London would prove to be as dangerous as the Battle of Agincourt? But just as the English triumphed over the French, we shall triumph over our conspirators. Will is beginning to find the whole conspiracy very amusing. He says it astonishes him how life imitates art. Our lives now seem like one of Will's history plays, in which enemies clash. Dear diary, they want to crucify my husband. Goodness and genius have always attracted greedy men who would undo the beauty of an outsider by causing them to act out vengeance.

AUGUST 15, 1606

The deed was done. The fire burned down the house and with it any belief that our concern was overwrought. When the conspirators walked into the Mermaid Tavern to celebrate the death of William Shakespeare, they were shocked to see us drinking ale and laughing. They are such pricks; I am glad they know that we are spying on them. I doubt if they will ever try another murder attempt since their stupidity is now out in the open. The King's Men have spoken clearly to Burleigh: He is not to frequent the Mermaid. He is not to visit the Globe. He may not be seen by our eyes again soon, and this does not displease me! It was pleasurable to see the conspirator quake in surprise. We greeted Will's would-be murderers with harmless mirth, so typical of the life of the Writer.

August 20, 1606

I can't abide my husband's unwillingness to see his enemies punished. I said to him today, "I implore you to report the conspirators to the king, Will. He will certainly throw them all in the Tower of London, because they are nothing but grizzled, hideous fools. The king will decapitate all of them."

Will replied, "I am not going to give the conspirators the satisfaction of being found out."

"Why not?"

He answered quietly, "I don't want to be involved in vengeance or scandal. Drama should remain in my plays. Why make them famous? England loves its villains. Guy Fawkes in the cellar of Parliament was a villain for a moment and now a legend till the death of the world. These I want forgotten, buried in the sands of history, not resurrected as martyrs."

November 15, 1611

It has been too long since I have written in these pages. As I look back upon my writing, I sense again the burden of sadness and despair that had descended during those days of death and danger. I was too certain that evening five years ago, too sure of triumph, too trusting in the broken will of those who failed to kill the Writer. The years are swift to pass, but the world is slow to change. We remain in London.

I have been busy helping the musicians learn the music for my husband's plays. Will has been working diligently on his new masterpiece, *The Tempest*, which was performed for King James in Whitehall Palace by the King's Men on Hallowmas Night. The noble gossip this week says that the king himself will host another party of the century to celebrate Shakespeare's great play. The preparation for the event is almost like a tempest in a teapot. It has taken the king as much time to plan the party as it took for Will to write the play.

The Tempest has all the familiar elements of a fairy tale— the magician with the customary spirit and the beautiful daughter—but even a fairy tale has to have a serious theme. The serious theme of *The Tempest* is actually the theme of Will's and my life. For my husband is soon to retire and rewind his life, like a clock, in Stratford with our two beloved daughters, Judith and Susanna.

The king plans to have *The Tempest* performed as part of the celebration of the marriage of his daughter Elizabeth. *The Tempest* uses stage machinery and grand scenery in such episodes as the storm at sea and the banquet that vanishes into thin air. My husband, as the head of the King's Players, has hired many extra actors for dancing, and if necessary, singing. Inigo has done a magnificent job on the scenery. With *The Tempest*, my husband has finally achieved mastery over words in the blank verse form. It is the king's favorite play, after *Macbeth*.

It was truly exciting to be at the final rehearsal for *The Tempest*, which Will directed. All the actors gathered around the stage, dressed in their costumes. Inigo Jones was there to ensure that his special effects worked properly. The play begins with a noisy scene, a ship at sea in great peril. Inigo Jones has created such a realistic shipwreck—with the sea washing over the stage and the sound of the ship colliding with the shore—that even the actors were amazed. A silence follows the shipwreck, and then an elderly man and his daughter enter. Burbage played Prospero and a young actor played Miranda. Burbage was brilliant. I could tell that Prospero, whom I had helped to create, was yet another specimen of Will's somewhat overbearing, tyrannical fathers, like Capulet in *Romeo and Juliet* and Polonius in *Hamlet*.

Ariel, a spirit of the air, appears. She is invisible to all except Prospero and the audience. Will stopped rehearsal several times to work with Ariel on how a spirit would move. The way Will directed the play was as part fairy tale, part comedy, and part tragedy. During rehearsal Will also spent a great deal of time with the character of Caliban, his portrait of the horrid savage.

The plot picks up as Prospero, the magician, makes everyone dance to his music. Prospero is rough and terrifying. Will, of course, gave Prospero many sexual puns and double entendres. My husband is very good at working with the actors to show them first-class low comedy.

When Trinculo, the jester, encountered the towering Caliban, Will worked with Caliban to demonstrate the body movements of a savage. He directed Miranda on how to progress from love and courtship to the pledging of troth. My husband made me so proud as he worked with the actors, showing them how to go from high romance to low comedy.

The Tempest is Will's farewell to his art. I began to weep during the rehearsal because I knew that Will would soon be saying good-bye to London and to his poetic genius. As I watched the actors onstage, our whole life in London flashed through my mind in an epiphany. We had nearly twenty marvelous years. I stood in the back of the Globe with tears running down my cheeks as I heard Prospero speak this magnificent epilogue, his farewell to his art:

Now my charms are all o'erthrown,
And what strength I have's mine own,
Which is most faint: now, 'tis true,
I must be here confined by you,
Or sent to Naples. Let me not,
Since I have my dukedom got
And pardon'd the deceiver, dwell
In this bare island by your spell;
But release me from my bands

With the help of your good hands:
Gentle breath of yours my sails
Must fill, or else my project fails,
Which was to please. Now I want
Spirits to enforce, art to enchant,
And my ending is despair,
Unless I be relieved by prayer,
Which pierces so that it assaults
Mercy itself and frees all faults.
As you from crimes would pardon'd be,
Let your indulgence set me free.

And so we work on, in London still, with the green of Shottery and Stratford only a memory and occasional visitation, our children grown and the world still turning as it did. *The Tempest* is Will's greatest masterpiece. He is Prospero, the magician, and the island is London. We must go back to our own Mirandas, Susanna and Judith, who love us.

NOVEMBER 21, 1611

The pages left herein are few, and our time in London draws to a heavy close. I shall not write much more from this city, this abode of fear and envy.

I saw my husband's blood last night, and his skin broken. I write it now to remember, and, hours from this moment's writing, to look back in triumph.

We were not particularly looking forward to King James's party last night. Will was toasted by the king, who sat at Will's right. I sat at Will's left. The king had spared no expense on the celebration. Royal musicians played several of the songs from *Twelfth Night* and *The Tempest*. All the great playwrights—Ben Jonson, Thomas Middleton, John Fletcher, and Francis Beaumont—were seated at the brilliantly lit table, as was the poet John Donne. The king had also invited the great painter Peter Paul Rubens to travel to London from Antwerp for the party. Rubens is a very polite, robust gentleman with finely chiseled features. He is extremely cultured. He has traveled in Italy and Spain. He sat next to me; it was delightful to talk about painting with him. I could tell he is a huge admirer of my husband.

Another important guest was the Spanish playwright Lope de Vega, who is sometimes called the "Spanish Shakespeare." A yellow-skinned man with huge, bulging eyes, this master of Spanish letters sat chatting with the Spanish ambassador. The ambassador, who looked like a stuffed elk, said how he wished to bring to Spain an octagon-shaped theatre, just like the Globe.

Before dinner, the king said to my husband, "It will give me much happiness, dear Will, if you stand and recite something from one of your works to my fifty dinner guests. All of them came to this feast to honor you."

Will answered, "I shall rejoice at doing so, Your Majesty."

"I am sorry that my dear friend the Duke of Buckingham is ill," the king commented. "Your play *The Tempest* gave the dear duke so much pleasure. He especially enjoyed the character of Prospero, the magician. He told me so several times."

"I am sorry he is not well. The court is full of jollity and revels. The duke is much missed," Will said. He continued, "I am so happy that the poet John Donne is part of the guest list and in very good health. I like John, Your Highness; he is a great Protestant."

The king couldn't tell if Will was serious or sarcastic.

King James then remarked, "I would like you to recite, from memory, the passage in *The Tempest* where Miranda greets her father, Prospero, for the very first time."

Will looked at me. I knew he was annoyed.

"If you don't mind, Your Majesty, I would rather the guests

wait until the play is presented with the actors playing their parts. I prefer to recite a sonnet."

King James seemed happy at the prospect that Will would recite anything.

I couldn't help but think, dear diary, that King James was not the most visually appealing of kings. His movement is very clumsy, and he has an annoying habit of playing with his codpiece when he talks. He wears extraordinary padded jackets to protect himself from any possible assassin's daggers. Still, for all his faults, James was a generous patron. One of his first acts as king was to award Shakespeare and his colleagues a royal patent, thus creating the King's Men. No honor came higher. Although Inigo had complained about James being a cheapskate, King James had paid the King's Men, Will's company, very well.

James asked his trumpeter to play a fanfare. The horn played out its music, and everyone came to attention.

"My dear guests," the king said, standing up and speaking in a very loud voice so he could be heard at the end of the table, where his wife, Queen Anne, sat, holding court. "My great poet, Shakespeare, who is a ruby in the crown of England, shall recite for you now, to sundry notes of music, a sonnet that is one of my favorites. You will find, by the way, as you leave the dining room, that I present as a gift to each of you a pamphlet of Shakespeare's sonnets, with your name embroidered in gold on the red leather cover. May it be a remembrance for you always of this dinner, which I hope will stay in your memories as a delightful royal event. Now I give you the great actor and poet, the genius, and my good friend, William Shakespeare."

Everyone applauded as Will stood to recite, just as if he were in a theatre.

When, in disgrace with fortune and men's eyes,
I all alone beweep my outcast state,
And trouble deaf heaven with my bootless cries,

217

And look upon myself and curse my fate,
Wishing me like to one more rich in hope,
Featured like him, like him with friends possessed,
Desiring this man's art and that man's scope,
With what I most enjoy contented least;
Yet in these thoughts myself almost despising,
Haply I think on thee, and then my state,
(Like to the lark at break of day arising
From sullen earth) sings hymns at heaven's gate;
For thy sweet love remembered such wealth brings
That then I scorn to change my state with kings.

More applause. Then it was time for the feast to begin. Many servants, theatrically dressed in costumes of country hunters, brought in platters of ducks with peacock feathers stuck in their glazed wings. I had never seen duck à la peacock, but it seemed to be a favorite dish of the king. After the duck came tiny vegetables, all imported from Belgium. Goblets were filled with wine. Behind each guest stood a musician, strumming softly. There were also strolling musicians, dressed in gold and velvet. One played the *viola da gamba*, another the lute.

I could not help but notice the magnificent dresses worn by the women of rank and wealth. The fabrics were richly embroidered; some were trimmed with fur. The gowns all had bodices. Unmarried women wore the front of the bodice very low. Many of the men wore double short coats, embellished in the front with numerous buttons. Some wore jerkins over their doublets. The Spanish ambassador and the poet Lope de Vega wore caps of velvet.

After the next course, the servants brought out golden platters of tender and miraculous fruit imported from all over the world specially for this feast. There were oranges from Bermuda, huge mounds of green grapes from the south of

France, and little apples plucked from the Dutch countryside. Everyone drank the finest wine and sherry.

Finally there came the pièce de résistance: a huge cake made of towers of different kinds of chocolate covered with white marzipan flowers. I almost cried when I thought of my mother, who had worked her fingers to the bone creating pastries to survive. Pastries that wealthy people ate in one minute took her hours to prepare. If it had not been for those pastries, I would not have been literate and Will would not have been interested in me. Dear diary, isn't it bizarre that my fate is tied up with whipped cream? As the music played and conversations about war and the colonies continued, I hoped my mother was looking down from heaven to see my husband being honored by the King of England himself, with me, his adoring wife, pretending to be his cousin. Here, under the candles of the king's magnificent crystal chandelier from Venice, I sat surrounded by brilliant artists, nobles, and knights. She would have been proud.

As I listened to the guests chatter, I heard the king laughing with great pleasure. I overheard Jonson asking the Spanish poet which of Shakespeare's plays was his favorite. The candlelight played on Lope's dark skin.

"Each play is more beautiful than the next," he replied in English tinged with a thick Spanish accent.

"But what do you think of *Hamlet*?" Ben Jonson asked.

"I think it's the greatest play ever written in English. I intend to translate it into Spanish so that people in my country can enjoy it."

"Brilliant!" said Jonson. "And perhaps you'd like to translate some of my plays too?" Jonson never missed an opportunity to promote Jonson.

Just then Will got up to take a short walk. I followed him. It was a chilly, dark night. The trees shimmered in the moonlight, and the air was perfumed with beautiful white gardenia blossoms that the king had had placed all around the palace, grown in the hothouse for this important event.

"How very aesthetic the king is," Will said. "What a celebration. I am overwhelmed that he has prepared this party in my honor." I stood close. "Gardenias always remind me of my youth because I would find them to give to my mother when I was a boy to alleviate the stink of my father's gloves floating in vats of urine and human dung. Gardenias are the sweetest flowers of all. They seem to come from another world. They are like white stars with an unusually sweet fragrance."

I looked up at the moon. I was so terribly happy to be the wife of William Shakespeare, but once I learned about the conspirators—some of whom, as it happened, were invited to the king's dinner—I always kept close to him. I shadowed him wherever he went, as did our spies, now Will's bodyguards. They were not far behind us. What misery it was to be at a party with the most interesting earls, painters, ambassadors, and poets, and to know in my heart that there is a design to take away the world's greatest writer, simply because traitors envy him. Talent and money, I understood only too well, can lead to envy and murder. I was now Will's bodyguard as well as his wife.

The wind was soft, brisk, and the air smelled strongly of wood smoke. I looked at Will and he at me. In another place, another life, we would have embraced beneath that moon, held one another, and breathed in the scent of evening, the smell of happiness. In another life, we would have found a private chamber and made love until morning.

But not in this life.

Suddenly, out of nowhere, a masked figure moved forward from the bushes, and a pistol shot rang out. Beside me, Will fell, pulling me down with him. He lay on top of me, and I looked into his eyes. He slumped over onto the grass. Blood was everywhere.

I screamed in my loudest voice, "Help! Help! William Shakespeare is dead!"

The guards reacted, but it was too late; the assassin had disappeared into the black garden, but I knew who he was. I had seen his shoes and I knew.

A loud shout went up from the crowd, and the garden was soon crowded with people. Everyone at the feast rushed through the open doors to see the spectacle of the dead poet. The guards calmed the guests and lifted Will to carry him inside. William Shakespeare wasn't dead; he was only shot in the leg. As the lords and intellectuals disappeared into the night, the guards carried Will in a stretcher to the king's physicians.

King James and I stayed all night in a private room to be at Will's side. I was glad to see that at least Will had a sense of humor. He laughed as he was being bandaged and taken care of.

"I am so glad to see you are alive and, according to my physicians, have only a slight wound in the leg," King James told Will. "You have added pomp and circumstance to my party, and as soon as you are better, my dear Will, I will give you the Order of the Garter to put above your wound. If you die, the theatre of the world dies with you."

I was impressed that King James was so concerned.

Will answered with a laugh. "This was one party I was dying to go to."

He loved to pun, even about his own wound. When I heard Will laugh I thought, "All's well that ends well."

I know that the assassin was none other than the Duke of Buckingham, because I had seen his expensive shoes when we last met: black-velvet slippers with gold rosettes—the same shoes that clad the feet of Will's would-be assassin. His shoes have given him away. He was the failed murderer. First the conspirators tried to kill Will. Now there has been an attempted assassination by the duke. The opening words of *Richard III*, spoken by Gloucester, keep running through my mind:

> *Now is the winter of our discontent*
> *Made glorious summer by this sun of York,*
> *And all the clouds that lowered upon our house*
> *In the deep bosom of the ocean buried.*
> *Now are our brows bound with victorious wreaths;*
> *Our bruised arms hung up for monuments;*
> *Our stern alarums changed to merry meetings,*
> *Our dreadful marches to delightful measures.*

Although the Duke of Buckingham does not have a hunched back, he has an emotional deformity. He is deformed by his lust for power and his love for the king. His is now our Gloucester. Thank God Will is alive. I want him home in my bed, where I can put my arms around him and protect him from evil men, like the duke, like the conspirators, like a million other men who are envious that he is the most gifted man who ever lived. Mediocrity hates genius. Nothing is so dangerous as being a great writer, especially one who makes money and whom everyone adores. Everyone? Only those who enjoy his words, words that they put in their hearts. As for those who are not able to write those words, there is something infinitely mean in the minds of those without great intellectual powers and whose language will never have Will's beautiful and unique music or magic.

NOVEMBER 30, 1611

Will is alive. I say it to myself again and again, with the thought that we were so close to hearing him no more. Will is alive.

I took good care of him so he could recover quickly. Now we plan our return to Stratford. Will is too much of a target for the conspirators and also for a jealous duke. His potential assassin, the Duke of Buckingham, frightens me as much as the conspirators themselves. A man who acts alone is even more dangerous than a crowd.

If the conspirators are like tigers, the duke is like a sly fox. He has no idea that I recognized his shoes before the pistol shot. The duke is a madman who has become a fool, but he is also a man who tried to kill my husband and botched it, which makes him all the more dangerous. He even had the nerve to pay us a get-well visit after shooting Will. We are living at Ben Jonson's house, and this afternoon the servant announced the Duke of Buckingham as a surprise guest. I greeted him at the door, pretending to be ignorant of his attempted assassination of my husband.

"How kind of you to call on Will," I said.

The duke replied, "Thank God your coz is on the mend."

He rushed to Will's bed, where Will sat with his leg bandaged and resting on pillows.

"The physicians have assured me there is no infection in the wound," Will said cheerfully.

"I can't imagine who would dare shoot at England's greatest playwright," the duke said. "The king is anxious to catch the villain, but he has disappeared into thin air. The unkindest cut of all is that we have no idea what his motive was. So the blame belongs to no one."

Will replied, "Never mind, Your Lordship, I will soon be well. 'Tis kind of you to come. How is King James?"

"Oh, King James is in fine fettle. Every day is merry. Every day we drink together and talk with nostalgia about the marvelous explorations of Sir Francis Drake. Did you know that we now have almost as many explorers going to the New World as Portugal or Spain has? The king considers the late Sir

Francis Drake a god, a combination of Neptune and Jehovah. I have to say, if I were in love with the king, which I certainly am not, I would be extremely jealous of how he feels about Drake's accomplishments. Drake was certainly one of the most honored men in England. A duke is noble, but an explorer is a legend."

"Every word you say is true," Will said, trying not to sound sarcastic.

"I want the king and me to purchase the *Golden Hind*, Drake's ship, which is for sale in the harbor. I want the king to go away with me in that famous vessel."

"You want the king to invest in a dead explorer's boat? Good God," Will said. "I hear the king is very frugal."

Buckingham agreed. "Yes, you are quite right. The king loves to stay in his palace and read. He hates to spend money. While he reads I sit in his royal chair and draw sketches of him. He loves to pore over old books about witchcraft. We are so compatible as friends because we are both quite interested in witches, but I know that the *Hind* is a great investment. If only we could just sail away together."

"So where would you go?" Will asked, encouraging the duke to dream.

"Oh, I don't know. To the city of kites and crows."

Will laughed. "You're quoting from my play *The Tragedy of Coriolanus*."

"I love that play. What are you working on now?"

"A poet speaks not of his art. Those men love least that let men know their love." Will paused and glanced imperceptibly at me. "But since your kindness is a font that spills over upon me, and you stand here so tall beside me after such a night, I will share a small secret. I now am revising another play."

The duke swallowed. I could see his throat move down and up. "And do you write it every day?" he asked.

"Every morning my cousin Arthur lends his hand, and we

together dive into words like they are water, and we swim and shape. Immersion, you see."

"Well, then. The best and kindest of luck to you. May your health increase as you create." The duke gathered himself to leave, his body leaning already towards the door. "I will share a secret with you, in return, as it were. I have an appointment to look at Sir Francis Drake's old galleon, as I told you. I am thinking of converting it into a museum. King James and I must make our visit in secret because we cannot have Queen Anne coming with us. The woman is a bore. And now, I must change my clothes and button myself into something more nautical."

"Thank you for your kind visit, Your Lordship."

"Fare thee well," the duke said. "And a pox on that madman who shot a pistol at your head. Thank God he missed."

The Duke of Buckingham left, and we stared after him. The greatest hypocrite in history, we thought. A murderer who comes to chit-chat, an assassin in the cloak of a friend.

"The duke would have made an extraordinary actor if he had taken to the stage," Will said. "As it were, he made for a bad assassin, having never learned to shoot straight."

DECEMBER 23, 1611

Today I wrote my last from London. I was not sorry to leave. I can't help but recall how we entered that putrid city with high hopes of achievement. Now we run away because our success has brought the conspiracy of evil men.

Mr. Buckman arrived at Ben Jonson's house to take us home. Jonson promises to visit us in a few weeks to report to us on the gossip of London. Tonight there is a revival at the Globe of *King Lear*, which is now Will's most popular play, along with *Hamlet*. We are sorry not to see the revival but had already decided to leave early. Will's leg has mended. King James has arranged for another carriage to take all our belongings to Stratford. That leaves only our personal things, which Will and I carry by hand.

The king gave us the gift of his understanding, and oddly enough has also promised to visit us in three months hence at New Place. This will be the first time a monarch came to Stratford since Queen Elizabeth was carried in a procession, like a bejeweled idol, to visit the estate of Lord Essex when Will was very young. We assured the king that he would be welcome at New Place by us, our daughters, and our son-in-law, John Hall.

Will explained to the king his reason for going home: "Like Prospero, I must give up my magical powers to return to the place from which I have come."

"London will miss your magic and so will I," said the king simply. "And so will the Duke of Buckingham."

He had no idea that we were not as innocent as he. We had to keep from laughing because the king had no idea it was his lover who had shot Will in an attempt to kill him.

As Mr. Buckman began the long journey, Will and I sat lovingly in the carriage, embraced in each other's arms, talking about the pleasures that await us when we shall live with our daughters and grandchild. We knew that at the very moment we were riding towards Stratford, *King Lear* was being spoken, with Burbage playing the mad monarch. We had nostalgia for the tragic play that we had worked on for so many years together.

"He was quite fine in rehearsal," Will said about Burbage. "I would say more than fine. He was his usual brilliant self. 'Tis true that he is the finest shadow in all of London. In *Lear*, Burbage becomes madness—that madness of King Lear, which holds no reserve of emotion or restraint. Lear, that fool, brings suffering upon his own head, as a weary runner dousing himself with water from a pail. And yet that bitterest of tragedies: were it not for one small mistake—no larger than a fruit—Lear could have saved himself the disaster of his daughter's death. Burbage—he bristles with arrogance and madness and..."

His words were cut. And he looked at me with wide eyes.

"But no more of this. The next act of my life is about to begin, and you, Anne, and I will find the forest again. Enough with cobblestone and multitudes. We are now citizens of the forest of Arden, where we first made love. Not even sonnets can say what that place is. We begin anew. Now starts our true collaboration."

"'I know a bank where the wild thyme blows,'" I said. And he smiled. I continued, "'Where oxlips and the nodding violet grows, / Quite over-canopied with luscious woodbine, / With sweet musk-roses and with eglantine.'"

"I love those lines," Will said. "'And in the wood, where often you and I / Upon fair primrose beds were wont to lie.'"

I looked out the window at the disappearing city.

"It seems much smaller now," I said to the window.

"In many and various ways."

"Let us not forget, as we take leave of London, to send love to all those who hate us. God will take vengeance on them."

"Forgiveness is our great act of self-love. Vengeance belongs only in my tragedies."

And with that he broke out laughing, the way he used to laugh as a young man, courting me in Shottery. We kissed each other passionately, forgetting that we were old lovers.

We are now rid of knaves and killers. We are off to the exhilaration of anonymity, of the countryside, of violets and gardens and sun on the fields. After years in London, we were going back to our roots. We both agreed that the great and exciting life of a playwright in the commercial London theatre is overrated. They say "nothing succeeds like success," but we have seen the darker side of the country of accomplishment, from which few return. Nothing impedes like success as far as I am concerned. 'Tis true. I have been secretly praying

227

to God all day to thank him for sparing Will's life. In Stratford-upon-Avon, everyone believes that Will was a hero in the world of royalty and theatre. No one knows the perfidy behind success as I do, how many wish to see the rich and gifted suffer death. Many people like to see heroes suffer.

June 30, 1613

Standing in the crowd last night, we watched the flames destroy the Globe for hours. And now the earth seems to have shifted its weight. The Globe is gone—that single monument to story and song, that hope rising from the muck and stone. Arson? I wonder.

We had returned to London to see a performance of Will's history play *The Famous History of the Life of King Henry VIII*. During the play, staged cannon fire ignited the thatched roof of the theatre. You might say that Will's career blazed in the heavens, and that was the end of England's greatest playwright. The loss is a tragedy; the Globe had the greatest plays that ever existed on its stage. But it is also a comedy, because it was Will's last play. It is almost as if the world said good-bye to Will in a puff of magical smoke. Of course a new Globe will be built, but it will never be the same. As far as I'm concerned, this day marks the end of Elizabethan theatre.

We attended the play in our disguises as priests, confident that neither Dekker nor Alleyn nor the Duke of Buckingham would have any idea we had returned to town; only Ben Jonson is privileged on our secret entrance. Unfortunately, the performance was a disaster because of the fire, causing everyone to run out of the theatre. So we stood with a thousand other members of the audience watching the Globe burn down.

The play had dramatic incidents that were not remote from our own time. The prologue of the play proved to be prophetic. Its first line reads, "I come no more to make you laugh."

What more can I say? As with the early history plays, the source of *Henry VIII* is *Holinshed's Chronicles*, although some facts were taken from Foxe's *Book of Martyrs*. The play opens with the meeting between Henry VIII and the French king, Francis I, in the Field of the Cloth of Gold, so called because of the magnificent display by all who took part. It ends with the baptism of Queen Elizabeth.

Will included in *Henry VIII* a prophecy of the glories of the long reign of King James, our king. Although King James was no longer our patron, it didn't hurt to flatter him. He had, in the end, been as much an admirer of Will's art as Queen Elizabeth. Will also writes about the bitter irony of Cardinal Wolsey's last speeches when he heard that Sir Thomas More had been chosen chancellor in his place. When the king marries Anne Boleyn, he discards More as chancellor, and when More rejects Henry as the head of the Supreme Church of England, Henry has him beheaded.

So Will went back to the most traumatic moment in the history of England—the unbelievable actions of King Henry VIII, who got rid of the Pope and Catholicism and declared himself head of the Church of England. He turned England upside down and launched Protestantism in the kingdom, which led to the *Book of Common Prayer* appearing in every church and, eventually, commercial Elizabethan theatre. Pageants about Jesus and his disciples were replaced by Queen Elizabeth and her playwrights. In the end, you could say that the playwrights were her armada of genius, and each brilliant play written for her was as wind in their sails.

AUGUST 9, 1613

Because God loves us, tragedies often flip-flop into miracles of good fortune. I am, in a way, grateful for the conspiracy against us. The country air is good for Will, for us. His mind and heart are healthy, and he writes with a freedom he had not known in years. Were it not for the conspiracy, we would not be home; all's well that ends well.

In the forest of Arden Will walks often, with his characters in his mind. I see him speaking, his hands and arms waving, in the fields beyond Stratford. Often I walk with him, and we improvise scenes and dialogue, working out the speeches in our imaginations. Will and I go back to New Place, and in his quiet writing room he begins writing.

In the afternoons we visit with our daughters, who live nearby. Susanna is happily married to Dr. John Hall, who is so besotted with Will that he has hosted small readings at his home of some of the plays. All the neighbors enjoy being actors and playing different parts. Last night, Dr. Hall arranged for us to read *Timon of Athens*. It was so well done that Will is arranging for it to be sent to the London, where we hope it will go into rehearsal.

Will has gone back to one of his favorite pastimes, gardening. Together we put flowers in the earth and watch them daily lean and spread.

In Stratford-upon-Avon, surrounded by the glorious nature of forests, wildflowers, and aging oak trees that he remembers from his childhood, surrounded by the swans of Avon, the bees of his own beehive, the laborers who doff their hats to him in respect, surrounded by his daughters, his mother, old friends, grandchildren, and the horizon—he feels safe. Today we walked in the forest of Arden and played a game identifying flowers.

"Field poppy! Greater celandine! Wood avens!" shouted Will.

"Round-leaved sundew," I parried. "Fool's parsley."

"Viper's bugloss," Will said.

He knew the name of every flower, but so did I. We loved to test each other.

"Self-heal," I said.

"Ah," said Will. "I win. That's not a flower, Anne. It's an herb."

The birds also provide great delight, but today, just as I felt joy, a deer leapt from the bushes, and my heart sunk— immediately I thought of the conspirators.

"Will!" I shouted in a panic. "They have found us."

Will laughed, rolling in the grass, unable to catch his breath.

"It's a deer, dear Anne," he punned.

I can't pretend that I have completely rid myself of my fears, but Will kissed me and put my fears to rest.

OCTOBER 7, 1613

We do like to entertain. Thank God the king has not kept his word and come to visit us, but many other illustrious friends from London have made the two-day journey and enjoy relaxing in the countryside. Our most recent guest has been the very pompous and snobbish Sir Francis Bacon, whom we never saw very much of in London since Will was always so busy acting, writing, and attending to the business of the Globe. Now that Will is older, more relaxed, and even house-proud, he is always willing to show the renovations that he has made at New Place, which turned our home really into Show Place. The furniture comes from very old craftsmen in Venice, and the tapestries come from Holland and look marvelous on the huge white walls.

"Gold mirrors are from Holland," Will says proudly.

We have settled Sir Francis comfortably in the bedroom for honored guests. He is a man who likes to talk about his life. He is known for having been a very precocious youth, and I think Will appreciates that he is a renaissance man, an English philosopher, statesman, and author. At Cambridge, at the age of twelve, Francis first met the queen, who was, it is said, impressed by his advanced intellect and was accustomed to calling him "the Young Lord Keeper." The ascension of James I brought Francis Bacon into great favor. Since he was always in debt, the king awarded him the office of solicitor, which pays quite handsomely. Bacon, with his beard, his huge brown eyes, and his hat, which for some mysterious reason he wears even in the house, is certainly a conceited character. He was very much in love with his second wife, who was younger than he was, and it is said he disinherited her when he discovered her secret romantic relationship with John Underhill. He rewrote his will, he told us one night when he was in his cups. Francis Bacon thinks too highly of himself. Methinks he has only written inferior verse.

Will, however, likes to read Bacon's book *Wisdom of the Ancients*. Many nights at New Place, we sit around the fire, talking about the philosophy of Aristotle. Unlike Will, I suffer the hours of Francis Bacon's company. We sometimes read Will's plays out loud, and Bacon could have been an actor. He projects the voice of an actor and loves performing. He is enthralled to be such a good friend of Will's.

"I wish," he tells Will, "I were you. I wish I could write a play as you do." He says it too earnestly, and Will only smiles like a sphinx.

But, sadly, I think he will remain in history a dilettante and minor poet.

November 3, 1613

Will spends much time with Susanna and Judith, talking of his past and telling them stories of London. I am reminded of Miranda in *The Tempest*. She knows nothing of her father Prospero's past, but she must learn.

Will wrote his own life into Prospero the magician. In

many ways, Will wanted to make *The Tempest* not only a comedy and a tragedy but a dramatic poem. By the time he wrote it, he had mastered perfect balance between thought, phrase, and meaning. *The Tempest* is also his apology to his daughters for our neglecting them and being away so long. I love *The Tempest*. I feel it contains some of Will's greatest lines.

> *A solemn air and the best comforter*
> *To an unsettled fancy cure thy brains,*
> *Now useless, boil'd within thy skull! There stand,*
> *For you are spell-stopp'd.*
> *Holy Gonzalo, honourable man,*
> *Mine eyes, even sociable to the show of thine,*
> *Fall fellowly drops. The charm dissolves apace,*
> *And as the morning steals upon the night,*
> *Melting the darkness, so their rising senses*
> *Begin to chase the ignorant fumes that mantle*
> *Their clearer reason. O good Gonzalo,*
> *My true preserver, and a loyal sir*
> *To him you follow'st! I will pay thy graces*
> *Home both in word and deed. Most cruelly*
> *Didst thou, Alonso, use me and my daughter:*
> *Thy brother was a furtherer in the act.*

JUNE 11, 1614

Will spends a lot of lime looking at properties to buy for tithes, but when he comes back in the afternoon to New Place for lunch, he plays his age-old game of thinking up double entendres for sex and filthy puns. I realize now that Will's ribald jokes are also a means of revealing character and exploring the moral world of his tragedy. Whereas *Coriolanus* was a potent mix of violence and male homoeroticism (the anus?), *The Tempest* is less bawdy, lusty, and slippery. The six thousand listening ears of the Globe were delighted with the sexual undertones of the character of the savage Caliban. Will's audiences are such skilled listeners and can decode a sexual pun instantly. Like *Hamlet* and *Lear*, *The Tempest* was one of Will's triumphs at the Globe for being bawdy, comic, and tragic.

The set designer Inigo Jones visits from London from time to time. He knows about the plots of the conspirators and brings us up to date on what is happening with those evil fellows. He loves to gossip as much as Ben Jonson. Dekker, Inigo tells us, is broke and very ill. Burleigh is now dead, as is Tilney, who spent his last years as an unwanted pest every-where he went. He lost his place at court and spent most of whatever money he had to peddle his influence at the whore-house, where, it is said, he picked up a most unpleasant disease. Edward Alleyn is stuck with his unattractive wife and worked to death almost like a clerk by his father-in-law, Henslowe, who makes him collect the money at the gate as if he were Henslowe's servant. I always try to change the subject when it comes to the conspirators. I am glad they are no longer in our lives or in my nightmares. Soon we will leave the sphere of this universe for another universe of heaven, where Will and I will always be one.

July 12, 1614

This day I saw Will sitting in our hollyhock garden with our granddaughter, Elizabeth. He is teaching her to write sonnets. She loves words. Will calls to me with his soft voice that is slightly weaker than it used to be.

"Anne, Anne, come and listen to this. She's a natural at rhymes."

I see the world of the alphabet dance in our granddaugh-ter's eyes, and I feel the secret bliss of being myself, and his.

April 15, 1616

Will is not well. Though he remains cheerful, I can hear the weight in his laugh. Because he is wise, I know he hears it too, and that he sees the worry on my face. But he sees, as he always has, the whole picture of humanity, and I fear he looks already to a farther place.

Today he told me three times that he loves me. We are, finally, very happy. What a great pleasure it is to forget about art.

April 24, 1616

My husband died a happy death yesterday. At the age of fifty-two he passed, and there was the sweet fragrance from white, long-stemmed lilies throughout the house, white lilies and white roses in silver vases. Will loved the fragrance of flowers. He breathed his last on our marriage bed, with the scent of flowers permeating the night air. It occurred to me that the fragrance was that of a great soul leaving its body.

The week before Will died, when word went out all over London and Stratford that the great William Shakespeare was dying, many friends came to see us. Our many-gabled house has been full of family and guests. They brought gifts, knowing that he was like a child and loved to open presents. The aging Sir Walter Raleigh visited, a puppet in his hand, with his explorers, men of fortune, and playwrights. I held Ben Jonson's hand one afternoon as we watched Will sleep. The gifts piled around Will—maps, juggling balls, pots of flowers. Great actors and so many wits, professors, and noblemen entered and exited the house. Will said he felt ever the king. Instead of sitting on a throne, he sat propped up by pillows on our marriage bed, greeting his guests, whether they were beggars or courtiers, with joy and verve. Even in his last days, actors subtly begged for parts in his plays. Jonson would shush them, and Will would laugh. "In the world of theatre, somebody always wants something from you," he said, "even when you're dying."

Will's close friend Will Kempe, the great clown, whom audiences loved to see dance the jig at the end of each play, was already dead, but other clowns, like Richard Cowley and Robert Armin, who played Touchstone in Will's *As You Like It* and also played *Lear*'s singing fool, came to keep their favorite playwright company and make him laugh. Our daughters, Susanna and Judith, helped in the kitchen and served food and ale while the guests chatted. Our granddaughter, Elizabeth, ran around our dwelling as a spectator to her famous grandfather's departure, looking at Will with childish awe. He sighed, "Ripeness is all." Will never feared his own death. He saw death as something else. As Prospero said:

> *Leave not a rack behind. We are such stuff*
> *As dreams are made on; and our little life*
> *Is rounded with a sleep.*

The king and the queen came and stayed for three days. It was a great honor for the family and exciting for our granddaughter—though it annoyed Will that the king stayed longer than two days. He said, "Like fish, guests begin to stink after two days. Despite his fancy soaps, I smell the king as much as anyone."

The apple orchards, cherry and pear trees, and mistletoe bushes—the many varieties of plants and flowers on our estate—bloom year round. Will loved his trees and bushes—pruning, cutting back the roots, getting rid of dead branches, and burning the fallen leaves in autumn. Will loved violets, their shape, their purple color, their fragrance, and their soft velvety petals. Our violet garden was the pride of my husband.

He once said violets were what God would have planted if He had the money.

I liked to laugh at Will's irreverent jokes, which I'm sure he never quite meant. His daring to say whatever he pleased made me believe that such impetuousness is the meaning of his genius. He found everything, even tragic things, slightly absurd, and was never afraid to say so in whatever words, new or old, emerged inside his mind. I think now of them, and smile as I sit alone.

We laughed together. This is what I am thinking of. How we laughed often at each other. In this house, how we laughed. Now as I walk through it, I see only him. In the things and the nonthings.

I cannot say how many people have asked where our books are. They all of them think there should be hundreds of volumes, that the house should creak beneath the weight of pages. A famous writer, apparently, should die with his library around him.

John Donne writes his poetry in a cottage where there are only books, a bed, a chair, and a small table. Will would have gone mad! Allergic as he was to dust, he was more impatient with those great dust collectors: books. He insisted that it was easier to borrow books from the bookseller and return them than to own them himself and sneeze to death. Over the course of our marriage we must have read aloud to each other thousands of books and chronicles. But he said if we kept books in our house there would be no room for our beautiful carved furniture. And for the ugly, broken chair.

These ancient Dutch tapestries on the walls were Will's beloveds, too. He loved everything he had first seen at the queen's palace, and also loved the dozens of drawings made by our three children when they were very young, and now those made by our granddaughter. Even as youngsters our children were encouraged by Will to paint, dance, write, act, and play musical instruments. The golden goblets and golden plates that were given to us as gifts by Queen Elizabeth and by the king—they rest in their places. As do the huge green-velvet pillows, the drapes of green silk, and the decorative furniture pieces that require the services of Raphael, our dear furniture-repair servant, whom we imported from Trieste. Rafi is constantly putting glue and stains on chairs and tables and clamping the broken items. He is kept busy night and day polishing, by hand, our many precious wooden tables and desks. It was he who failed to tell Will of the broken chair.

During the last days of Will's life, poor Rafi was sentenced to the cellar with his glue pots, his brushes, his chemicals, and his inevitable cloves of garlic and chunks of mutton. Will could not endure the garlic on his breath. "No poet," Will said, "wants to die in a cloud of Italian garlic."

Will hated anything broken. And he appreciated a master craftsman, being one himself. When I once suggested that we sit on wooden stools instead of our delicate chairs, he said, "Are you mad? English gentlemen do not sit on stools!"

It was one of the few times during our long marriage that Will snarled at me, but I did not wince. I understood this man, my husband. The pride he found in his social status, not for a thing in its own right, but for how it demonstrated that his genius and hard work had made him a wealthy man. That crest above the mantle, that ring he never removed—now held in my palm, it looks a strange emblem of a past life. Prestige motivated Will all his life.

The fields outside the window speak of him. How he enjoyed walking for hours alone, or, if with me, in silence. After a bit of hobnobbing, he would grow bored—he would crave silence and the secret thoughts of his own mind. I suspect he was always writing in his brain, singing silly nursery rhymes to himself.

"All poetry begins with nursery rhymes from your childhood," he once told me. "Poetry. It all comes down to the head of a child."

It took Will a week to die. A high fever held throughout. Despite it, he made his own last days almost like a party. Will loved the drama and the comedy of dying. He saw everyone coming to visit him on his deathbed reflected in the huge gold-leaf mirror that hung in our bedroom. He enjoyed watching the entrances and exits of his guests and delighted in everyone making a big fuss over him. He would look at me with laughter in his eyes.

A zest for life and a zest for death. He stayed awake the last few days so he wouldn't miss anything. Dying was something he found interesting, and it seemed he wanted to bear witness to his own departure, watching himself sail away in a mirror held by a friend on the shore.

Before he left us, he begged me to sit on our bed next to him and read aloud "The Seven Ages of Man"—Jacques speaking of the stages of life, wherein man goes from infant in birth to infant in death. At the end, in the seventh stage, "sans teeth, sans eyes, sans taste, sans everything." Will laughed until he had not the strength.

He put off making his will until the last, when Coglin insisted. Will hated lawyers, even his own. He made a list of small gifts to leave to friends, almost as if he were making up a Christmas list. Two years ago, Heminges and Condell, those kind actors, helped me sort out the plays in chrono-logical order. They, out of the goodness of their hearts, took the trouble to help me retrieve, with great difficulty, the sides that Will and I never bothered to keep. Collecting the sides of all the hundreds of characters that were still in the hands of the players who kept them was an enormous task, and I never would have been able to do it without the assistance of those two. Will left the theatre with no copies of his plays. "What difference does it make?" he said. "I'll only be immortal for my poems."

He knew every line of every play by heart, but I knew that when he died those lines must not be forgotten. Thank God I made it my business to paste the sides together so he could correct them while he was still alive. Thus his plays remain. I gave Ben Jonson the collected plays to publish someday.

In his bequest, Will also left special gifts such as pieces of jewelry, swords, and costumes to various actors. He left a decent amount of money to the poor. To me he left his second-best bed. The first-best bed was the bed we had in the guest room for visitors, and the "second-best bed" was our personal marriage bed. It was a great compliment to me that he left me this treasure as a token of his love. I am sure he expected me to sleep in this bed and remember our passionate lovemaking, which lasted almost up to the end. He also left me our beautiful estate to live in for the rest of my life and a secret chest with drawers filled with hundreds of pounds to keep me comfortable so I didn't have to depend on our children. Will was generous to everyone, but above all he was most generous to me.

As I look back with love at our life together, I see more clearly what it was like to be married to a genius. Often the greatest literary persons seem ordinary on the outside and are not particularly eccentric or articulate. Not Will. Even though Will was extremely polite and well mannered, he had a raging and spectacular inner life, filled with his own demons, shadows, and sunsets. He attracted people with his elegant manners as well as with his often-bawdy wit.

In many ways Will was a very private person. He never allowed me to keep any traces of his notes, notebooks, or scribbled thoughts. Everything was burned at his request and turned to ashes before he died. He wished only for his polished plays and poems to remain as his written legacy. Another reason for our setting on fire and destroying any letters we sent to each other was that during our long marriage we both remained secretly Catholic, even if we weren't practicing our religion, because for that you could lose your life in Protestant England.

"Anne knows every word I have ever written," he told our daughters before he died. "And I've memorized every poem or song your mother has written also."

It was true. We truly loved each other. It is impossible to now analyze the interdependence of our relationship. I can only tell you that Will was not particularly interested in inventing stories and doing research at the bookseller's. That was always my job. I did all the "dirty work," sniffing out sources. I spent hours studying on his behalf. I borrowed a lot of material from Latin plays, old chronicles, and even myths of Ovid and Homer. He was the master, and I served as his apprentice and assistant. We borrowed freely from other writers, just as people borrowed from us. Every playwright in Elizabeth's England believed that plagiarism was the highest form of flattery. Will had the genius to take even the most banal lines, ideas, and stories that I found for him and make them sing in his own voice. I was his student as well as his helpmate and wife. No one could imitate his writer's voice. You always knew it was William Shakespeare. Why? No one else sounded as he did. He had a unique voice and his own madness, which were, I guess, the things that made him a genius. Also, like me, he loved new words and names. He loved trivia and details.

"The voice of the angel is in the details," he told me.

Together we were a team of poets. I was always happy to defer to him and be his silent partner. We shared the same views that we did not want to write religious plays or plays with moral judgments. We both loved comedy, making fun of people, silliness, and dramatic bombast. We both put some of our zany and tragic personal experiences into every character, be it a fool, a pompous ass, a clown, a queen, a servant, a jealous Moor, or a gatekeeper. We enjoyed being opaque and not always giving reasons for our character's actions. In *Othello*, Will never gave a reason for Iago's evil plan to destroy Othello; he wanted to let each person figure it out for themselves. Don't tell too much. Will was particularly good at imagining what our Elizabethan audiences wanted to see for their money. He was not only a superb playwright but a genius at understated self-promotion and at predicting the tastes of the London audiences. These two qualities made him the most successful playwright in England under Elizabeth I and James I. In my opinion, William Shakespeare was not only a great lover and a great husband. He was also a great clairvoyant of what was right for his time.

I used to say to Will, "All these feelings are inside of us, and all you have to do is remember them. Like those who play the flute, our mission on earth is to blow our personal experiences into the musicality of the English language."

"Yes, but make sure we are making music, not just breaking wind," he would say.

"What do you mean?"

"I write poems; others just write farts."

"You're right darling," I would say. "Musicality of poetry begins in rhythms of magical words in your brain, and you're not afraid of being vulgar. In fact, you're not afraid of anything. You take risks. Other people try to be correct. You dare to be incorrect."

In London, I noticed, as we grew older we were constantly deepening our experiences, and we took more risks and put them into the motives and ambiguities of our characters. As we grew older, our characters grew older. When we were young, there were Romeo and Juliet; when we were older, there were King Lear and Prospero. As husband and wife, we always worked together, helping each other try to find a flow of words that would express what we knew to be true in our lives. "To thine own self be true," Will would tell me, but who was my own self? In my heart, I was more wife than poet. In Will's heart, he was more poet than husband. We always admired each other's opposite qualities. By holding up the madness of our inner lives to a mirror, we felt we could hold the audience members' lives up to the same mirror. Holding a mirror to the human nature created art.

"O tiger's heart wrapped in a woman's hide," said the malcontent playwright Robert Greene, who was jealous of Will and slandered him in a pamphlet. We ignored Greene. In fact, we ignored everyone but Marlowe and each other.

Will said, "Two is a magical number. Two is the number of the openings in the body. Two halves create a space between each other in the image of a doorway. Two people procreate, and in our case, two people write plays."

The day that my husband, Will, died is the day I began seriously writing poems again as a way of distracting myself from the sadness I felt at being only one. Even before he died I wrote a poem that expressed my pain:

I know that one should speak in time of death.
But how should I begin?
I was not shown a way to speak of pain when I was young,
Although I listened to the lizard's tongue,
And heard the stars lamenting as they glide
Into the foaming zodiac to hide.

As Will lay dying, I spoke out loud this poem I had written just for him. He held my hand in his and looked at the gold wedding band he had given to me on the day of our marriage, which he often said was the happiest day of his life.

"What a magical poem, Anne. If you had been born a man, you would have been my rival, with your poet's soul. You are my Ariel."

It felt yesterday, as the funeral neared, that London had come to Stratford. No one had ever seen anything like it in Stratford-upon-Avon. Thousands of people traveled from London and mingled with the common folk of our town. Tinkers and tailors, nobility and priests, the great actor Robert Burbage, as well as minor players and dreamers who had sat in the audience of the Globe and experienced the pure spirit of Will's comedies and tragedies. Property dealers, Sir Walter Raleigh, pawnbrokers, Oxford students, poets and pamphleteers, John Donne, members of Parliament, the poet Chapman, serving maids, Elizabeth's old Cockney coachman, leading his ancient horse—we all paraded to the church.

The great age of English drama was over, and everyone knew it. Some sobbed, tears rolling down their cheeks. Players and gentle ladies walked silently as we marched in the funeral parade through town to the Holy Trinity Church. Of course Will was buried as an Anglican, not a Catholic. There was never such a glorious funeral for any player or poet in Stratford-upon-Avon or anywhere else. Poets were no longer rivals. The jealousy the other playwrights felt towards Will ended with my husband's death. The curtain had dropped on the greatest of all bards. Ben Jonson spoke with tears in his eyes at the funeral: "He was not of his age but of all time."

I am now a widow. As the funeral guests trudged slowly back to our house, I cannot help but see flashes of my husband's life before me. How we had gone to London together, conquered and loved it, and finally left it for this place, this home. As I walked in Will's funeral parade, I imagined that our characters, those spirit friends, were walking with me. I saw Falstaff, Hamlet, Rosalind, Iago, Lear, Macbeth, Cleopatra, and Antony. Walking slowly behind me were Henry IV, Richard III, the two Gentlemen of Verona, Kate of *Taming of the Shrew*, King John,

Richard II, Troilus and Cressida, Othello, Coriolanus, Timon of Athens, Pericles, Cymbeline, Ariel. There were thousands of characters, major and minor, some speaking poetry and some speaking prose. All our characters surrounded me, and I looked in their eyes and bade farewell. Beside me walked the ghost of Christopher Marlowe. His laugh was in my ear, the smell of his whiskey breath in my nostrils, his hand upon my shoulder as it had been so many times. When he whom you have loved is gone, the sadness expands into the past, and all you have lost arrives at one moment, marking for you the life you once lived, showing you all you've gained and lost.

He is gone, yes. And not. He is here, ever here; no one and no time may take his legacy. I will see to this.

It seemed for a moment that our life together was all an illusion. "Such stuff as dreams are made on."

MAY 15, 1616

Beloved Will. I have not become accustomed to living without you. The smell of the world is different. I am alone. And I feel lonely. Today it is raining. Where have all the days gone? We had so many, and I know not where I have placed them. I asked the face in my mirror who I am, but there is no one to answer me.

I have not died, but I have seen my soul fall from the ceiling down the bedroom wall. And so when I say *death*, I mean the time of now, where there is no one to whom I can show my verse. I hear your voice at times, saying again and again and again, "Come live with me and be my love and we will—"

A Poet's Epilogue

I have always been in love with Shakespeare. Finding the diary in the soiled wheelbarrow fulfilled my dream in some ways, my dream of finding connection to the greatest poet who ever lived. Much as Philippe Petit walked that wire in the clouds, suspended between the earth and the heavens, between one giant tower and another, I have found my thread of connection, a way to float between the now and the forever. Through Anne, I have known and loved the greatest poet this world has known.

Last week, exactly two years and three days after I gave the diary of Anne Shakespeare to the scientists, forensic experts, and bibliophiles at Harvard, I was awakened by a phone call at eight thirty in the morning. The secretary announced that it was the president of Harvard University, Drew Gilpin Faust, waiting to speak with me. Her words changed my life forever.

"It's real," the president said, getting right to the point.

"Excuse me?"

"Good morning. This is President Faust of Harvard University. I must congratulate you and tell you how important the discovery of this diary is for Harvard University, for Her Royal Highness, Queen Elizabeth of England, for the British Museum, and for the world."

Was I dreaming? I tried to stay calm.

"My dear, you have given the world a modern treasure. Anne Shakespeare's diary has proved to be authentic. It is the most valuable literary manuscript in the world. Even more precious than the First Folio of William Shakespeare, recently stolen and returned to the British government after the Folger Library almost bought it by mistake for a fortune. You have discovered the key to the life of William Shakespeare.

"The Oxfordian theory, the Baconian theory are now of the past, shown to be what we at Harvard have always known, conspiracies to deny the talent of the greatest bard who ever lived. We will now have to consider the quill of Anne Hathaway Shakespeare and her presence in the life of her husband as having major importance in the Shakespeare canon, which until now has totally swept her under the rug of Shakespearean studies. Now we know from the diary that the undoubtedly greatest writer in the English language, or perhaps any language, did not beg, borrow, and steal alone. Anne participated in his crime of genius. And thanks to your discovery, we also know that Shakespeare was as hated, hunted, and threatened by those who wished to destroy greatness as Jesus or Gandhi or Martin Luther King or Mozart. The diary shows brilliantly that goodness and genius inspire malice."

"Oh yes," I said into the phone. "I am sure of that. Genius not only inspired envy and malice; it inspires madmen. Look what happened to John Lennon."

I am, I admit, not really at my best in the morning, before coffee. As I pressed the phone to my ear, all I could think of (as a Yankees fan) was that by mistake I had hit a home run for poetry, playwriting, authenticity, and women, all at the same time.

President Faust continued, excitement growing in her voice. She no longer sounded like the first female president of Harvard, responsible for raising money for the endowment fund, but like an animated girl at a surprise birthday party.

"The diary has passed thirty carbon-dating tests. The type of binding and stitching on the cover of the manuscript could only have been produced in the seventeenth century. The precious yellow writing paper has been tested and authenticated. The dark-blue ink has passed five tests to prove it is the same ink used in 'Hand D' of the *Sir Thomas More* manuscript, now under glass at the British Library. The paper and ink are without doubt over four hundred years old. The quill marks match exactly the signature of Anne Shakespeare found in the parish house records in Stratford-upon-Avon and also on her marriage certificate. Forensic experts have proved that the handwriting in the diary is the same handwriting that appeared on baptismal documents that bear her name. Her handwriting has been analogized and confirmed to be authentic by our own handwriting analysts, who studied with the great Dr. Clara Roman, the expert in graphology who broke many codes during World War II."

"Really?" I managed.

I was thrilled and amazed. Will wonders never cease? I not only discovered Anne's diary; I have exposed the conspiracy against Shakespeare. We were interrupted by another phone call in President Faust's office. I heard the secretary saying that the Queen of England was on the phone. President Faust courteously came back to talk to me, keeping the queen waiting.

"Excuse me, it is the Queen of England on the phone. I have to go, but my secretary will tell you the rest."

Her secretary continued, "The president is sending a limousine this afternoon at five p.m. to your address in Manhattan. It will bring you to Cambridge for a ceremony with all the deans and professors in the humanities department, as well as the head of the Schlesinger Library on the History of Women. The president will announce this discovery to the media, who have already been alerted and have begun to arrive. Dan Rather, in Washington, who remains a consultant to Harvard, has said this discovery is as important to Shakespeareana as the Dead Sea Scrolls were in establishing the authenticity of the Essenes. The Queen of England is so grateful that you will be donating the original diary to the British Library. As soon as it arrives in the diplomatic pouch of the American ambassador, it will go under glass. It will be viewed, as long as there is an England, by millions of grateful tourists, scholars, and even young people, all of whom will see the handwriting of this great and little-known heroine. Not only did she preserve Shakespeare's plays, which would have been lost forever, but she also preserved his sonnets and his long poems for a miraculous legacy. According to the diary, she also preserved his sanity." She stopped to catch her breath. "Thank you so much. I look forward to meeting you later this afternoon. Congratulations."

The president's secretary hung up, and I quickly dressed and packed.

I did not go to the ceremony. Instead I bought a first-class ticket to the Galapagos Islands, where I've always wanted to travel but could never afford to before receiving the generous honorarium from the Harvard Endowment Fund, which I admit was in the six figures. On the plane, I mused upon the fact that I had exposed three conspiracies. The one against William Shakespeare in the seventeenth century; the one against his reputation that began a hundred years after he died, saying he was the Duke of Oxford or, even more ridiculous,

Francis Bacon; and the one against Anne Shakespeare herself. Even the greatest modern scholars such as Stephen Greenblatt and Peter Ackroyd buried her without reason in the attic of Stratford-upon-Avon. Now the world would know Anne was not a neglected older housewife whose husband didn't care for her, but a female poet who lived out a great love affair and kept a diary.

On the plane, looking out at the clouds, I excitedly reflected that I would soon be alone in the Galapagos Islands, snorkeling in the water with sea lions and other watery creatures. I opened my laptop and went to the homepage of the *London Times*. The headline read, "American Poet Discovers Diary of Anne Shakespeare in a Wheelbarrow." I smiled to myself. I had created a legacy and a new identity. I had, unwittingly, discovered a diary everyone now and in the future would know is authentic.

I will not have to go through life remembering with bittersweet sadness how Mr. John Sweeney, the head of the Lamont Library in 1963, had exhibited my manuscripts after I won the Yale Younger Poets Award. Mr. Sweeney recorded my voice reading my own poems, but then he explained, somewhat embarrassed, that I wouldn't be allowed to see the exhibit of my poems or even be allowed in the library, sadly, because I was a woman. At that time the Lamont Library at Harvard University was open only to men. As Shakespeare said, "Revenge is for minor poets."

Mr. Sweeney is dead now. The world has changed. Writing well is the best revenge.

Biographical Resources

Scholars are sure of certain facts about William Shakespeare's life, culled from sources that include parish registers, court records, title pages of first editions of his poetry, thoughts recorded on his tombstone, and his last will and testament. Readers interested in learning more about the Bard's life can begin by consulting the following books.

Chambers, E. K. *William Shakespeare: A Study of Facts and Problems*, vols. 1 and 2 (Oxford/Clarendon, 1930). Considered a definitive resource by some scholars for factual elements such as dates, etc.

Harrison, G. B. *Shakespeare: The Complete Works* (Heinle and Heinle, 1952). Contains a biographical essay.

Holland, Peter. *William Shakespeare* (Oxford University Press, 2007). Short and "precise."

For more, check out the entry on Shakespeare at the website Five Books: https://fivebooks.com/interview/james-shapiro-on-shakespeare-life/.

Acknowledgments

The first person I must thank is Anne Shakespeare herself. Being in her company has been a privilege. The fact that her beloved husband, William Shakespeare, knew so much about the human condition and was such a great master not only of human psychology but of poetry, music, and the underbelly of the bawdy mind takes my breath away. According to Professor Pauline Kiernan—whom I wish to thank, above all, for her decoding of sexual puns in her book *Filthy Shakespeare*—Shakespeare must have been mercilessly ribbed all his life. He was a walking, talking, breathing sexual pun. According to Professor Kiernan, his surname meant *wanker*—to shake one's spear. His Christian name, William, was a pun of *prick*, *cunt*, and *sexual desire*. But the Anne of my imagination, like Will, stood for someone unafraid to shake others out of assumptions about politics, sexual identity, and morality. I am grateful to

Professor Kiernan; her book enlightened me and saved me a great deal of time researching sexual puns.

I wish to thank Professor Stephen Greenblatt for his thoughts expressed in *Will in the World: How Shakespeare Became Shakespeare*. He did an excellent job, considering the shortage of information we have about Shakespeare's life.

I wish to thank the late Arthur Schlesinger Jr., the late Sandy Richardson, the late Norman Mailer, and the late and beloved Kitty Carlisle for believing in my writing. Also my late mother, Mae Barnett, and my sisters, Linda Barnett and Ellen Ivy Barnett, who were always behind me with love.

I wish to thank Janet Gushin, Gary Kupper, Colleen Primerose, Francis X. Clifton, Gabe Pagano, and Jason Ashlock.